D1426686

014413563 6

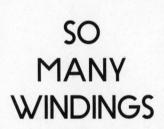

SO
MANY
WINDINGS

SO
MANY
WINDINGS

Catherine Macdonald

WINNIPEG

So Many Windings

Design by M. C. Joudrey and Matthew Stevens.
Layout by Matthew Stevens and M. C. Joudrey.
Map by Greg McCullough.

Published by At Bay Press May 2021.

Library and Archives Canada cataloguing in publication is available upon request.

ISBN 978-1-988168-46-3

Printed and bound in Canada.

This book is printed on acid free paper that is 100% recycled ancient forest friendly (100% post-consumer recycled).

First Edition

10 9 8 7 6 5 4 3 2 1

atbaypress.com

For my father, Donald Bruce Macdonald,
unabashed Scotophile.

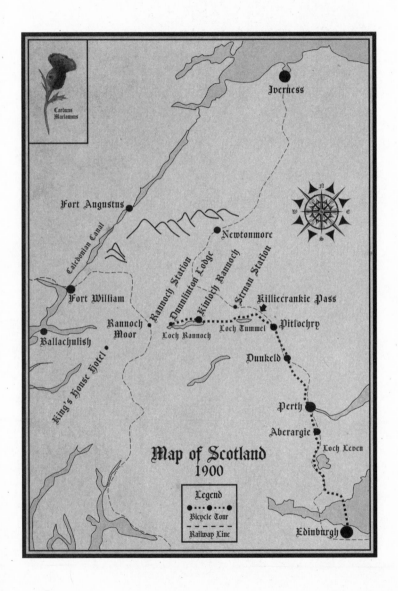

Map of Scotland
1900

Legend

· · · · Bicycle Tour
– – – Railway Line

The heart is deceitful above all things.
The heart is deep and full of windings.
The old man is covered up in a thousand wrappings;
Therefore keep guard over yourselves.

Lancelot Andrewes

PROLOGUE

Scotland, 1900

The dog trotted ahead of him, snuffling the ground and look-ing intently around. The animal seemed to know that their rescue mission was in doubt. The old ewe had not come back to the fold with the rest the evening before and if left on her own, maybe sickening from something, she'd be no match for foxes or wild dogs. There was talk of big cats too, here in the hills round about, though he had never seen one or known anyone who had set eyes on one. He turned his collar up against the chill of early morning.

Mist hovered above the surface of the weir pond for the sun had not yet risen over the hills to chase it away. The dog halted on the other side of the weir, suddenly stiff-legged, muzzle pulled back. When the barking started, he readied himself to find the ewe dead and bloated by the side of the pond. But there was nothing on the bank and what he saw tangled up against the weir would not assume the form of a sheep no matter how hard he stared at it. He called to the dog to be quiet and moved closer. That was when he saw an arm, floating lazily just below the surface, the hand a bluish white.

1.

Geneva, 1889

May 7, 1889
Miss Annie Gairdner
c/o Hôtel d'Angleterre,
Geneva, Switzerland

My Dear Miss Gairdner,

I'm afraid I must renege on my promise to walk the Sentier du Rhône with you and Miss Hagan this afternoon. In fact, with great regret, I must leave Geneva today. My father has been asking more pointedly in his recent letters about the date of my return to Boston. He complains that I have resisted my obligations in relation to our family's business for too long. There are dark hints regarding my financial wherewithal should I elect not to return. And so I take the express train to Paris later this morning.

I like to think that you will miss me, Annie. Don't miss me too much. Don't waste your tears on someone who can never live up to the high ideals you have set for yourself. I admire you for them and always will. But I am made of baser stuff. I wish it were not so, but there it is.

Still, I can't regret those sweet hours we spent together. If they led you to believe that my regard for you is of a different kind, I am truly sorry. Please be assured that whatever you do and wherever you go, you will have the friendship and admiration of,

Yours very sincerely,
Emmet Lathrop

2.

Edinburgh, 1900

Aug. 1, 1900
Sergeant Andrew Setter,
c/o John Mowat
Skerries Farm
Stromness, Orkney Islands

My Dear Setter,

Delighted to get yours of the 15th from Stromness. Are your Orkney relatives treating you well? And is your leg mending as it should?

I'm writing this in the drawing room of Miss Semple's Hotel for Young Ladies while waiting for Maggie to change for dinner. The drawing room is the farthest that members of the male sex are allowed to venture at Miss Semple's. I'm staying up the way at the Cockburn Hotel and changing for dinner is a simpler matter for me. No clerical collar since Germany as I am now officially on holidays. Hurray! (My last "official" duty was to wave goodbye to my little flock of theology students at the London docks.)

Things are certainly more formal over here. Had to rent a dress suit—white tie, tails, stiff front and the whole malarkey—in order to attend a dinner given by Mrs. Thorburn and Miss Gairdner in Berlin last month. The entire theology faculty of the university was there. I've observed that nothing inspires a professor of Systematic Theology so much as a free meal.

We arrived in London two weeks ago and "did" the sights. Then came up here to Edinburgh, where I'm hoping for some time alone, just the two of us, away from the all-seeing eye of the matron at Miss Semple's. We have about 3 weeks before we have to start making our way back to Canada and I want to show Maggie all the haunts I frequented here as a student in '93 when I was at New College.

Charles paused in his writing. Then, stretching and leaning back in his chair, he looked around at the other occupants of Miss Semple's drawing room. He thought about how uncomfortable his friend Setter would be in this too-pretty room and almost burst out laughing. Poor Andrew was painfully bashful around females, especially young, eligible ones. But Charles had found him excellent company over the last year while Maggie had been away from Winnipeg, studying in Germany.

The bond with Setter had been formed in a crisis when a close university friend of Charles's, Peter McEvoy, had been arrested for murder and Setter had been the policeman in charge of the investigation. If Setter had not formed an unorthodox alliance with Charles so that together they could find the real murderer of Joseph Asseltine, Peter might very well have been sentenced to hang.

Thoughts of that time inevitably brought Charles to the turnoff to another one of the darker roads in his mind, the one sign-posted "Trevor." He was saved from going down that well-worn path by Maggie, who appeared, clothed in her best dinner dress and pulling on her evening gloves, her tall, slender form theatrically framed by the archway into the drawing room.

"I'm not late, am I?" she asked, peering at the grandfather clock across the room.

"No, not yet, but we'd better make haste if we're going to walk."

"Agreed. The sisters are not given to long preambles at meal times. When they say, 'dinner at seven,' they mean exactly that, so we'd best be off."

Charles folded up his unfinished letter, stuffing it in his jacket pocket, and followed her to the door.

Later that night, snug in his room at the Cockburn Hotel, Charles spread the letter out on his desk and began writing again.

Midnight, same.

Dinner with the Burning Bush sisters—the Mrs. Thorburn and Miss Gairdner mentioned above. All did not go as planned. The sisters are leaving in three days on a bicycling tour of the Highlands. They were describing the trip in the most exciting terms—and we were quite enthusiastic on their behalf. Until they asked, wouldn't we like to come with them? Maggie, who ignored my kick under the table, said why, that would be so grand. Another kick. We'd be thrilled, wouldn't we, Charles? Charles did his best to look thrilled.

So much for walking arm in arm on Corstorphine Hill and intimate suppers at that little restaurant near the Grassmarket. We had one of those conversations while I walked her back to Miss Semple's. Why on earth did you say yes? Well, they took me by surprise and I couldn't say no and they've been so kind to me and they're really such dears and besides it's only 10 days and wouldn't you love to see the Highlands from a bicycle and it will be an adventure and there'll be no questions about propriety with them there to chaperone us.

I ask you, Setter. Consider the plight of the engaged man. His intended so near; the appointed day so far off. A beautiful old city full of history and romance. Especially romance. I suppose it's for the best but I can't work up much enthusiasm.

Say, Andrew! Couldn't you cut your time in the Orkneys short and join us? I could use another man to even the odds. After all, nothing so rehabilitates an injured leg like trudging a bicycle uphill. And I've got my travelling cribbage set. What do you say? If necessary, I could drag you in a cart behind.

Yours in supplication,
Charles Lauchlan

Aug. 3, 1900

Dear Charles,

Yours to hand of the 1st.

Sorry I can't help you withstand the tender mercies of the Burning Bush sisters. The bicycle tour idea is a fine one. And some people here would be only too happy to see the back of me. But the leg is blasted slow to heal. I'm still having to use a cane, though I can see the improvement daily when I'm not feeling sorry for myself.

Here's an idea though. I could meet you for a few days at the end of the tour, wherever that will be. I had planned to come south in about 3 days anyway.

I've had to get used to planning my day anew each morning. Keep wanting to go down to the local constabulary and see if they want any help. Such is the case of the policeman on sick leave.

The people here are interesting. So many Spences, Linklaters, Moars, Isbisters and Fletts. Just like at home, really. So far, I've found only a few people who actually knew my grandfather. Not surprising. He signed on with the Hudson's Bay Company in 1819 and never did come back here.

The older people, strangely, have greeted me like the prodigal returned and thumped me on the back and fed me till I explode. They talk about people who lived a hundred and fifty years ago as if they were just in the next room. One old toothless woman said that the next time I come I must bring my squaw wife. I tried not to take offence for these dear old people don't mean any harm. I've never thought of using that word for the girls from home—or for my own mother, for that matter. But that is the word they use here for an Indian or half-breed wife. A few fellows from home did come back to the Orkneys after they were done their service for the Company and they brought their wives and children with them. As far as I know, they were treated well enough by the island folk.

But in Kirkwall, especially, I do stand out from the crowd and that is not always a comfortable feeling. I'll be in Edinburgh at the Queen's Hotel from the 7th on. You can reach me there. My best regards to Miss Skene—and the Burning Bush sisters. (Interesting name. Is there a story there?)

Yours,
Andrew Setter

Aug. 5, 1900

Dear Andrew,

Disappointed but not surprised that you won't be joining us on the tour. And I didn't mean to deprecate the Burning Bush sisters. They are remarkable women and you would like them very much, as I do myself. I call them that because they organized their own expedition to St. Catherine's Monastery in the Sinai Desert. Rode camels and swatted flies and discovered in the library there one of the earliest manuscripts of the Greek New Testament in existence. The next year they went back to the monastery and painstakingly photographed each page and then *transcribed it all when they got back home to Scotland. And between them they know all the biblical languages—Greek, Latin, Hebrew, Aramaic, Syriac, Coptic and dear knows what else. It has set the airless little world of biblical scholarship on its ear, not the least because the discoverers are female and lack the letters after their names that these learned professors bear. You can just imagine what Maggie has to say on this subject.*

Once I got over my sulk, I began to quite like the idea of the Highlands by bicycle. Mrs. Thorburn has us organized and kitted out to a fare thee well. Having dealt with dragomen and desert marauders, she is undaunted by the prospect of midges, flat tires, terrain with more ups than downs, and the mysteries of the MacBrayne's Steamship timetable.

As a matter of fact, Maclaren's Travel Itineraries Co. are so impressed with her skills that we are to have two additional members that were cast adrift when their bicycle tour was cancelled. Mrs. Thorburn was initially somewhat resistant to this plan, but Maclaren's wife is a fellow women's suffragist and prevailed on Mrs. Thorburn to help her husband out of a ticklish situation. We have yet to meet these new comrades of the way, but both are men, which frankly is something of a relief. We are also to have a young friend of the sisters, a Miss Pitkeathly, another late addition, which swells our number to seven.

We'll end up on Skye, if not killed by the effort, and take a steamer from Portree to the mainland on the 16th. We can meet you in Edinburgh on the 17th. I'll be at the Cockburn Hotel again.

Yours,
Charles Lauchlan

3.

Cambridge, England, 1900

The Master stood at the window in his rooms trying to see down into the quadrangle through both the rain and the wavy distortions of the seventeenth-century glass. Cordwainer scuttled unsteadily across the grassed expanse, forsaking the neat pathways but heading in the general direction of the porter's lodge. The Master took out his watch, flipped it open and scowled.

"Almost three o'clock. Confound the man!" he said, though there was no one in the room to hear. He turned and was rifling through some papers in the drawer of his desk when there was a knock on his door. A head appeared around the door, and a gowned arm.

"Oh—it's you. Come in, Taplow. Have you talked to Cordwainer?"

"Cordwainer? No. Not since this morning at any rate. Why?"

"I suspect he's taken his luncheon—and then some—at the Quail and Quince."

"Again? I thought he told you he'd signed the pledge."

The Master made a harrumphing noise at the back of his throat. "As if I don't have enough to worry about. Fleeming returned well after the college curfew again last night. Along with his other demerits; we simply can't overlook it. I'm afraid we're going to have to send him down. I hate to distress his father this way."

"Yes, most unfortunate, Master. Not to add to your burdens, but have you had a chance to think about my application to the library fund to purchase that manuscript fragment I was telling you about?"

The Master walked over to his desk, every square inch of which was covered with piles of paper, stacks of books and more than one half-drained teacup with a stale looking biscuit on its saucer. "Ah, now let's see." He moved a pile of books and began flipping through the papers underneath it. "Yes. Here we are." The Master squinted at the page for a moment. "Didn't you say that the fellow who is selling it has an unsavoury reputation?"

"Yes, but that is often the case for dealers in Egypt these days. Now that the American universities have entered the fray and their newly minted plutocrats have started buying antiquities by the barge load, we have to take a few chances or be left behind."

"But are you even sure he wants to sell? Didn't he just want your help in authenticating the manuscript?"

Taplow smiled. "Well, yes. But these tactics are quite transparent, aren't they? He wants to appear reluctant to sell so that we'll up the price."

The Master looked again at the page in his hand. "In that case, he has succeeded royally."

"I grant you, it seems quite a large outlay. But, unfortunately, that is the way the market is going. That is the price I feel we must offer him in order to persuade him to part with it."

"You've taken a good look at this manuscript, have you?"

"Yes, well, I got quite a good look—"

"Quite a good look? Is that sufficient to be sure?"

Taplow fussed at the sleeves of his gown. "Well, I got as good a look as he was willing to give me." He looked at his shoes. "I asked him to leave it with me for a day or two, but he declined to do so."

"Surely that is a rather bad sign? Perhaps the fellow is afraid that more prolonged appraisal will reveal it is not genuine?"

"Well, yes, but it could equally mean that, knowing its true value, he is unwilling to let it out of his sight."

The Master gave an involuntary sigh and looked again at the paper. "But as far as what you have seen is concerned, you feel it's genuine?"

Taplow looked uncomfortable. "Yes—well, it looks very promising. It may well be what he says it is. That is—it looks genuine. I can't in all conscience make a firm pronounce-ment on it. But if we don't act now, Cambridge may lose out to another university. For example," he screwed his mouth up as he pronounced the word, "Chi–ca–go."

"Chicago," the Master repeated, his lips curling. "I see the problem."

"And he's even mentioned those annoying Scottish sisters. What if he ends up offering it to them?"

"Worse and worse," the Master mumbled. "But I need hardly remind you, Taplow, that if we purchase this manu-script, we use up the acquisition allotment for the whole year. We have many calls on these funds. What if we buy it and it turns out to be a fake?"

Tiny droplets of moisture had appeared on Taplow's upper lip. "Well, it is clearly an uncial manuscript fragment of the Gospel of Mark, Master. Very possibly fourth century. We would, of course, want to look at the parchment and the scribal hand and the text most closely to determine its age and relation to other manuscripts. The probability is high that it is what he represents it to be. If it turns out not to be fourth century, then its monetary value is indeed lower. But there are significant finds occurring with great frequency now. It may well be discovered to be important in the light of future finds. As the person in charge of building the college's manuscript collection," Taplow cleared his throat, "I feel that we should not let this opportunity go by."

"Well, this is not my field and I am relying on your judgment. But I take your point. We wouldn't be left with nothing if it turns out to be just another orphaned fragment. But it could be a very expensive orphan."

"No manuscript can be considered unimportant, Master. We are, after all, trying to trace the chain of copies back to the original, the very first manuscripts of the gospels that came direct from the hands of the great evangelists themselves. Every scrap, every tiny piece of the puzzle brings us nearer to that end."

"Yes, quite. Quite," said the Master, and squinted again at the figure on the sheet in his hand. "But the trustees will want assurances, and I don't think—"

"Oh, but—"

"My dear fellow, I can see that you very much want to get your hands on this manuscript. You are in the grip of that passion for your field that does you credit. But to go ahead without a solid authentication? Without an opportunity to further verify? And especially from a fellow with his reputation? Too many unknowns, dear chap. Too risky in the end." He held up his hands to forestall Taplow's next argument. "I will take your request forward to the trustees' meeting next week. That is the best I can do. Regrettably, I find that I am unable to lend the request my personal support."

"I see, Master," said Taplow, sounding as if there was sawdust in his mouth. "You must, of course, act as you see fit."

"Don't take it too hard, Taplow. There'll be other opportunities. Good heavens, look at the time." The Master pulled his gown off a hook on the back of his door. "Will you excuse me? I have to meet with the bursar over the beginning of term accounts. Oh, by the way, have a good holiday. Norfolk again for the shooting?"

Taplow hesitated for a moment, then answered with sudden determination, "Er—no. No, I've changed my mind. Somewhere further afield, I think."

4.

Charles and Maggie walked up the steps of the house in Greenhill Gardens and knocked using an immense door knocker that seemed to be made from the horseshoe of a Clydesdale. They were to have dinner with the sisters, receive final instructions on the itinerary of the bicycle tour and contribute a parcel of clothing each to the communal steamer trunk that was to precede them via rail and coach and be there waiting for them at their inns and hotels every night at the end of a day of invigorating cycling.

The sisters' solicitor father had worked primarily for an eccentric Glasgow steel industry magnate who, being a bachelor, left all his money to his faithful legal advisor. Since Mr. Gairdner was already comfortably fixed at the time of this generous bequest, he became a very rich man, indeed. But rather than build or buy an estate in the country, he decided instead to build this behemoth of a house, which loomed over the smaller houses in Greenhill, the Edinburgh neighbourhood where he had lived since his marriage. Perhaps this was to honour the memory of his late wife, who had died young and left him to raise their daughters on his own. The girls had taken over the running of the house as soon as they reached their late teenage years, first Janet, the eldest, and then the younger sister, Annie, who actually enjoyed running the house, unlike her sister.

The heavy oak door swung inward and Charles and Maggie were greeted by a small grey-haired woman in an apron and cap.

"Good evening, Mr. Lauchlan, Miss Skene." She motioned them to enter. "I'll take your hat, sir, and your bundles, too, Miss. I'll be packing those in the wee trunk out the back."

"I hope we're not late, Emmie," Maggie said as they stepped up from the entrance into a richly carpeted hallway. "We walked in order to enjoy the evening."

"Aye, it's lovely to see the sun. The ladies are expecting you, but…" At this she peered around at the double doors to the library, which were closed. "But they're entertaining a foreign gentleman, who seems to be staying a little beyond his time."

Emmie led them down the hall, through a vast sitting room full of overstuffed furniture and through a set of French doors that led to a conservatory at the back of the house.

"If you'll just wait here, I'll bring some refreshments," Emmie said. "The ladies will join you presently, I'm sure."

The conservatory was filled with palm trees and other exotics, many of which the sisters had acquired from Palestine and from Egypt. Two lemon trees with bright green, shiny leaves and fruit that was just beginning to ripen, grew in enormous pots. This ample greenery was sustained by the warm, moist air, provided by a hard-working boiler and set of radiators that clanked and periodically hissed with steam. In front of a set of French doors leading out to the back garden there was an open area where a metal rack holding a set of Indian clubs, a rubber floor mat and other physical culture apparatus was set up. By the scuffs and scratches on the equipment, Charles and Maggie could tell that it was well-used. Charles grabbed a skipping rope off the rack and began to whirl it around, alternately skipping and getting the rope caught around his ankles.

Maggie watched this performance with some amusement. She was glad Charles liked the sisters, for she was very fond of them herself. She'd first met them in Berlin during a lecture by Professor Von Harnack on the nature of Christ. Maggie had been seated behind them and heard their soft Edinburgh burr. Since there were few other women in the hall, she sought them out during the break. They seemed quite charmed by the idea that she had come all the way from Winnipeg to study in Germany, where they were themselves spending the winter months. They were cultivating contacts among the biblical scholars and attending lectures at which, as Maggie had also discovered, ladies were not always welcome. You had to develop a thick skin over things like this, which Maggie felt she was doing, but when the sisters took her under their wing, inviting her to their flat frequently and on outings like bicycle trips through the countryside, she accepted this maternal treatment gladly.

Charles was now attempting to chin himself on a high bar apparently set up for this purpose. After the third clean repetition, he began kicking his legs frantically to assist in getting his chin up and over the bar and Maggie called out encouragement between giggles.

Emmie returned with a green concoction served in crystal wine glasses and a plate of small biscuits spread with an unidentifiable paste. She set the glasses and plate on an oval-shaped wicker table surrounded by fan-backed wicker chairs that would not have been out of place on a balcony in

Cairo. Charles dropped to the floor with a sharp exhalation of breath, shook the fatigue out of his arms and came to join Maggie at the table.

As she got to know the sisters better, Maggie could not believe her good fortune in finding such compatible friends. Their father had been a great believer in the value of education, even for girls. He provided his daughters with the best schooling available in Edinburgh and any inclination they showed for further learning was encouraged with tutors, extra lessons, and enriching trips abroad. Though they knew little science themselves, the sisters believed as Maggie did, that many of the world's ills would be solved through scientific investigation. They were instantly full of encouragement over her new-found interest in physics.

Like her, they had lost their mother at a young age. Then the death of their father when they were in their early twenties deepened the already close bond between the sisters. They were parted briefly when Janet had married, set up house in England with her new husband, only to endure his sudden illness and death. Since then Janet Thorburn and Annie Gairdner had lived together in the house in Greenhill Gardens, pursuing their interests in women's suffrage and physical culture. They were especially interested in the study of early New Testament manuscripts, which they furthered with hard work and determination, utilizing their complementary talents and their considerable fortune.

After Charles and Maggie had sat in the conservatory for more than twenty minutes, Janet and Annie burst in, overflowing with apologies.

"So sorry we've kept you waiting."

"Are you almost perishing with hunger? Really, that man—"

"That foreign gentleman?" Charles said.

"Yes, Mr. Radulescu. He's a dealer in antiquities," Janet said. "We met him in Egypt last year."

"We bought some excellent items from him, though what he had on offer was rather mixed," Annie said. "Quite interesting Coptic papyri and some obviously overpriced rubbish. We've learned to be very careful."

"Not like some of those American gentlemen who come into the Khan el-Khalili market in Cairo and scoop up job lots full of items indiscriminately," Janet said.

"Was he trying to interest you in another manuscript?" Maggie asked.

"No, not at all," Annie said. "In fact, he was trying to buy back one of ours. A fragment that we bought from him last year."

"Yes, and he was quite insistent," Janet said. "He kept upping his price, but we told him in no uncertain terms that after we publish our facsimile edition, we're going to donate the manuscript to the New College library."

"But never mind that for now. Bring your kale and carrot juice with you to the dining room," Annie said.

Charles, who had been prevented by Maggie from watering a palm tree with the contents of his glass, dutifully picked it up and followed the ladies to the dining room.

5.

Two days later Charles followed Maggie down the greasy cobblestone incline from Granton Square onto the middle pier of Granton Harbour. The ride from the bicycle rental shop across from Waverley Station had not been entirely without excitement as they dodged uneasily between omnibuses, coaches and dray wagons, while being jarred by the uneven joins in the stone paving. Maggie had bicycled every day while studying in Tübingen and Berlin and was instantly at ease in the saddle of her sprightly red Swift. Decked out in a light woollen suit with a skirt short enough to reveal the riding spats she had borrowed for the trip, she seemed at one with her metal steed. But Charles was now regretting the long layoff since his last ride on a bicycle, particularly when sharp turns were required.

The pier was dominated by large cranes that unloaded the fishing trawlers of their silvery burden of herring. Ferry passengers felt like interlopers here and no particular effort was made to provide for their comforts as they waited to board the smallish side-wheeler *William Muir* for the five-mile passage to Burntisland across the Firth of Forth.

Amidst the general confusion, Charles spotted the trim, upright figure of Janet Thorburn holding her bicycle with one hand and waving at him with a folded newspaper. Annie Gairdner, smaller, blonder, had leaned her bicycle against the railing and was in the process of tucking her hair into a stylish felt hat with a small, iridescent green feather in its satin hatband. She looked up, caught sight of Charles and Maggie, and waved happily.

"There you are! Isn't the day a marvel?" Annie called out. "I can hardly wait to get to the other side."

Janet pulled a small watch on a chain from the hip pocket of her tweed riding skirt. "We'll have to board in about ten minutes. But I fear Miss Pitkeathly will be late. I don't know how she could be ready this morning when she only came up from London yesterday."

"Don't fuss, Janet," Annie said. "Violet is the most organized young lady we know. Not at all like so many of those empty-headed creatures who go down to London for the season."

"That's true enough. I should give her more credit." Janet scanned the square, shielding her eyes from the morning sun with the folded newspaper. "I must say I was surprised she'd choose to come away with us rather than stay and finish out the season in London."

At that moment, an open carriage turned briskly around the corner of the Granton Hotel and halted in front of the pier. A young lady in a riding suit with an elegant divided skirt alighted and immediately began to pull a fully loaded bicycle down from the carriage with her driver's assistance. She gave a little excited hop when she saw the rest of the group on the quay and waved before mounting her bicycle and directing it down onto the pier.

"Hello, hello!" She brought the bicycle to a stop and jumped down all in one neat motion.

"Most impressive, Violet," Janet said, "I don't think I could have pulled everything together in just a few hours."

"Not so hard, really," the young woman said, blushing and busying herself with straightening her skirt. "I stayed with my aunt in Moray Place last night. And I telegraphed home for Hutton to send my bike on the train a few days ago when I knew for certain I was coming with you. Did you get the bundle of extra clothes I sent you for the trunk last night?"

"Yes, all duly tucked away by Emmie. But it's a pity you had to cut your season short," Annie said. "I'm glad your mother could spare you to come along with us."

"As it happens, *Maman* was not so pleased," Miss Pitkeathly said. "But I expect she'll get over it. I couldn't endure one more dance or dinner making inane small talk with men who aren't really listening to me anyway."

"Well, you're of age. We don't see why you shouldn't be able to decide these things for yourself," Janet said and turned to Charles and Maggie. "Now. Introductions all round."

Charles waited his turn while Maggie was introduced. Miss Pitkeathly was very pleasant looking with a striking combination of glossy, dark hair with a glint of auburn, fair, almost pearlescent skin and blue eyes. She appeared to be about Maggie's age or perhaps a little older. He had been expecting a genteel Edinburgh accent, like the sisters, but there was nothing of that in her speech. Though he had been told that Violet Pitkeathly was from a very old Perthshire family, to him she sounded English.

"And here is the Reverend Mr. Lauchlan, also from Canada," Janet said.

Charles doffed his cap to her and extended his hand.

"How d'you do, Mr. Lauchlan." As she held out her hand, her handlebars turned sharply, causing her bicycle to flop over sideways. "Oh…dear. Just a—"

Charles immediately reached over and righted the bicycle, bumping his head against hers in the process.

"Oh—do excuse me—so sorry," she said, and blushed a deeper red, unable to meet his eyes.

He laughed. "Well, you should at least call me 'Charles' now that we've bumped heads."

A look of bafflement flashed across Miss Pitkeathly's face at these familiarities. After a few moments of paralysis, she said, "I'm so sorry, Mr. Lau—Charles, yes. And, um, well, then—I suppose you should call me 'Violet', too, I think. Yes. And so should Miss Skene." She gestured toward Maggie.

"Yes, of course," Maggie said. "And I'm 'Maggie.' I'm sure we're going to be great friends."

"Well—that is— Yes, I hope so. As long as I don't cause you an injury on the way. I have a reputation for clumsiness, I'm afraid. *Maman* is always saying so. You all have been fairly warned."

"I've not heard of this reputation," Janet said, "And saying things like that to a child only makes the child wish to fulfill such expectations."

Before anyone could react to this staunchly declared precept, two more bicyclists glided down onto the pier, bearing large bundles on their carriers.

"Ah," Janet said. "Here's the rest of our party, perhaps." She dropped her voice lower. "Maclaren was supposed to send me their names, at least, but there was nothing in the post yesterday."

The two riders swung their legs off their bicycles and walked toward their fellow travellers. The man in the lead sported tweed knee breeches with matching Norfolk jacket that had been well-worn but, perhaps, not worn lately. As he pulled his cap off for introductions, there was a faint odour of mothballs and pipe tobacco.

"Hullo. Are you Mrs. Thorburn, by any chance? I hope we're in time."

"Yes, I'm Janet Thorburn. I'm afraid I've not been given your names."

"Pollack, Mrs. Thorburn, Gordon Pollack. So nice to meet you—and thank you for allowing me to join your party."

"Welcome to our little gathering, Mr. Pollack. And this is…?"

Pollack turned to the man behind him, who seemed to be hanging back. "I've only just met this gentleman this morning, so I'll let him introduce himself."

As the second man advanced slowly, touching the peak of his cap with his free hand to greet the ladies, there was an expression on his face that Charles hadn't expected. What was it? Something like irony with a touch of resignation?

"I'm not sure that you will be so delighted to see me, Mrs. Thorburn. But I am nevertheless grateful to you for welcoming me into your tour."

Janet narrowed her eyes. "I don't quite— Have we met before?"

"Only metaphorically. In the pages of the *Journal of Biblical Literature* and the *New Testament Review*. My name is Taplow. Alfred W. Taplow."

"Taplow! You?" For a moment Janet seemed to be struck dumb.

Annie's eyebrows shot up. "Merciful heavens!"

"I can assure you, Mrs. Thorburn, that I did not know you were the tour leader until late yesterday evening. And then it was too late to contact you."

Charles had no idea what was going on, but he was rather enjoying this. Just at that moment, the *William Muir* blew its horn and the purser on deck beckoned all to board.

Janet looked relieved to break off, or at least delay, the

rest of the conversation. "Right, everyone. Gather yourselves together and let's away. Mr. Taplow, perhaps you would join Annie and me on deck once our bicycles are properly secured on board."

Taplow gave a little bow to her. "Certainly, Mrs. Thorburn."

Charles, with a quizzical glance at Maggie, began to steer his bicycle toward the gangway.

6.

There was a room aft of the main deck passenger lounge on the *William Muir* in which racks were provided for securing bicycles. Charles and Gordon Pollack had been deputized to make sure that all of the party's bicycles were in the room and safely stowed and that everyone had what they needed for the voyage before the room was locked.

That duty accomplished, Charles put his hands on his hips and stretched backward and to each side. He knew that his nether parts would be troubling him before the day was out. "I don't know about you, Mr. Pollack, but I'm now wishing I had done a little more cycling in the last few months to prepare for what awaits."

"I know what you mean, Mr. Lauchlan," Pollack said. "I've been an indoor man for far too long. The solicitor's life encourages it, I'm afraid." He turned his face to the sun, savouring it. "My wife and I used to be very keen on hill walking and cycling when we were first married. But then came the children and the house and the schools." He cocked his head in mock resignation. "And the need to pay for them. And, well, you know how it is."

"As a matter of fact, those happy obligations are in my near future." He pointed to Maggie, who was standing by the railing with Violet.

"Ah, how very nice," Pollack said, with a wistful smile. "My congratulations to you both."

"Thank you. Your wife will not be joining us, then?"

"No. She died two years ago."

"Oh. I'm so sorry. I can't imagine the pain of such a loss."

"Yes," Pollack said.

Charles knew that men always find it easier to talk about difficult things when there is something to hand, so he was relieved to see that Pollack had a pipe to concentrate on, which he did, carefully filling and tamping it from a small, red leather tobacco pouch.

"I escaped into work, I suppose. In fact, that's rather much why I'm here. The children virtually ordered me to take a holiday. I saw Maclaren's advertisement in *The Scotsman* and well, here I am."

"And here we all are. Though I'm not sure if we'll have the pleasure of Professor Taplow's company once that little conference over there concludes."

"Yes. Curious business that."

A growing expanse of lightly churning blue-green water appeared between the ship and the pier as Charles and Pollack crossed the deck toward Maggie and Violet, who were standing against the starboard railing. The four formed themselves into a tight quartet while trying not to gawk at the tense trio of Janet, Annie and Taplow at the opposite railing.

"Do you have any idea what they're talking about?" Charles said to Maggie.

Maggie leaned further toward the others and said in a low voice, "I have some idea but I don't know details. I think it's about that manuscript they mentioned at dinner—the one they bought in Cairo when they were there again last year."

"Was it related to the one they discovered at St. Catherine's?"

"I don't know. It's just a fragment—of the Gospel of Mark, I think. But even so they had to pay quite a bit for it. They're convinced it's quite important. They've managed to get a paper on it published in some journal or other. The editors made the usual objections but one of the sisters' friends at Oxford put in a good word for them."

"What does Taplow have to do with it?"

"If he's who I think he is, he teaches at Cambridge. At a college with some important biblical scholars and I guess he's one of them."

"Shouldn't he be encouraged by what they found, then—if it's important?" Violet said and Pollack nodded in agreement.

"You'd think so. But it seems that the conclusions the sisters draw from their manuscript fragment contradict opinions Professor Taplow has been dining out on for several years. He's quite the upcoming man in his field, apparently. And he's been counter-blasting in every journal and at every scholarly meeting he can get a foot into."

"Yes, I see. It's an uncomfortable situation, then," Charles said. "But don't they leave these disputes in the lecture hall? I thought scholars were terribly chivalrous about such things, especially English scholars." He did his best to give the words a terribly English flourish.

"You should know better than that, Charles." She shook her head at him. "University politics are almost as brutal as church politics."

"As bad as that?" Charles said.

"Yes. And there's a lot at stake. He's a leading opponent

of full membership for women at Cambridge University," She said, as if that explained everything.

"The true enormity is brought home to me."

She gave him a playful push. "Silly. This is no joking matter."

"I suppose it mustn't be, if you won't even consent to having your leg pulled."

"The fact is, the sisters have been working hard for ten years at least to be taken seriously as New Testament scholars—and facing all kinds of obstacles thrown in their path—and just as they were making some headway, along comes Professor Taplow. They know this isn't just about themselves. It's for the women who come after them."

"Look sharp," Charles said, touching her elbow. "The parley has concluded."

The sisters and Taplow, as far as he could see in relative amity, joined them at the starboard railing. The introductions that had been interrupted on the pier were completed a little stiffly. When Charles greeted him as "Professor Taplow", Taplow set him straight. Apparently Cambridge dons are addressed as "Mr." until they reach the very highest rank. In the ensuing conversation it was made clear by inference that Mr. Taplow would be continuing with the tour and not, as Charles had thought more likely, making his own arrangements once they reached Burntisland. Nothing was specifically mentioned about the basis for the decision but Janet said something calming about being on a holiday and leaving workaday vexations at home. It seemed that all three were making a determined show of magnanimity.

It was an odd beginning for a holiday, Charles thought, but it would be intriguing to see how this uncomfortable threesome would deal with their obvious differences while on the road.

"Excuse me, sir?" Someone was jostling at Charles's elbow. He turned to see a young man in worn black corduroy breeches with leather patches on the knees, a rough collarless linen shirt open at the neck, and a grey waistcoat, the whole ensemble set off with a red neckerchief.

"Would you like a copy of the *Workers' Clarion Call*?"

"I don't know," Charles said. "Would I?"

"I think you would. It's free." The young man smiled and tucked a pile of papers under one arm and opened a copy to show Charles. "Published by the Scottish Workers' Cooperative League. We're working toward a united front of industry and farm. Everyone who's under the heel of bosses whoever they may be—capitalist factory owners or proprietors who stole their land from its rightful owners."

"Well, I'm sure it's very interesting but—"

"Not only very interesting, sir, but vitally important. You'll find things in here that the so-called quality newspapers would never touch in a million years. Why? Because they're all beholden to the—"

"Hey! Did I not tell ye ta keep yer blasted newspaper ta yersel?" A brawny hand appeared and clamped heavily on the young man's shoulder, pulling him around none too gently. The hand belonged to the purser, who had a muscular seaman in tow. They pinioned the young man between them and started to hustle him away almost lifting him off the deck.

The young man twisted around and seemed remarkably cheery, given his predicament. "Don't mind them," he called back to Charles. "Once they realize that they're dupes of capital, they'll be buying me a drink, not shutting me up with the bilge!"

Charles could not help but smile back at him and since the young man had left him the newspaper, he began to leaf through it.

An older gentleman in a bowler hat and clutching a briefcase peered over Charles's shoulder. He sniffed. "Godless radicals and anarchists, sir," he said and fixed Charles with a baleful eye. "I blame the schools. They give fellows like that ideas above their station." He sniffed again and took off in dudgeon, in the direction of the refreshment bar.

Maggie, who had been at Charles's elbow while this scene played out, said, "That lad wasn't doing anyone any harm, was he? Where do you suppose they're taking him?"

"I don't know, but I think I'd better find out."

7.

The purser was none too happy about the situation but he selected a key from a chain attached to his broad leather belt and bent to open the locked door of the baggage storage room.

"Dear knows what the captain will say ta me if he finds out I'm lettin' this poor excuse for a man go free."

"You've nothing to worry about there, Mr. Cumstie. He won't hear about it from me," Charles said.

"Aye, well, that's as may be. It's only for the sake o' the kirk and your office that I do this. Mind you keep an eye on him, though. I wouldnae be surprised if he slipped the knot and started spreadin' his nonsense abroad again."

The purser opened the door and motioned Charles to go through ahead of him. The young man, who had been sitting on a brass-bound trunk, jumped to his feet.

"Well, I wasn't expecting company! Had I known, I would have ordered tea for us."

"No tomfoolery," Mr. Cumstie said. "You're to go free with the Reverend Mr. Lauchlan here. And no more funny business or you'll get the back o' ma hand." Cumstie turned to Charles. "Just pull the door to when you're done, sir. And I'll leave ye to it." With a shake of his head in the young man's direction, he strode out of the room.

"Reverend?" the young man said. "Do you not wear the uniform in America?"

Charles was puzzled for a moment. "Oh, yes. I see." He put his hand up to his collar. "Well, actually I'm in mufti as befits a man on holiday. And I'm from Canada." Charles shook the hand that was extended to him.

"I'm Riddoch. Ben Riddoch. Call me Ben and I'll call you—?"

"Oh, ah, Lauchlan. Charles Lauchlan."

"Charles it will be then. I try not to pander to outmoded notions of social superiority. I'm as good as any person I meet but no better, so I like to deal in first names. Well, Charles, I was hoping to have a word with the sailors, but I suppose that's not on now?"

"Probably not." Charles was a bit embarrassed. "I'm afraid the purser could only be persuaded to let you go if I acted—I guess you could say—as your babysitter."

"Ach, well, it doesn't matter. We'll be docking at Burntisland in half an hour anyway. And the purser threw the last of my newspapers overboard. The gulls will be very well informed."

Charles laughed. "Well, Ben, you certainly know how to bounce back after adversity. But, if you really believe the things you were talking about when we met, you must get a lot of practice."

"Aye, I do that. A lot of people don't like to hear or talk about those things. Money, economic relations…they're not for polite conversation, it seems."

"But all that *dupes of capital* business, isn't it just a little—"

"Strident? Lacking in nuance? Misrepresenting through

overstatement? Maybe. I admit that sometimes my enthusiasm runs away with me. But the thing you've got to understand, Charles, is that I have to talk in broad strokes to startle people out of their complacency. Once I've got their attention, it's time for the finer points and the shades of grey."

"You think there are some then. Shades of grey?"

"Yes, of course. But I do believe—deeply—that our economic life in Scotland is based on the exploitation of those who actually perform the work so that the owning class and those with inherited privilege can accrue disproportionate wealth. That's a reality that is not susceptible of shading or nuance in my view."

"I think there's a lot of truth to what you say—in Canada as well as Scotland. But you're not going to do much to change things if people like me have to keep bailing you out of places like this. Come on, let's get out of here. I'd like to introduce you to my fiancée."

When they joined the party on deck, Ben Riddoch insisted on wrestling first names from everyone. The sisters and Maggie surrendered theirs easily after Ben declared that he was for the broadest possible extension of the franchise and that this would involve women gaining the right to vote. He lingered over the handshake with Violet and asked if he could call her "Vi" which shocked her into speechlessness and before she could forbid it, he went on to Pollack. Pollack gripped Ben's hand warily and wished to be known as "Gordon." Only Taplow proved resistant to Ben's charms and remained resolutely "Mr. Taplow" to the likes of him.

Charles suggested they explore the rest of the ship and he and Maggie, arm in arm, and Ben, alternately asking questions and holding forth, began a slow circling of the decks.

"Forgive me for saying this, Mr.—I mean, Ben," Maggie

said, "but you don't sound very much like a working man."

"Aye, it's true," said Ben, sighing. "I've had all the Pollokshaws beaten out of me. That's what happens when you get a scholarship to a so-called good school."

Charles smiled. "So it really is the fault of the schools?"

"Maybe so. My father didn't think I'd make a cooper like him so he sent me off to Hutcheson's to apprentice as a member of the middle class. I finished Manchester University before I realized I was now neither fish nor fowl—talking too posh for the works yard and not posh enough for the Writers to the Signet."

"If you're not making barrels, what do you do?" Charles said.

"I disturb the comfort of my former classmates," Ben said, with a hint of glee. "But in a more mundane vein, I'm a reporter for the *Clarion*. And my bicycle and I are on our way north to gather information for a series of articles on the state of the crofters now that the Crofters Commission has been in force for a while."

"Now you see!" Maggie said, suddenly intense. "That's just the kind of thing we want to learn about. Real things, not things out of guidebooks. If you're going by way of Perth, we'll see each other on the road. Perhaps you could even give us a lecture or two—"

Ben held up his hands, "I don't know about that. I won't be travelling in quite your style. I've a blanket and a mac and a length of rubberized canvas to tent over me if it rains." He gestured at the heavens. "The stars will be my ceiling when I put my head down. So I won't be joining you in the sitting room of your hotel—and I doubt your party would welcome my company even if I could."

"Is that wise?" Charles said. "It could get pretty cold at night I hear."

"Not much choice, I'm afraid. The *Clarion*'s expenses

don't run to hotels. I'm lucky they pay me anything at all."
He noted the concern on Charles's face. "Don't worry. I feel
like all of nature is just waiting to embrace me."

Charles said something hopeful about the weather. But
he thought to himself: here is the difference in our ages.
Twenty-three looks ahead and sees only temperate, star-
filled nights. Thirty-three is glad to look out on the inevitable
torrents from the window of a room with a well-stoked fire.

8.

The *William Muir* eased into its berth at the Burntisland ferry pier where the passengers lining its rails had a privileged view of cargo ships in the inner harbour from Germany, Sweden, Holland, France—all there to be loaded with coal from the nearby Fife collieries. Once the tour party had retrieved their bicycles and they were once again on firm ground, a few errands had to be attended to before they could set out in earnest. The womenfolk fanned out to various greengrocers, bakeries and shops to buy food, drink and sundries for the road ahead. Charles and Gordon heaved the communal steamer trunk onto a cargo wagon and accompanied the wagon to the nearby train station so that they could direct it along its way to the Ayton House Hotel in Aberargie, where they were to spend their first night. Taplow was conspicuously left without much to do and he was therefore the one who was in charge of guarding the bicycles until everyone returned. They left him sitting on a bench near the High Street, reading, while the seven bicycles were ranged around him in various attitudes of attention.

After a half hour, they reassembled and packed their

saddlebags with the food they had bought for lunch. Maggie and Violet had found an inviting tearoom on the High Street and as the men, in particular, were in favour of arming themselves with tea and scones before tackling the lengthy hill road that swept around and above the town and headed northwestward to Kinross, the party moved off toward the Binn Tea and Sweets shop, wheeling their bicycles and chatting happily.

"I've read about 'the Season'," Maggie said to Violet, once they were seated with their milky tea and buttered scones, studded with raisins. "But what's it like? Have you really met the Queen?"

"Oh, you don't really want to hear about that, surely," Violet said. "Why don't you tell me about Canada, that place you're from, Winnee…Winni…?"

"Winnipeg. Gateway to the west and all that. I'd love to tell you all about it sometime but, really, this is probably the only time I'm going to meet someone who's met the Queen face to face. Is she really as stern as her portraits make her?"

Violet made a face. "To tell you the truth, I don't look back on the experience of being presented to her with much in the way of pleasure. It was terrifying. Not in my line at all. I wanted to give it a miss altogether but *Maman* insisted. That was four years ago and I still have nightmares about falling into the Queen's lap while making that awful low curtsey they make you do."

Charles joined them at the chintz-covered table, juggling a plate with two scones and a piece of cheese along with his teacup. "Is that what really happened?" he said.

"No, thank heavens. We all had to take classes from Madame Valayevska in curtseying and backing away from 'the Presence.' We practised for hours and, I suppose, sheer repetition overwhelmed my natural tendency to trip over my own feet."

·"The rest of it must be amusing, though," Maggie said. "All those parties and dances—and handsome men in uniforms and white tie and tails."

"It's exhausting, actually. And as it's my fourth go at it—and my last, I vow—I'm viewed as rather an antique. It's like the Perthshire Agricultural Society Fair. All the eligible young ladies are paraded around, showing all their best points to the gentleman buyers." She looked off into the distance and shivered. "I'd much rather *be* at the fair in Perth than be one of the exhibits up for auction in London. There at least I could be doing something positive for the estate."

"Is it large, your estate?" Maggie said.

Here Violet seemed to come alive. "Not huge, really. Only seven thousand acres but some of the best land for cattle rearing. We've been improving our Angus breeding stock over the last five years and we've won several prizes. And there's our sheep. And we grow barley and wheat and potatoes. Really, some of the cultivating methods coming out of Germany could double our yield if only I could persuade my tenants to take them up." Violet's cheeks had flushed with excitement. "There's so much more we could be doing to increase efficiency, both on the animal husbandry side and with our crops. And that would benefit my tenants, as well as improve the income of the estate."

"Goodness, you seem to know a lot about farming," Maggie said.

"Oh, yes. It's my passion." She noticed an amused look exchanged by Maggie and Charles. "It really is though. There's only me, you see. My parents neglected to have a son. So it's all down to me. But that doesn't matter because I've always loved knocking about the home farm and working with the tenants." She fixed them with a determined look. "And I mean to learn all I can, and do all I can to hand it down to my children in a much improved condition. Papa has been rather—um—*distracted*."

Charles swallowed a mouthful of scone. "Maybe farming just isn't his passion."

"That much is true," Violet said with sudden vehemence. "He can usually be found at the gaming tables in Monte Carlo." She blushed and looked down at her cup. "And *Maman* says that these matters should be left to my husband." She looked over at the window and said, almost to herself, "But where to find such a creature who feels about Storbrae as I do? Not in London, I've decided, but where?" She turned toward them again. "Of course, *Maman* accuses me of having impossibly high standards."

Maggie was quick to reassure. "I'm sure he must be out there somewhere. You must have met men in London who run their own estates and who, who…"

"Who are looking for wealthy heiresses whose money they can tap until it's all tapped out? Or men like Dwight Cavers, who are more interested in my grouse moors and my deer ranges than they are in me? No, thank you. I'd rather be a spinster and raise bulldogs than see Storbrae become one large shooting lodge for my husband's business cronies."

"Dwight Cavers?" Maggie said. "Isn't he something to do with shipping?"

"Yes, something like that. He's a Canadian, like you." Too late, she heard how that sounded. "Well, not like you at all really. You seem very nice. Heavens, what must you think of me! I've been talking too much about myself. I'd much rather talk about you two. You're getting married?"

"Yes, indeed. The sooner the better," Charles said at exactly the same time that Maggie said, "Oh yes, eventually."

He looked sidelong at Maggie, who, oblivious, said to him, "Oh, Charles. Before I forget. I think I want my saddle raised about an inch before we set off, but the bolts are too tight and I can't budge them. Would you mind doing it?"

Charles started to say something to her, stopped and then said, "Of course. I'll do it now. Would you excuse me?"

Both girls nodded, Maggie a little puzzled at the slight chill in his response, as he stuffed the second scone into his pocket and picked his way through the crowded tables to the door.

Eventually, she had said. Just how long might she consider "eventually" to be, Charles wondered. Outside the tea shop, he slumped against a lamppost to consider this question. He was surprised at how low that one little word had brought him. He was almost sick with love for her. Didn't she know that? Had he not already been more than patient?

He knew that her father had been right in letting her go off to Germany. She had needed time to recover from the shock of witnessing her beau Trevor Martland's death last year. And he, Charles, had needed time to sort through his own guilt over Trevor's death. He still wondered, in darker moments, whether he could have done something more to save Trevor, whether in some black corner of his soul he had wanted Trevor out of the way so that the path to Maggie's heart would be unobstructed. But he always came back to one hard fact in the end: Trevor had been cruelly torn from this world. And his soul, Charles hoped, had found rest in the loving arms of his Saviour. But his claims on those still living in this world had died with him.

Charles had stoically endured, therefore, almost a year being parted from Maggie while she sampled the banquet of study offered at Tübingen and Berlin and he remained dutifully at home. Just give me this one year, she had said, and I will follow you to Timbuktu, if necessary. Well, she had had her year. And it seemed only to pour gasoline on the fire. She went on and on about this fellow Max Planck in Berlin whose impenetrable physics lectures she longed to understand fully. She talked about cathode rays, Braun tubes and the "inner universe of matter" and almost nothing about the wedding at Christmas they had talked of once they returned to Winnipeg. She said she loved him. And in every precious unchaperoned moment they had, she had been by turns sweet and yielding and so hot-blooded that he wondered if he would be able to govern himself. Why would she not put an end to his misery and name the day?

These thoughts put him into a state of, almost, somnambulism. The dray horse pulling a wagon steadily by; a man standing over by their bicycles, whose clothing suggested the alpine mountaineer rather than the tweedy Highland tourist; a pigeon alighting on the bollard across the street. All were present to his mind but did not penetrate the dark cloud enveloping it. *Get going, now. Time to make that adjustment. Stop moping; it won't help.* As he moved slowly toward the bicycles, the alpine man caught sight of him, then turned on his heel and walked briskly off down a side street and the pigeon, with a loud flourish of wings, flew off to find another perch. Charles got out a small case of wrenches from the triangular leather satchel strapped within the frame of his bike. With no enthusiasm whatsoever, he began loosening the bolt underneath Maggie's saddle, trying to banish the word "eventually" with every turn of the wrench.

9.

After tea, Janet insisted that she must make a formal portrait of the group to mark the beginning of their journey together. Annie lined them all up in a pleasing configuration in the High Street while Janet removed her new camera from her rucksack and assembled a portable tripod which she carried strapped to the carrier behind her saddle. She inserted a film plate, sighted through the viewfinder and made some adjustments.

"Right. Now. Smile everyone," she said, and drew a large imaginary smile in the air with her index finger. "Steady..." She clicked the shutter button decisively and there was a whirring and resounding click from the camera as its shutter opened and closed again. Everyone cheered and clapped and they were off.

The road to Kinross began with a two-mile uphill climb, not steep, but long enough that the effort gradually sorted the group out by fitness level with the devotees of physical culture in the lead and the less fit bringing up the rear. Violet was first, smiling, determined and showing no sign of effort except a becoming rosiness of face, followed, surprisingly, by

Taplow, who had exchanged stories of undergraduate athletic pursuits with Gordon over tea. Gordon's sporting career belonged to his youth whereas Taplow was presently coach of his college's rowing team and regularly took to the oars with them. He kept up a steady pedalling cadence regardless of the steepness of the climb. Janet and Maggie came next, riding almost abreast and Charles struggled to keep up with them. Annie and Gordon trailed behind this middle group by about twenty feet. It was pretty clear that Annie was capable of riding up with her sister, but she hung back with Gordon, who had begun to labour slightly, his handlebars swaying with the effort of every pump of his legs.

"That's the spirit, Mr. Pollack. If you keep this up, you'll be riding in the lead by tomorrow."

"That's hard to believe, Miss Gairdner. I could do with an extra set of lungs at this point. But I do appreciate your belief in my powers."

"Not at all. You're doing really well."

Charles heard Maggie broaching the subject of Taplow with Janet and he pulled abreast of them so that he could hear better.

"I must say," Maggie said, "I was quite surprised that you didn't suggest that Mr. Taplow might be more comfortable joining some other party."

"Well," Janet said, "we may yet wish that I had done so." She looked ahead to confirm that Taplow was out of earshot. "But we did rather see it from his point of view. He came all the way up here only to be disappointed about his tour. And it would probably have taken him a couple of days to arrange something else. And—well—does Christ not say we must love our enemies?"

"He does, indeed. But is it really that bad between you?" Charles said.

"Well, our St. Catherine's manuscript and also the fragment of Mark's gospel that we bought last year both support Mr. Renshaw's contention that the last twelve verses of Mark are not original."

"And Taplow differs from Renshaw?" Maggie said.

"Oh yes. Taplow's theory holds that the twelve verses somehow got separated from the original version and that they were then restored by a later editor somewhat dressed up and with emendations. That's how he explains the differences in style between the last twelve verses and the style of Greek found in the rest of Mark."

"It's all fascinating, and I learned a lot from the lectures I attended in Berlin," Charles said. "But what are the people in the pews going to think of all this? I'll bet ninety-five percent of my congregation thinks that every word of the gospels comes directly from the mouth of God without any intermediary. That's what our catechism says, after all. What are they going to think when I tell them that the last part of Mark may have been tacked on by some scribe feeling creative on a slow day at the scriptorium?

"I can see your concern," Janet said. "Ordinary folk are not used to the idea that God's word did not come directly to us. That those who knew Christ in the flesh and heard his preaching remembered what they heard and that later these thoughts were written down. So his words have come to us by human agency. But I don't believe any less that God was present, moving the hands of the great evangelists. I think there is nothing to fear in learning as much as we can about the fine details of that process."

"Even if the fine details include apparent mistakes?"

"Yes, even so—and I grant that there is much we still don't understand. But scribes made copying errors. Editors made insertions that were not in the text being copied. These things happened and cannot be wished away. But Annie and I truly feel that God is working through us, just as he worked through Paul or John or Mark."

"All well and good. Let's just hope that he's working through me, too, when I give those lectures at the YMCA that I've agreed to when I get home."

Janet laughed. "I've no doubt of it at all, Charles. No doubt at all."

The terrain was now flat and rolled by as if unwound from an unseen but endless spool. The group revelled in the fact that the sun had not abandoned them and that the wind was just high enough to keep them cool. The road was easier after Loftheads and was agreeably pastoral, though they passed through several grimy industrial towns—Cowden-beath, Kelty, and Blairadam. After a couple of hours, they were approaching Loch Leven to the northeast. Janet called out to Violet and Taplow to stop and gathered the party for a conference by the side of the road.

"Well," she said, pulling her watch out of her hip pocket. "Almost one-thirty. Now, we have the wherewithal for a picnic lunch. We could find a suitable park in Kinross or we could look for a path to the loch. What does everyone think?"

The loch, everyone said. Maps were pulled from saddle-bags and spread wide across handlebars.

"Look, here," Gordon said, pointing to a place on his crisp new ordnance survey map. "There's a road going east at Gairneybridge that crosses the railway tracks and heads toward the loch. And after Vane Farm there seems to be a path leading to the water."

They crowded around, peering over his shoulder. "Oh, that will do splendidly," said Annie. "It's about a mile out of our way, but it will be well worth it since the weather is so fine."

They returned to the road with thoughts of food, rest and scenery pushing them onward. About a quarter mile before their turnoff for Vane Farm, they encountered Ben Riddoch by the side of the road. He had his sleeves rolled up and a small tool and patching kit lying open as he worked on the front tire of his bicycle.

"Hello, Ben. What have you got there?" Charles said.

"Charles. Hello." Ben acknowledged the rest of the party with a wave. "Afternoon ladies. Lovely day for a puncture, isn't it?"

"Do you need some help?" Charles said.

"No. No. Just about done, thanks. It's the curse of buying second-hand. These tires have been to more places than Marco Polo."

Charles looked in Janet's direction, trying to read her expression, and then turned back to Ben. "Tell you what. We're stopping for lunch up the way. Why don't you join us?"

Ben gave a quick glance at rest of the company and said, "Oh, I don't think so, Charles. You don't want to be—"

"Yes, please do join us Mr. Riddoch. Em, I mean, Ben," Janet said. "We've bought more food than we need. An extra person at the table would help us to lighten our load."

Taplow's jaw muscles tightened, and Gordon looked a bit disconcerted. But Violet smiled. "I—I'm sure we have plenty, Mr. Riddoch. We went rather overboard at the confectioners," she said.

Ben laughed. "Well, if it's an appetite you need, I'm your man. Thank you. That's very kind of you all. I'll add my ham roll and milk soda to the feast."

Retreating glaciers scraped out a broad and shallow valley between the Cleish Hills to the southwest, the Ochils to the northwest and the Lomond Hills to the northeast.

Loch Leven nestled in this sandstone basin. Once they reached the southern shore of the loch, Taplow and Charles scouted out a nice flat place in a meadow halfway up the hill above the water. It was probably a meadow owned by the proprietor of Vane Farm, but everyone felt there could be no possible objection to a respectable party of travellers looking for a pretty place with a high prospect to rest and drink in the beauty of the loch. In no time several rubberized canvas capes were spread on the grass for a tablecloth and the sandwiches, sausages, carrots, fruit, cheese and pastries, whose weight had been equitably distributed among all the riders, were produced from various saddlebags and carriers. Annie pulled out two small spirit lamps and two compact kettles and asked Ben to go down to the lochside and get some water for tea.

"I may need some help in knowing where to draw from," he said, taking the kettles. "Perhaps Vi could come with me?"

Violet looked a bit alarmed. "Oh, I'm sure that you… well, em…" She looked over at Annie.

"We do need decent water. We don't want to be chewing our tea," Annie said. "Perhaps you could assist Mr. Riddoch?"

"Well, I don't see…that is, yes, certainly, Mr. Riddoch."

Ben smiled a smile of sweet innocence and gestured for her to go ahead of him. Violet took off her hat and removed her jacket and with a look of slight concern flashed to Annie, she led the way down the meadow.

10.

When Violet and Ben got to the shore of the loch, after following a path down from the road, they found that the shoreline was not well suited to drawing water. There were mud flats for at least fifty yards before deeper water could be accessed.

"Strewth, I'll have to wade out in mud up to my knees," Ben said.

"Oh, well, no. That is, I don't think that's a very good idea, Mr. Riddoch."

"It's Ben. And why isn't it a good idea?"

"Because you'll just stir up the mud and—er—whatever is in the mud. I wouldn't doubt that the cattle from the local farms are watered here and I know that waterfowl are here in abundance."

"Ah. I see. Well, I'd hate to come back to the picnic empty-handed."

She shielded her eyes from the sun and scanned the landscape to the east. "If our map is correct, the mouth of the River Leven is just over there about 500 yards. It's now a canal."

"Excellent. So that's where the water enters the loch?"

"No, no. That's where the water leaves the loch and drains down the Leven and into the Firth of Forth. That will be the sluice house over there. If you'll just come this way, Mr. Riddoch, I think we'll get the cleanest water in the inlet to the sluice where it's deeper."

"It's Ben."

She was already ten feet ahead of him, striding toward the sluice house at the inlet of the canal. He had to rush to catch up. "You seem to know a lot about this sort of thing, Vi."

"Well, the drainage of Loch Leven is probably the most famous agricultural reclamation project in Scotland. You see, they simultaneously increased the amount of arable land and provided a consistent water supply to the mills downstream by reducing the level of the loch by several feet, digging a deeper outlet and adding a control structure—" She paused mid-flight to look at him. "I—If you don't mind my saying so, Mr. Riddoch, you're looking at me in a rather peculiar way."

"Sorry, Vi! I've just never met a girl who knows the things you appear to know."

"Well, it's just that—Oh! I suppose you think that it's unseemly for a woman to take an interest in agricultural matters. I hear that from most—"

"No. No! I think it's magnificent—"

"Frankly, I would consider myself to be most irresponsible if I did not take an interest in matters that affect my farming. What? I'm sorry, I didn't catch—?"

"Magnificent. You. I think it's wonderful to meet someone who's knowledgeable in just the areas where I'm deficient."

"Oh, well, um…really?"

"Yes. Really. Say, I don't suppose you know anything

about the Crofters' Holding Act of 1886?" .

"Of course. I've got a copy in my study at home and my copy of the Napier Report is also very well thumbed, I can tell you."

Violet's exposition of the Crofter's Holding Act and of land reform in general lasted well beyond the drawing of the water near the sluice house and its conveyance back up to the picnic site. During lunch Ben peppered her with questions between mouthfuls, and took copious notes in a small ring-bound notebook.

"Look at them," Charles said to Maggie. "They've barely come up for air."

"Yes, I don't think Ben often finds himself in the role of student, sitting at the knee of wisdom."

"He doesn't look at all unhappy. Let's investigate the rest of the meadow, shall we?" He untangled his long legs from their cross-legged sitting position, rose up and stretched. The rest were still splayed out in various attitudes of relaxation, storing up energy for the afternoon ride. Charles and Maggie walked up the meadow until they were over the brow of the hill and out of sight of the other picnickers. He took her hand and gently pulled her around to face him. She was ready for a kiss, but instead he held her a little away from him.

"Is something wrong?" she asked.

"I want to talk to you. I want to have the conversation we've been avoiding since Germany."

"Charles—dear—I don't know if this is the time."

"This is exactly the time. It can't wait any longer. In fact, I can't wait any longer. Darling girl, don't you want to marry me? I thought you wanted this as much as I do. But every time I try to get an actual date out of you, you change the subject or tell me that there's time enough to talk about that later."

"That's not fair, Charles. You know that I've been preoccupied with my studies and trying to find a practical way forward. If you'll only be patient a while."

"I've been nothing but patient." He broke off and rubbed the back of his neck. "Maggie, men and women who love each other get married. Why is that notion so difficult? To me it seems simple."

"Simple! Oh yes, it'll be simple for you, all right. Things falling nicely into place. Your life will expand to include me and our children. But mine will shrink."

"It needn't be that way at all. You can find many outlets for your talents. You have so many. There's the church—"

"Really, Charles? Do there seem to be so many outlets for my talents? I see only the ones that are sanctioned by propriety. Only the ones sanctioned by my husband. Once we're married, I'll lose whatever ability I had to choose for myself alone."

He was wounded. "I thought that we were going to build a life together. Can't you see any fulfillment in that?"

"Of course!" She took his face in her hands. "I love you so desperately. I want us to be together. I'm just afraid that I will make the worst wife for you—make you and myself miserable—unless I can somehow pursue my own way at the same time."

"Wait…! This has something to do with Trevor, doesn't it?"

"What do you mean?"

"You think you have to somehow make up to him for what he's lost by dying. There's some notion you have of living *for* him. But you have to let him go and live for yourself. Don't you see that?"

"But that's exactly what I'm trying to do! When Trevor died I did feel guilty that I was alive and he was dead. And that I was never in love with him the way I am with you. But what I've come to realize these last few months is that he'd want me to grab life with both of my hands."

"Well, let's get down to specifics, then. No more beating around the bush. What is it you want to grab?"

She took a step backward and set her feet firmly. "I want to continue my studies after we're married. I want to work on improving my mathematics and then I want to study physics at the university."

Charles was almost struck dumb. "B...but what about, um, babies? How will you—"

"There's a woman named Madame Curie in Paris. She's a physicist and so is her husband. They have a lab together and she has a child. They manage somehow and so can we! I'll study when the baby is sleeping and we'll have to hire a maid to help me. It can work, Charles. I know it can."

"You two?" A shout from below, from the picnic. "Halloo? Maggie? Charles? We're packing up now." It was Janet's voice, all business. "We should get back on the road if we're to reach the inn by seven."

She kissed him hard, pulled back and laid her finger on his lips. "Our marriage can't be the same as our parents' was, Charles. We need to be a little bit brave and not care so much about what other people think. As long as we know what's right for ourselves. I'll only be able to find that courage if you believe in me, if you support me."

"Haven't I always supported you? But this is a lot to take in. What about the church and my work?"

Janet appeared over the brow of the hill and they had to break off and paste smiles on their faces. But Charles was relieved to have an excuse to end the conversation. Maggie had put him on the spot, testing his love, he thought, unreasonably. He wasn't entirely comfortable with the direction she was tugging him in. Didn't he have some say in these matters? Most men would simply lay down the law and that would be that. But he had seen that defiant set of her chin; she was in earnest and laying down laws had never been their way of being together.

11.

The rest of the ride from Kinross to the inn at Aberargie passed happily as the level road passed through the town of Milnathort and the fields swept away to right and left until they met the low hills of the Ochils to the northwest and the Lomond Hills to the east. After Glenfarg, they descended in a long, glorious freewheel with wheat and barley fields on either side. Then the road followed the winding, stony course of the River Farg, small, dark and red-tinted with its rich organic load. The trees hugged the road on either side now, providing shade from the late afternoon sun. They reached Aberargie at about seven, a little ahead of their expected time. Ben said goodbye to them at the gate of the Ayton House Hotel and went in search of a likely farmer's field in which to make his Spartan bed.

"I hope we won't be saddled with that fellow for the rest of the journey," Taplow said as they wheeled their bicycles to a barn at the back of the hotel. "What he's spouting is uncomfortably close to sedition as far as I'm concerned."

"Oh, I don't know about that, Taplow," Charles said. "I find him quite stimulating. In fact, it's alarming how much sense he makes." He smiled and half winked at Violet, who inadvertently pushed her front wheel over her foot, when she turned to reply.

"Drat!" she said. "Well, he doesn't know much about farming, that's quite evident. But at least he's willing to learn."

"Hmphhh," Taplow said, and cast his eyes heavenward.

The Ayton House Hotel was a small, whitewashed country inn dating from the 1840s. A wing had been added since it was built but still it slept only fourteen at capacity. The late additions to the tour party had necessitated doubling up in the bedrooms and even at that the landlord had been hard-pressed to accommodate them all. Gordon was assigned a servant's quarters off the kitchen while Taplow and Charles were to share a bedroom. The women were paired in a similar fashion: Violet and Maggie in one room and the sisters in another.

Dinner was served in a small but comfortable dining room. They expected the obligatory stag's heads and plaid swags but were surprised to see French silk curtains, Turkish carpets and a surprisingly adventurous menu. It turned out that the landlord's wife was from Lyon. At Janet's request, they were all seated together at one table while the other guests sat at smaller tables around the periphery of the room. Like all the hotels that Janet had booked, the Ayton House Hotel was a temperance hotel. No alcohol was available on site for purchase, which made Taplow sniff with annoyance. But he had come prepared. He had produced a bottle of wine from his saddlebag and persuaded the girl waiting at table to open and serve it. The rest of the company declined his offer of a glass, though Gordon had looked rather longingly at the bottle. But he perked up when the serving girl came around with a jug of the local Elderflower cordial.

Once Gordon's glass had been filled with cordial, he

turned to Annie. "I saw you examining flowers in the meadow today, Miss Gairdner," Gordon said. "Are flowers a particular interest of yours?"

"Yes, indeed," Annie said. "I've collected them and pressed them since I was a child."

"I used to know the names of many of the flowers around about my home when I was a boy. Always meant to take it up seriously but—well, you know—life got busy."

"Oh, but you should. Flowers can be so consoling." She looked down at her plate. "When I'm on the hunt for a particular flower or plant, I have no worries or cares. They all seem to be left at the gate of whatever field or path I'm on."

Janet looked concerned at the melancholy tone of her sister's remark until Annie gave her a reassuring smile.

"Perhaps you could help me get started," Gordon said. "I have a small book I could use as a press."

"Of course. Mind you, Janet here prefers to immortalize flowers in photographs."

"Oh, I take the odd photograph of flowers," Janet said, "But ruins and runes and scenery are more to my taste. What about you, Mr. Taplow? Have you any hobbies?"

Taplow considered the question. "Well, you know, I find my work so absorbing that I don't really have much room for leisure pursuits. A bit of rowing, of course, a bit of shooting in season and walking in and around Cambridge. But I usually have to force myself to take some time away."

"Well," Janet said, with a wry smile, "We must consider ourselves fortunate to have your company."

Annie looked a bit alarmed but Taplow said, "Aha. Yes. I deserved that. I'm afraid pomposity is a hazard in my profession."

Janet laughed. "Well, you're not too far gone if you can recognize it in yourself."

Taplow inclined his head to her. "Thank you. I suppose I can count on you for continued assistance in the matter?"

"You can. But I expect you will return the favour."

"I am beginning to see, Mrs. Thorburn, that you and I will have a very interesting time." Taplow's smile was unexpectedly roguish.

"Really, Mr. Taplow," Annie said. "I must apologize for my sister."

"Not at all, Miss Gairdner," Taplow said. "We are rivals and cannot be otherwise. There can be no harm in acknowledging what we all know to be true."

"I'm afraid I am inclined to be straightforward," Janet said, "I feel it is the best way. If you are just as straightforward with us, we will deal well together."

Taplow raised his wine glass. "I cannot ask for fairer grounds to begin the game. *Palmam qui meruit ferat!*"

"Let *she*, who has earned it, bear the palm," Janet said teasingly, raising her water glass to him.

"Hah!" Taplow said and laughed as he raised his glass to meet hers. He took a sip and swirled it around in his mouth. "Mmm. It will serve. Now, what have you to say about my note on 1 Corinthians 34–36 in the latest issue of *Studien des Neuen Testament*?"

Janet gave a questioning glance at Annie, who nodded. "On women maintaining silence in church? We have of course read your note with great interest; however, your Cambridge colleague Mr. Renshaw's work on alternate translations of those verses seems to yield to us some very fruitful insights on—"

"Excuse me, Madame. I do beg your pardon for interrupting." It was the proprietor's wife. "But there is a telegram which has arrived for Miss Pitkeathly. I am not sure which of you ladies…?"

"I am Miss Pitkeathly," Violet said and all other conversation at the table stopped.

The woman handed the telegram to Violet, who held it in her hand and stared down at it. "I don't know…I hope nothing is amiss at home. Oh, dear. Could be that foal, I suppose."

"I'm afraid you won't know until you open it, my dear," Janet said.

Violet had lost some of her accustomed colour. With a look of determination, she slit the telegram open with her butter knife and read it. "Oh, really, this is most—I thought I was shot of— Really, it's quite vexing—"

"Has something bad happened," Maggie said.

"Oh—not really, I suppose. The cable is from *Maman*. It seems that we—she and I—are invited to Mr. and Mrs. Hart-Menzies' hunting lodge near Comrie for the weekend upcoming. A shooting party that includes—conspicuously—Mr. Dwight Cavers."

"I see. Well, we will quite understand," Annie said, "if you want to cut short your trip with us and accept the invitation."

"Of course, I won't accept!" She had regained her lost colour and then some. "*Maman*, I'm afraid, is quite keen on Mr. Cavers." She dropped her voice lower. "Or at least keen on his money. He's been insinuating himself into her good graces and obviously has enlisted the Hart-Menzies into the cause as well." She shivered suddenly.

Annie put her hand over Violet's. "You needn't go, if you don't want to. Tell your mother that we are depending on you to stay with our party and take your share in carrying our equipment. It's close enough to the truth."

Violet crumpled the telegram in her hand. "Yes. I'll send a reply in the morning. Though I doubt whether they'll stop at this. Mr. Cavers seems a rather determined person."

After dinner, Charles went for a walk by himself in the gloaming. But he was weary and could no longer put off his return to the room he was sharing with Taplow, where they were to share a bed. When he entered the room, Taplow, stripped down to his drawers and undershirt, was already under the covers and reading by the light of the coal oil lamp on the bedside table. He had claimed the side of the bed closest to the door and had left Charles with the side that abutted the wall.

"I hope you don't mind an open window, Lauchlan. I like a well-aired bedchamber."

"Er. No. Not at all. It's refreshing."

Refreshing it certainly was, and Charles got out of his clothes quickly before it got even more refreshing. He clambered awkwardly over the footboard and crawled up the bed until he reached the place where he could ease himself under the covers. Once settled, he opened his small, battered copy of the New Testament to the place he had ended his habitual reading the night before. His fingers felt the reassuring texture of the suede binding where it had been worn down to a shiny patina. After the allotted five verses, read squintingly in the low light, he closed the book and, without a night table on his side of the bed, put it gently under his pillow. He looked over at Taplow's reading material and saw an illustration with Greek letters arranged in two narrow columns.

"It must be very satisfying work to delve so deeply into the biblical texts. I took the required Greek when I studied theology, but I never developed much facility."

Taplow laid the book down on his chest. "Yes, indeed. Not everyone has the capacity to master the language; I mean, really master it so that it almost is absorbed through your skin and becomes a part of you. In my experience most divinity students study just enough to pass their exam and that's an end of it."

"Well, it's a question of where best to devote your energy, isn't it? I've always found the pastoral part of my job extremely rewarding, but demanding too. Studying and preaching are important, but I always come back to the people in the pews. What is it they need to hear from me; how can I reach them best."

Taplow looked puzzled. "But surely they must consent to be led and instructed by you. Not the other way round. Otherwise they will all too soon fall into error."

Charles laughed. "My parishioners have more often saved me from falling into error. You talk as if they are passive vessels waiting to be filled with the exalted fruits of my knowledge. I can assure you that they have minds of their own."

Taplow looked as if he had suddenly been transported to the most foreign of foreign countries. "It is perhaps well that I never took holy orders," he said. "Though my father was a parson—of the low church persuasion, I'm afraid. His was an example I never wanted to follow."

Taplow returned his gaze to his book and Charles realized the conversation was over.

12.

"'Week', 'sowp', 'saft.' Oh, and in the Orkneys, I think they say, 'bleeter' or 'skirp',"" Gordon said to Charles as they wheeled out of the village of Aberargie heading toward Perth the next morning. "Yes, we Scots have many words for rain in all its guises and intensities."

In fact, they were enveloped in a light mist and the tops of the hills had disappeared from view. With yesterday's sun just a memory, it seemed to Charles that no weather of any kind stayed for long here.

"Never mind," he said to Gordon. "Two miles from here they might be enjoying tropical breezes, for all we know."

Gordon laughed. "Yes. Let's hope that's the direction we're going."

When they came down the hill and into Perth after about an hour of riding, however, the mist had coalesced into a spitter of rain. It settled lightly on the surface of their clothes. Charles was for breaking out his waterproof cape.

"It's hardly even a mist, Charles," Annie said. "Not worth the bother." Charles wiped his face with his handkerchief and soldiered on, too.

Perth looked inviting even in the rain and they could not resist a small detour to investigate. They pedalled down the High Street toward the dark, rushing breadth of the River Tay but the lowering mists foiled Janet's attempt to take a photograph of the beautiful tapering spire of St. Matthew's Church with Smeaton's famous bridge in the background. As they rode down Atholl Street on their way to Dunkeld Road, Charles looked wistfully at the people sipping tea in the warm amber light of a café window.

Although at first he had resisted pressing his most tender parts into the hard saddle of his bicycle, the pain and stiffness had soon ebbed away and he was riding strongly today, well able to keep up even to Violet, though she still maintained the lead. Where possible, he and Maggie rode abreast, but they did not say much. The parting words of their conversation yesterday hung between them. It was true. He had been assuming that their marriage would fall into the familiar pattern set by their parents. He had thought that after Maggie had sown the female equivalent of her wild oats during her year in Germany, she would be happy to settle into an uncomplicated life with him, taking care of the house, and the children when they came along, and that she would be a partner with him in building up his church and in everything God was leading them to do. If she wanted to follow this path of her own, how would that fit within the tight confines of his ministerial calling? As it was, he was asking his congregation to deal with a great many new ideas, modern ones, necessary ones. What would they make of an unconventional wife?

These were not comfortable thoughts but the road to Dunkeld was soothing in its slow relatively flat terrain traversing through the towns of Bankfoot and Waterloo with low, pastured hills on either side. Then the road itself became more hilly and treed as they began passing through the beautiful forests belonging to the Duke of Atholl. A short distance ahead they would see Birnam whose woods were so famed in *Macbeth*, and also said to be the dividing line between the Lowlands and the Highlands.

Violet had ridden ahead of them by about twenty yards and disappeared over the brow of a hill. When they crested the hill themselves, they could see that it was a long, steep and winding drop to the valley below. Violet was freewheeling round the curve ahead, the wind raking back wisps of her hair. Charles and Maggie went back to single file. He was backpedalling to engage his brakes and was wishing Violet would use hers a little more. As they rounded the next curve, she continued to gain speed. *Blast the girl.* He looked back at Maggie and saw a mirror of his own concern.

"Violet! Slow down!"

"Can't! Something's wrong—"

He eased up on his own brakes and sped up as much as he could without totally losing control, but he was already too far behind to overtake her. Then he saw someone standing in the middle of the road below. *Oh Lord, it's Ben!*

"Look out! Can't stop!" the girl screamed.

Whether Violet ran him down, or he tried to catch her as she went by, Charles couldn't say. But Ben somehow grabbed onto the back of her carrier and held on, dragging his weight behind to slow her down while trying to keep the bike upright, desperate for any purchase, scrabbling and scraping, now on his feet, now on his knees on the wet pavement, the strange two-person creature they made swaying and swerving wildly. By some miracle they made the curve as the road swept under a railway bridge at the bottom of the hill. But not the curve on the other side. They flew off the edge of the road, disappearing completely from view down the slope.

13.

Charles hit his brakes hard, the back wheel of his bicycle skidding out sideways behind him as he came to a stop at the point where Violet and Ben had gone over. Maggie was right behind him. They half ran and half slid down the bracken-covered embankment till they reached the bottom. There Violet, the bicycle and Ben lay all tangled up together in a heap. Maggie went to Violet, Charles to Ben.

Violet was just raising herself to a sitting position. "Are you all right!" Maggie said. "Here, let me look at you." She began at once to run her hands along Violet's arms and legs. "Does that hurt?"

"No, I don't think so."

"That?"

"No...no. I'm all right, I think."

"You could have been killed!"

"Stupid of me. I couldn't seem to work my brakes. My pedals were going backwards but nothing was happening. And then Ben was there— If he hadn't grabbed hold of me, I don't know what..."

"You heard her, Charles. You are my witness." Ben

grimaced as he sat up.

"What do you mean?" Charles said.

"I had to have her run me down before she would call me Ben." He looked over, suddenly concerned. "Are you all right, Vi? Are you hurt?"

"Oh, Ben. I'm so awfully sorry! But I did shout for you to get out of the way."

"Ach, never mind. I knew six miserable years at school as a rugby forward would be useful for something."

At that point the rest of them came sliding and shoving down the embankment together, shouting. In a minute they were able to conclude that Violet was amazingly unscathed; a few scratches to her face, some tenderness in one hip but otherwise miraculously unharmed.

"What a relief!" Janet said. "It's a miracle you didn't hit any trees on the way down."

"Rather," Violet said, "But—oh Janet—your poor new bicycle." She pointed at the bicycle, which had clearly received more punishment than Violet. Its front wheel was noticeably bent.

"Never mind that. It can be repaired easily enough," Janet said. "I never would have traded bicycles with you if I had known this would happen. And what about Mr. Riddoch?"

Mr. Riddoch was in a similar state to the bicycle. His breeches were torn at both knees—the leather patches gone altogether—revealing raw, scraped and bleeding skin underneath and in places the unearthly whiteness of abraded cartilage. The middle finger of his right hand was pointing at a distinctly odd angle and now that the initial shock had worn off, that finger was causing him considerable pain. Charles helped extricate him from the bicycle and he rose gingerly to his feet.

Taplow elbowed his way to the front. "I may be of some

assistance. Show me your hand, Mr. Riddoch."

Ben was not keen on letting anyone handle his finger.

"It's all right," Taplow said. "It's probably just dislocated. Come now, let's get a look."

Ben gritted his teeth and held out the injured hand.

Taplow took a grip on Ben's wrist with his left hand and lightly encircled Ben's injured finger with his right hand. "Right, Lauchlan, will you brace Riddoch's shoulders for me? That's right, a bear hug, a good strong hold. Best if you look away, Riddoch."

Violet turned her head into Maggie's shoulder. Taplow gave a sudden firm pull on the finger.

"Arrrrgh!" Ben screamed, "Ah! Ah…ah…oh!" He looked down at his hand and saw that the finger had come back into position. "That's—well, I'll be damned. It's sorted. Thank you. Thank you very much, Taplow."

"Right. Good." Taplow said. "Now, could somebody get me two small sticks to serve as a splint? And ladies, a piece of cloth of some sort to bind them with?" In no time, the wood for the splint was found and Violet tore three small strips off her petticoat to strap the splint to Ben's finger and stabilize the finger and hand with further wrapping.

It was clear that they would not be able to repair the damaged bicycle by the roadside. Plans shifted to ways to transport Violet and the bicycle to the Ben Vrackie Inn at Moulin, near Pitlochry, their destination for the night. Since Dunkeld was only a mile away, they decided to walk there with Violet and put her and the bicycle on the train for Pitlochry. Charles and Gordon removed the deformed front wheel from the bicycle and Taplow slipped it over his shoulder. They made Gordon's bicycle into a kind of mechanical pack horse by strapping the damaged bicycle onto it and Charles, Taplow and Gordon took turns pushing this contraption along. At Dunkeld Station they left a rather forlorn looking Violet, with the ruined bicycle, to wait for the afternoon train and, reluctantly, continued on their way. The weather had deteriorated, with pelting rain heavy enough to convince even Janet and Annie to pull on their waterproofs and as they turned onto the Pitlochry Road they faced into a headwind. Ben had declined to go with Violet on the train, saying that he was fine and could ride. But Charles thought it more likely that Ben could not spare the money for the fare. Though they had a first aid kit, Ben's knees had been left open to the air, since he would have to flex them so much while riding that bandages were bound to chafe and make things worse. And for the same reason, Ben had decided not to change into his other pair of trousers. Looking at Ben, Charles winced in sympathy and persuaded him to ride at the back of the pack for maximum wind protection. But even so, Ben pushed on doggedly, rain dripping from the peak of his cap his injured finger held straight over the handlebars, the frayed knees of his breeches exposing the raw flesh beneath.

Tourists flocked to Pitlochry seeking the healing waters of its large hydro resort and sportsmen of all types convened in the vast halls of the Pitlochry Hotel. But the sisters were allergic to sportsmen and had booked their party instead into the small but ancient Ben Vrackie Inn at Moulin, a sleepy village a mile to the north of Pitlochry. The old Inn was a welcome sight when they pulled into its yard just after seven. Violet met them at the desk.

"Thank goodness, you've finally arrived." She surveyed the party, all of whom were impersonating drowned rats. She frowned. "Where's Ben?"

Charles looked around and realized that Ben must have silently gone off in search of a place to camp for the night.

"Oh—Charles?" Maggie said.

Charles looked at Violet and then at the equal distress in Maggie's eyes. Without another word he put his waterproof cape back on and set out again. He found Ben crouched under a tree in a corner of the graveyard belonging to the church across the road from the hotel. He was trying to light his spirit lamp but his hands were shaking from the cold and his splinted finger wouldn't cooperate. Ben put up a token resistance to the idea of sharing Charles's room at the hotel, but he was too banged-up and cold to persist. Once in the room, a rather small one but warm and comfortable, Ben sat on the bed and exhaled a sigh of pure relief.

"I'll see if I can get us some tea from the kitchen. And I'll ask the landlady for some bandaging for your knees." Charles said, and made for the door.

"Charles, hold on a moment."

"Yes?"

"Did you get a look at the chain on Vi's bicycle?"

"Yes. The chain was broken. That's why her brakes failed. She couldn't activate them with a broken chain."

"Yes, but did you look at the break?"

"No. Not that closely. Why?"

"The chain didn't fail at the join between links as you'd expect. A link was partially cut through with a hacksaw."

14.

The next morning before breakfast, Charles and Ben made their way to the storage room at the back of the inn where the bicycles had been stowed for the night. Charles moved the damaged bicycle out into the yard so that he could see clearly. He removed the chain guard then took out a handkerchief and laid first one end of the broken chain and then the other on the handkerchief. Then he fit the broken ends together.

"Well?" Ben said. "What do you think?"

Charles did not answer right away. He fit the ends of the chain together again. "I see what you mean. A very straight, regular cut to a point between half and three quarters of the way down the width of the link. And then a jagged edge—presumably where the link weakened and finally broke through."

"Someone did this deliberately. Someone who wanted to hurt Vi."

"It certainly looks suspicious. But it's not a very efficient way to hurt someone. The chain could just as easily have come apart on a level stretch."

"But much more likely on a hill. Don't you see? The chain would have been stressed while pedalling up the hills. Then backpedalling on a steep downhill to engage the brakes could have finally forced the link to break. You couldn't be sure, but it would more likely happen on a hill. And this is Scotland, not your Canadian prairies."

"But who would do this? I suppose it's the sort of thing a young hooligan would do for a prank. Someone who wouldn't necessarily realize how dangerous it could be."

"I doubt that. I think this is too nasty a piece of work for some local plowboy full of beer and empty of sense. Doesn't this seem to you like the sort of thing a rejected suitor might pull—especially the kind of man who has no real sense of fellow feeling. Like that fellow Dwight Cavers. You've heard the way Vi talks about him. There's something not right there. Something not right at all."

"Has she told you about Cavers, then?"

"Yes! He's everything she despises—no feeling for the land or the people here. And, though she's made her feelings clear, he continues to pursue her."

"But—look— if Cavers is trying to persuade Violet to marry him, why would he deliberately cause an accident in which she might be killed or badly injured? It just doesn't—"

"But his charm has failed, hasn't it? She's not interested. Now he's trying to frighten her into marrying him. Expect him to turn up at any minute like a white knight on a charger. He'll beat his chest and tell her that no harm could possibly come to her while he's around. She just might be so upset that she'll fall for it—and for him."

Ben was looking a little wild-eyed at this point and Charles was more than a little dubious about his theory. Still, Ben's assessment, though improbable, was at least clever. "All right. All right. I grant you that something is funny about this whole business. But all we have right now is a bicycle chain that might have been tampered with. We need to alert the police and we need to gather some facts. Agreed?"

Ben had calmed down a little. "Agreed."

"Right. Here's how I think we should proceed." Charles laid out a plan with which Ben largely concurred and they began making their way toward breakfast. But before they entered the dining room, Ben pulled Charles aside.

"But, Charles. The police aren't likely going to take this very seriously. What if he—or whoever it is—tries again? I think I should ride with you now. Stay close. What do you think?"

"Good idea." He was humouring Ben, of course. It seemed completely far-fetched that Dwight Cavers had gone to the trouble of sabotaging Violet's bicycle. And yet. What if it wasn't just one of the local hooligans out to make mischief?

Reactions around the breakfast table were mixed:

Violet: "Oh, surely not? Are you quite sure? I could have broken the chain myself, you know."

Taplow: "Don't you think you're overreacting, Lauchlan?"

Janet: "Of course he's not. We must get to the bottom of this."

Annie: "But who would do such a thing? It's monstrous."

Maggie: "How do you suppose a person like that thinks?"

Gordon: "If it's true, this is a serious offence under the law."

Charles and Ben described the length and dimensions of the cut in the chain link. They debated possible explanations. The link came defective from the factory. But then, Gordon said, the technician who readied the bicycle for the trip last week would have noticed it. Then, the link could have had some internal weakness that caused it to fail, said Janet. No, Ben said. If the metal was faulty, the edges of the broken pieces would have been irregular, not straight.

"But, wait a moment," Janet said. "The night before the accident, Violet and I arranged to exchange bicycles the next day."

"Yes, that's right," Violet said. "I ride a chainless and I wanted to try Janet's new bicycle to see what the fuss over chains is all about."

Charles drew his brows together. "Yes. We've been thinking about that too. Then how did the fellow know which bicycle to fiddle with?"

"If it was just some local idiot, perhaps he didn't really care which bicycle he chose." Taplow said. "He grabbed the nearest chained model because it was the easiest to damage without anyone noticing. And" —His face registered distaste— "perhaps there was an added *frisson* to choosing a ladies' machine."

"So it was just Violet's rotten luck to have been riding that particular model the next day," Maggie said. "Unless—" She stopped to think.

"Unless what?" Charles said.

"Unless someone overheard the conversation between Violet and Janet and knew that they would be switching bicycles the next day."

"Oh, but that's impossible," Janet said. "Violet and I were, well, sharing a sink while we discussed the matter."

"Yes, that's right," Violet said, "Janet made a rota, and she and I were last. We were getting ready for bed. There was no one else in the room."

"So unless our friend had his ear to the door" —here the female members of the group screwed up their faces— "or was hanging from a tree branch outside the window," Charles said, "he couldn't have known about the exchange of bicycles."

"So then…" Maggie stared into the distance as she always did when thinking hard. "That would tend to support Mr. Taplow's conclusion that the tamperer just chose a bicycle at random."

"Or…" Charles hesitated before he spoke. "Or the fellow intended to harm Janet and not Violet."

"That's preposterous!" Janet said.

"Lauchlan's right, Mrs. Thorburn," Taplow said. "Speaking logically, that must be admitted as a possibility." Then he assumed a look of stagey evil. "By Jove, I suppose I'd better prepare my oddments for the inevitable hacksaw search."

"Hardly a joking matter, Mr. Taplow," Janet said with a tart expression. "And besides, I would have expected a more direct method from you."

When Charles and a still unsure and self-conscious Violet reported the crime at the Pitlochry police station later that morning, Gordon's prediction proved to be accurate. The lone sergeant on duty informed them that due to the seriousness of the alleged crime, attempted assault, possibly attempted aggravated assault, the County Police in Perth would have to deal with it. Having, with great difficulty, persuaded Ben, who still harboured dark suspicions of Dwight Cavers, to stay in Pitlochry and see to the repair of Janet's bicycle, Charles and Violet took the train down to Perth, where they spent two hours giving statements to Inspector Hector Storrs.

Storrs, a fifty-ish man, lean, moustachioed and dressed in a slightly rumpled grey suit, ushered them into his small cubbyhole of an office.

"Now then, Miss Pitkeathly, take a seat here—oh—ah, let me just remove my satchel…Aye, there now." Storrs held the chair in front of his desk while she seated herself and motioned to Charles to sit in the other chair. "There, good. Em, would you care for some tea?"

Without waiting for them to reply, Storrs leaned out of his office door. "Seivright? Get us some tea, will you? Och, never mind what you're doing. Yes, that's right, three cups, please."

Storrs returned to his desk, sat down, flipped open the brass inkwell in front of him, dipped his pen in, and steadied it above a fresh sheet of paper. "I've had a telephone call from Sergeant Curran at Pitlochry giving me the bare bones of the incident. He concurred with your assessment that the bicycle chain had been tampered with. Very concerning, I must say. Now, suppose you start at the beginning, Mr. Lauchlan. What exactly occurred while you were cycling yesterday?"

Charles described the accident and the subsequent discovery of the hacksawed link in the chain of the bicycle that Violet had been riding. He was interrupted by Constable Seivright, who knocked on the doorframe and entered with a tea tray containing two heavy mugs, slightly chipped, and one delicate cup bearing a likeness of Queen Victoria and her much lamented husband. It was clear from the constable's anxious demeanour, as he carefully set this cup in front of Violet, that tea was not often served to members of the public there on police business. Once they were settled with their tea, Storrs returned to the matter at hand.

"You see, Mr. Lauchlan, what we have to do to get a conviction in cases like this is to prove, firstly, that the perpetrator actually tampered with the bicycle chain, and, secondly, that when he did so, he intended to inflict grievous harm on Miss Pitkeathly here."

Violet stirred her cup, looking a mixture of vexed and amused. Up until then Storrs had directed his attention only at Charles.

"Now," Storrs continued, "you say none of you actually saw anyone suspicious at your hotel in Aberargie Tuesday night or Wednesday morning before you set out?"

Charles began to speak, but Violet broke in. "That's right, Inspector. Our rooms all faced the front of the inn, except for Mr. Pollack's, and he didn't have a window. So none of us had a view of the barn where the bicycles were kept and I'm not even sure it was locked for the night. In any case, it was open when we went to get the bicycles that morning. The fellow could simply have got to the bicycles before us."

"And, Miss Pitkeathly, you say that you can't think of anyone who might wish to harm you?"

"No, Inspector. I believe, that is, I think, I'm quite well regarded on the whole."

"There's something else that's a bit odd, Inspector," Charles said. "The bicycle Miss Pitkeathly was riding wasn't her own. She and Mrs. Thorburn had arranged to exchange bicycles the night before."

Violet described how the arrangement had been made with Janet while they were preparing for bed at the Aberargie Inn.

"So then, Miss Pitkeathly, you're quite certain that no one was likely to have overheard this conversation while you were—em—attending to your ablutions?"

"It seems very unlikely, Inspector. But it seems equally unlikely that anyone would wish to harm Janet."

Storrs pulled out a sheet from the file folder on his desk. "I see that Mrs. Thorburn and her sister are rather prominent Edinburgh folk." He removed his pince-nez spectacles. "And involved in university pursuits, too?" His eyebrows lifted.

"Yes, indeed, Inspector," Charles said.

"That is a bit…out of the ordinary, but not usually an incitement to violence." The inspector fished around in the pages on his file. "Well now—em—a Mr. Riddoch, who I believe is known to you, told Sergeant Curran that we ought to be making inquiries about a Mr. Dwight Cavers, who I believe is also known to you?"

"Oh, for heaven's—Yes, I know Mr. Cavers, but this is really quite ridiculous. Mr. Riddoch is…he's…well, rather sweet, really, but—"

"Mr. Riddoch, as you know, Inspector," Charles said, "saved Miss Pitkeathly from almost certain injury yesterday. Understandably, he is very zealous after her welfare. And perhaps lacking anyone else to blame, has fastened a little too readily on Mr. Cavers."

"I have danced with Mr. Cavers a number of times in London. And attended several balls and parties where he was present, and talked with him at dinner two or three times. That is the full extent of my acquaintance with Mr. Cavers, Inspector. I…well…I rather doubt that he has made a special trip to Scotland to tamper with my bicycle chain."

The inspector smiled for the first time. "Well, Miss Pitkeathly, we generally limit our initial inquiries to people who have actually been in the country where the alleged crime took place. But I will make a note about Mr. Cavers."

The smile was fleeting. "And Mr. Riddoch, I believe," the inspector continued, "is a somewhat troublesome person. We'll be taking particular note of his activities. Take care where he is concerned, would be my advice."

"Really, Inspector," Violet said, "I am surrounded by people who think they know what is best for me. But I can assure you that I am quite capable of choosing my own friends."

Storrs was impelled backward in his chair by this volley. "Of course, Miss Pitkeathly, that is clearly your right. I'd no intention to offend you. I meant only a word of caution from one who has seen too much wickedness in this world."

Violet, somewhat mollified but still resolute said, "Thank you, Inspector. I appreciate your concern. Have you all the information you require?"

"Well, there's the matter of statements. I'm going to ask Constable Seivright to come in while we prepare written statements for you to sign. After that you are free to go. Sergeant Curran at Pitlochry has been preoccupied with a robbery investigation today. That will mean that the rest of your party will not be able to give their statements to him until tomorrow morning. Will that be convenient?"

Charles looked at Violet and then said, "I suppose it will have to be, Inspector."

"We'll also send a constable to Aberargie to make inquiries of the staff at the inn. And we'll locate and interview the other guests that were present." He took off his spectacles and rubbed his eyes. "I've no doubt that the perpetrator's actions could have resulted in very severe injury to Miss Pitkeathly. This is a matter that we take very seriously." He sighed and leaned back in his chair. "But I must caution you that even if we find the man, unless someone actually saw him lurking around the inn with a hacksaw in his hand, we are going to have great difficulty in proving the charge."

On the train back to Pitlochry, Charles kept turning the matter over in his mind, veering between two opposite conclusions: surely the accident was simply a prank gone horribly wrong; or: someone deliberately tried to hurt Violet… or Janet. If not Cavers, then who? Unwanted thoughts of what the inspector had said about Ben came to him. Ben, who had been camped out somewhere near their hotel the night before the accident. Ben, who had, conveniently, been fixing a flat tire at the bottom of the hill where Violet lost her brakes. *No. Couldn't possibly be. He's a good lad. And yet.* He wanted some kind of resolution of the issue in his own mind, for his own sense of unease. Police can be very tight-lipped about this sort of thing, he thought. And then he thought about his friend, Andrew Setter, who was now in Edinburgh.

15.

Violet and Charles did not arrive back at the inn until six o'clock in the evening, and since it had quite early in the day become apparent that they would have to stay an extra night at Moulin, some adjustments to the schedule were necessary.

Janet and Annie had telegraphed ahead to their friend Harald Dibbage, who had kindly invited the whole party to stay at his hunting lodge near Kinloch Rannoch. A return telegram from Dibbage confirmed that he would not expect them that day as originally scheduled but rather at the end of the following day. But when Charles and Violet told the sisters about the necessity of everyone giving police statements in the morning, the chance of their reaching Dibbage's estate by nightfall that day seemed remote. Guidebooks were flipped open and maps spread on the dinner table. The Loch Tummel Inn was only ten miles from Pitlochry and almost at the halfway point between Pitlochry and Dibbage's house.

"Right," Janet said. "We'll see if there are rooms available there for tomorrow night. That should be a reasonable cycle for the afternoon tomorrow and then we'll go on to Harald's the next day and have a think about the rest of the schedule when we get there."

Plans were laid over dinner as to who would give their statement to Sergeant Curran first and who would buy provisions for the day's cycling.

"I would like to give my statement last. That is, if nobody minds," Annie said.

"Why so, dear?" Janet asked, drawing her eyebrows together.

"Em, well, there's an errand I've got to do after breakfast. Just a small thing that needs attending to. I'm sure you can go before me, Janet, can't you?"

"Certainly, I can." Janet looked as if she expected further information, but Charles broke in with an announcement that he needed to go to the post office in the morning, and he was then delegated to mail letters on behalf of the group.

POST OFFICE TELEGRAPHS
34 SB 572 Pitlochry 10 Aug 1900
Andrew Setter Queens Hotel Edinburgh
Need information. Can you help? Please confirm employment Ben Riddoch at Workers' Clarion Call newspaper, Glasgow. Anyone there vouch for him? No need for alarm but want information quickly. Reply to post office Kinloch Rannoch.
Letter to follow.
Charles Lauchlan

10 August, 1900

The Hon. Hugo Trublowe MP, Holtings, Wisby le Marsh, Lincolnshire

My dear Trublowe,
*   I hope you are having a restful summer and are recharging your*

energies for the fall sitting. You will wonder at the postmark. I decided to get right away—to Scotland—as you can see. A tour of the Highlands by bicycle is proving to be most refreshing—even surprising.

Perhaps you have heard my name bandied about in connection with the election for the Millbankian Professorship. I won't deny it. Several of the leading men of the university urged me to put my name forward. Of course, I felt that it was too soon and that others stood higher in general esteem than I. However, they persisted and it would have been ungracious to refuse. Accordingly, I have been communicating with members of the university whose opinions are highly valued by their fellows. (And also by their Fellows!)

I count you among that select group, Hugo. And because of our long acquaintance, I am taking the liberty of urging on you the merits of my candidacy. I will not stoop to vulgar campaigning, unlike the ever-ingratiating Mr. Jabez Renshaw. But I do ask you to consider my standing in philological and palaeographic circles generally and among those who study New Testament manuscripts specifically. And consider, too, my two books on the travesty that is Westcott and Hort's "New Testament in the Original Greek" which—not by my own account, but by that of other eminent scholars in the field—have defended the Authorized Version, particularly as concerns the disputed last twelve verses of the Gospel of Mark—and have constituted a substantial corrective to ill-considered theories advanced by those who lack a deep understanding of the extant manuscript evidence.

If you do this—and I ask it with a sense of utmost humility—perhaps you will speak well of me should you cross paths with members of the Millbankian Board of Electors. I would consider it an honour to be so well regarded by a man of your sterling qualities. Believe me, my dear Hugo,

Yours truly,
A. W. Taplow

Aug. 10, 1900

Rev. Dr. James C. Skene
154 Balmoral Street,
Winnipeg, Manitoba, Canada

Dearest Father,

    I'm writing in the sitting room of the Ben Vrackie Inn, near Pitlochry. It is more than 200 years old but very comfortable and welcoming for all that, which is lucky because we have had to stay an extra day. There was an accident involving one of our members, Violet Pitkeathly. She lost her brakes on a hill and would have crashed if a young man hadn't broken her momentum by holding onto her bicycle and using his weight to slow her down. And now it turns out that someone tampered with Violet's chain beforehand, causing it to break on the hill!

    So, we've been dealing with the local police today. Charles and I get the distinct impression that the police think the perpetrator is likely just a local boy who had no idea of the consequences of his act. That's probably what happened but just in case, we're on the lookout. I'm finding those lectures in Tübingen on exceptional mental states quite useful.

    But I'm avoiding your question. In reply to your last, we haven't yet set a date for the wedding. In fact, Charles is getting more than a little impatient and I suppose I can't blame him. I've gained so much strength and confidence in myself in the last year and so many doors in the world of science have opened up for me, particularly in physics. And I feel that I could be useful by pursuing physics—useful to humanity—if that doesn't sound too pompous. Each time I think about coming home and giving all that up, I feel such frustration and anger. But then Charles is so wonderful and understanding and I do love him so very much. I simply can't become one of those vestal virgins of science that I met occasionally at Tübingen and in Berlin. Assisting in laboratories run by professors. Working away quiet as mice, afraid that too much notice might be taken of them and cause them to lose their little toehold. One or two had published work in their own name, though not as senior authors, and two had actual positions in the university, but without pay! None were married except one and she had been widowed.

Oh father. If you could only see Fraulein Sonnenberger. She can't afford to eat properly and the cuffs of her shirtwaist have been turned more than once. But all she can talk about is the work, just the work, and when she does there's such a light in her eyes. That part is inspiring. But to give up Charles and home and children for that? No. That is not what I want either. Is it so wrong of me to want to have both?

Oh dear. I have written rather more than I intended and can only trust that you still love me even though I am apparently becoming a notorious blue stocking. Please tell me that you do!

Your loving daughter,
Maggie

10 August, 1900

2nd Lieutenant James R. Pollack
Highland Light Infantry
Maryhill Barracks, Glasgow

My Dear Jamie,

Day 3 of our trip and it has already been quite an experience. You and Christiane and Robert were right, of course. I badly needed a break and I am certainly getting it! I can still ride a bicycle but it seems to require twice the effort it did when I was your age. And it's so long since I had to muck in with new people, I wondered how I might fare. But everyone is very congenial and they've made me feel welcome. Mrs. Thorburn is a most impressive woman, almost too impressive. She's very strong on logistics and planning. (Perhaps you should recruit her!). She and her sister have rather extreme views—votes for women and that sort of thing. But both are good churchwomen, which is reassuring. And also Mrs. Thorburn is kind and can both make a joke and take a joke, if you know what I mean. Miss Gairdner, her sister, is of a rather softer nature, but just as intelligent. She knows a great deal about the natural world and we share an interest in wild flowers.

I'm enjoying myself more than—well, really, more than I can remember since your mother was alive. But even here I can't totally get away from the law. Someone played a stupid and harmful prank on one of our members, so we've been dealing with the police today and tomorrow and this will set us behind two days in our itinerary. Now we don't expect to reach Mr. Dibbage's until the day after tomorrow, the 12th. You can reach me by post or telegraph at Kinloch Rannoch then.

Is there any news about when the regiment will set sail for South Africa? The War Office doesn't listen to fathers, but if I had my way, the whole damn business would be finished before you get there. Let me know as soon as you have word, as I would like to wave you off at the docks. Until then, work hard and listen to the older officers. And be careful about standing the others to drinks at the mess. One round a week is standard, but more and you'll find yourself short at the end of the month. Must close to get this in the post.

Affectionately,
Father

16.

Once Maggie had given her statement to Sergeant Curran and Charles had sent the telegram to Setter and posted the letters, they had a few hours to put in before lunch, which the group was scheduled to have in the dining room of the Fisher's Hotel, located on the Atholl Road across the street from the post office.

Maggie said, "My guidebook says there's a nice little waterfall close by. It's called the Black Spout."

"That sounds promising. Let's see."

They looked at the map and the directions to the falls and decided it would do very nicely. They could take the short leg of the circular walk and just retrace their steps to the Atholl Road and be back in time to join the group for lunch. They followed a path through the grounds of the Hydro and toward the Black Spout Wood. It was a pretty path through farmers' fields and then into deep woods and, there being no one in particular on the path, they walked companionably arm in arm or hand in hand except where the path narrowed and forced them into single file.

"What are your current thoughts about who really did the deed?" Maggie said.

"Hack-sawed Violet's bicycle, you mean? I suppose, in the absence of any evidence to the contrary, the simplest explanation is probably best. A prank gone wrong."

"Then I suppose we needn't fear another incident since we'll be leaving the area this afternoon. Still…"

"Still what?"

"Well, I was just thinking about our trusty little cycling group. We're cooperating together and making an effort to get along for the greater good of the whole party. But we don't know each other very well at all, do we?"

"Your point is?"

"Well, why, for example, did we never consider that someone in our group might have tampered with Violet's bicycle? Take Ben, for example. Wasn't it a little odd that he should be there at the bottom of the hill, fixing a flat tire? Suppose he engineered the whole thing to rescue Violet and prove himself a hero."

"Well…funny you should mention that." Charles looked a little abashed.

"What do you mean?"

"Well, that same thought occurred to me, so I just sent a telegram to Andrew to do a little checking on Ben. Confirm his employment, ask his co-workers a few questions. That sort of thing."

"But that's terrible!" Maggie said. "I like Ben and I'm sure he didn't do anything wrong! Why are people so quick to suspect someone who's a little unusual?"

"Wait. My head is spinning. Didn't you just say that we shouldn't be so trusting of people we've just met? And didn't you just cite Ben as a for instance?"

"Well…yes, but—that's not fair." She stamped her foot. "I didn't mean for you to take me so seriously!"

"Look, I don't like it any better than you do. But lay

your emotions aside and consider the possibilities. Ben's a little bit excitable and he has a kind of feverish intelligence. Suppose his fondness for Violet is just a cover. Suppose his resentment of the landed gentry has tipped over into some kind of mania? And this mania has fastened on to Violet as an exemplar of her class."

"Aha!" Maggie said, popping in front of him on the path and stopping his forward motion. "But here's the flaw. He couldn't have known that she was going to switch bicycles with Janet the next day. And!" She put her hands on her hips, triumphant. "How did he know that the chain would break on that particular hill?"

"Well. There is that." Charles took a moment to consider these things. "All right, it's explainable. That was the steepest downhill of our day's cycling, so there was a good chance of it breaking. He just stationed himself down at the bottom of the hill on the off chance. And if Janet was the real focus of his resentment, the argument still works. Janet and Annie are rich and, by his lights, who knows what vile deeds were done to workers to accrue their father's wealth. Low wages, deplorable working conditions, punishing hours."

Maggie cocked her head to the side and gave him a look. "Come on now. You don't really believe he could be that deranged, do you?"

"No, I don't. Or, I don't want to. It makes only slightly more sense than Dwight Cavers being the culprit. But isn't the fact that *someone*, some unknown person, actually did take a hacksaw to that bicycle chain just as shocking and outside the realms of our normal experience?"

"I suppose, when you put it like that, we might as well reach out and encompass all possibilities, no matter how absurd they may seem at the moment. Oh, look, there's the spout. How lovely!"

The narrow column of water cascaded down the rock face of dark basalt from a height some seventy feet above the forest floor, casting a light mist over the bracken and gnarled bushes that clung to the cliff side, before subsiding into a deep pool at the base of the cliff.

"Yes. Wonderful. Let's get closer. Wait. Isn't that Annie up ahead?"

"Yes, I think so," Maggie said, craning her neck to see more clearly. "But who is she with? A man, but he's not one of ours."

Charles started to move toward the falls, but Maggie caught his arm. "Hold on. Let's wait here a moment."

"Why?"

"Well, silly, suppose we're about to interrupt some tryst. Think of it. Annie—a secret lover! Talk about still waters running deep."

"Well, if that's what it is, shouldn't we just leave?"

"I suppose so… Look out—they might see us."

She dragged Charles off the path and into the underbrush. They could still see Annie and the man standing close together where the path opened out opposite the spout.

"I feel very awkward," Charles said, "Let's—"

"Shhsh! Something's not right here."

By peering carefully around the bushes, Charles was able to see. This was not a meeting of lovers. The slightly wicked fizz of arousal that went along with watching a liaison unobserved was quickly dispelled by the anxious lines on Annie's face. She was almost imploring the man. Maggie and Charles could not see the man's face, since he had his back turned to them, nor hear their conversation but his movements and the low, urgent tone of his voice revealed tension, even anger. It was clear that these were not words of endearment. Annie suddenly turned her back on him and covered her face with her hands. He came close to her and addressed the back of her head in a cold, flat tone, then turned and headed back down the path toward Charles and Maggie.

By reflex, Charles drew Maggie further back into the undergrowth pulling her down into a crouch and drawing her close. Two impressions played in his mind simultaneously. He did not like the look of what had just happened nor the look of this stranger, and yet he wasn't entirely sure that he was a stranger. The man was almost level with their hiding place. Surely the whole world could hear their heartbeats and the loud intake of their breath. But the man passed by without looking their way and continued down the path.

When he was out of earshot Maggie made a move to go to Annie. Charles grabbed her arm.

"You go to Annie. I want to follow him."

"But—oh, all right. But be careful."

Charles walked down the path quickly but not so quickly that he would overtake his quarry. When the path began to wind, he lost sight of the stranger's retreating back. He simply wanted to know where the fellow would go and, if possible, observe him at a distance. But when he reached the point where the path emerged from the forest, he couldn't see any trace of the man in any direction.

Lost him. Blast! Charles took off his cap and smoothed down the hair on the back of his head. *How odd, if he is a friend of Annie's, that we haven't heard her mention him. And if he's here, and he's a friend, or even more than a friend, why have we not seen him before? But wait now.* The feeling returned—that he had seen the man before—but dear knew if he could think where. There was only one person who could supply answers to these questions. He turned around and headed back toward the Black Spout. About halfway down the path, he saw Maggie and Annie heading in his direction.

"There's Charles," Maggie said. "She's says she's all right, Charles. But I'm not sure." This was in answer to the look of concern Charles had not quite managed to erase from his face.

"Look, no need to make a fuss about this," Annie said. "It was just a slightly unpleasant encounter with an acquaintance. I'm sorry you had to see it. But, frankly, I prefer to deal with this myself."

"It looked more than slightly unpleasant, Annie," Charles said. "We couldn't help but see that he upset you a great deal."

"Yes. And he had a rather threatening manner," Maggie said. "What did he want from you?"

"It's a private matter," Annie said. "And must remain so."

Charles said, "We certainly can't find out from him. I lost him, I'm afraid."

"Please, Charles!" Fear broke through Annie's look of strained composure. "Don't try to find him. That will only make it worse."

"Annie! What is this about?" Maggie said. "Now you're making me really concerned. Why won't you confide in us?"

She broke away from Maggie and turned her back on them. "I wish I could." She struggled to compose herself, then turned to face them again, fierce now. "But everything depends on my dealing with this alone. Understand? Everything!" She took a deep breath. "Please stay out of it. For your own sakes as well as mine. And I must ask you not to speak of what you saw with anyone."

"But Janet will surely—"

"Especially Janet!"

There was no budging her when she was in this state. They walked in uncomfortable silence back to the centre of town, to the Fisher's Hotel, where the rest had sifted in from giving their statements at the police office and from various errands and excursions around Pitlochry. Janet greeted Annie with more questions than usual but almost immediately Taplow diverted her attention by asking some niggling questions about the prices at the Loch Tummel Inn. Throughout lunch, Charles and Maggie took turns trying not to look at Annie, and failing. For her part, Annie, seated as usual next to Janet, seemed glad for the distraction of discussing wild flowers with Gordon, which she did with a determined concentration.

17.

After the day and a half of enforced layoff, no one was in a mood to linger over their tea at the Fisher's Hotel and so sharp at one-thirty the tour party headed for their bicycles. Ben, having eaten a meagre lunch at the pub across the street, was sitting on a bench outside the pub and writing in his small notebook when they all came around the side of the hotel wheeling their bicycles toward the street. He put his notebook away, mounted up and quietly joined the group as they turned onto the Atholl Road heading north toward Loch Tummel.

"Ah, Riddoch," Taplow said. "I see your route takes you our way...again."

"Yes, well, Taplow, there are only so many roads up here," Ben said, smiling broadly. He pulled in alongside Violet, who had resumed riding her own bicycle. He lifted his cap to her and she smiled in acknowledgement.

"I've decided to make my way to the Western Isles in a more strategic way, by way of Skye," Ben said.

"Have you, Ben?" Violet feigned surprise, rather badly. "That's where we're headed as a matter of fact."

"Aye, that's what I understand. I hope you don't mind if I tag along for a wee while. After all, we've hardly touched on—em—the revival of the seaweed trade, and I'd like to have your impressions of those legislative measures that Norway is enacting."

Charles and Maggie, riding behind them, smiled to each other as Ben and Violet launched themselves happily into the obscurities of the market for seaweed. Charles motioned to Maggie to follow him. He pulled out beside Ben and Violet and then passed them in order to pull in behind Annie and Janet, who were riding abreast and deep in their own conversation.

"But I don't understand, dear," Janet said. "I thought we were four-square on the subject of our fragment of Mark. Why ever would we sell to Mr. Radulescu?"

"Well, it's just that I'm having second thoughts about it, that's all. Is publishing a facsimile of that manuscript really the best move at this stage? We need to be careful from here on in, or we'll lose the ground we've gained."

"Yes, but we're convinced it's fourth century, aren't we? And Mr. Renshaw is too, so at least we have one Cambridge don on our side. Publishing the facsimile with our commentary should be a substantial feather in our cap."

"I—It's just that, I think we might be opening ourselves up to more ridicule, if it turns out that we're wrong about it. Radulescu is offering us a good price for it. Why not sell and concentrate on the St. Catherine's manuscript? There's so much more there, so much we haven't explored."

"But it needn't be one to the exclusion of the other, surely." Janet peered at her sister. "We can return to the St. Catherine's manuscript after we've published the facsimile. What's gotten into you today? You don't usually indulge in second-guessing once we've made up our minds."

"Nothing's gotten into me. I don't know why you would say that. Just—if you would just consider the idea of selling the fragment, Janet, on its merits—"

"I would be glad to do so. But the idea has very little merit, frankly."

"Janet, please! I am serious about this. Don't dismiss this out of hand. I…I hope I still have some say in our decisions."

"Of course, dear. Of course." Janet reached over and placed her hand over Annie's where it rested on her handlebars. "Don't go upsetting yourself over this. We'll talk about it further after supper and I promise I will hear you out fully."

Annie swallowed and simply nodded.

Charles and Maggie exchanged furtive looks of concern but they were unable to voice any of this for fear of making things worse for Annie. Charles chaffed under the promise they had made; surely they could help Annie if only she would be more open about what had happened between her and the strange man at the Black Spout. He couldn't help wondering if the tense exchange they had just overheard between the sisters was related in some way to what the man had said to Annie. Or was it just that Annie was so upset that it was spilling over into other areas of her life? Maggie had wondered if what they had witnessed was a man brought to great anger through jealousy. Of another lover? But if so, Charles said, where is the other lover? Maggie had to admit that in the time she had known the sisters—almost a year—she had never seen any evidence of a man courting Annie—though Annie was still an attractive woman and merited such attention.

The weather, at least, was cheering. The sun was high in the sky and the heat shimmered on the road up ahead in a way that was quite out of character, or so the locals were quick to tell them. They stopped by the side of the road just south of Bridge of Garry so that all of them could remove their jackets and the ladies could pull scarves over their hats to better shade them from the sun. Gordon took a look at his guidebook and suggested they take a slight detour in order to see a site called Soldier's Leap on the River Garry.

"It's very picturesque," Gordon said to Charles. "And very historic. You know—'Bonnie Dundee' and all of that. I haven't seen it in twenty years but it will be a deal cooler down there by the river than it is up here with the sun beating down."

Since they could easily make the Loch Tummel Inn by nightfall, and since it sounded like a good place for a photograph, Janet declared herself in favour and the others were easily persuaded. They crossed the beautiful arched bridge over the Garry at the foot of the Pass of Killiecrankie and, instead of heading due west toward Loch Tummel as they had initially intended, they took a smaller road northward that followed the west bank of the Garry and crossed the Garry again just below Killiecrankie Station. This road ran through the heavily forested valley of the Garry and was certainly cooler than the Perth–Inverness road had been but it was hilly and winding and the recent rains had washed the soft surface into deep ruts that were not yet dry. It took them almost two hours, alternately riding and walking their bicycles, to reach the head of the path leading to Soldier's Leap.

There they found a clearing and a small cottage where a local woman was busy selling tea and cakes and a map showing the way down a wooded trail to the river. They leaned their bicycles by the side of the cottage and put their heads together over the map. Janet went back inside to ask the woman about one of the turnings on the path and when she had satisfied herself, she found that Taplow had waited for her while the others, impatient to be off, had disappeared around the first bend in the trail.

"Kind of you to wait up for me," she said and, after a pause, "but I fear you may regret it."

"How so, Mrs. Thorburn?"

"Because I intend to take you to task over that pamphlet you published deploring the notion that women students at Cambridge should be offered full membership at the university."

"Yes. I was wondering when we might get to that. And before you flair your nostrils at me, let me say that my position is based on a sound interpretation of Holy Scripture. 'Male and female, created he them.'"

"Yes, the Almighty went in for a strange bit of syntax there—not the only infelicity of King James's translators." She sniffed. "Eve was created out of Adam's rib. Yes, yes. I know. But is it not a monstrously unwarranted leap of logic to deduce from this passage—which may be nothing more than a literary device—that Cambridge's women students are incapable of shouldering the great responsibility of full membership?"

"Aha! Allegories of convenience! This is just the kind of dangerous claptrap that is undermining the committed study of scripture. You've imbibed the poisonous brew of Harnack and his ilk, my dear madam. If there's something in the holy books that you find inconvenient, that is a painful stricture— why, it is simply a literary allusion that need not be held to be true."

"My dear sir, what is really undermining the committed study of scripture is the bloody-minded stubbornness of people like you who reject new insights, new technical advances, new ways of looking at textual problems on the grounds that the whole edifice of the revealed word will come crashing down should any of these things be given the floor for honest and disinterested debate. And another thing— Is something the matter?"

Taplow's expression was half-puzzled, half-amused. "It's just that—I know you're wrong. You're fatally misled by mistaken notions, and yet…"

"And yet, what?"

"I don't know. Having only met you before in print and by reputation, I had pictured you as a humourless scold with only the thinnest veneer of actual learning."

"Well, I hope I live up to the 'scold' part."

"Indeed, you do. But I don't find you sour at all. And I must grant—reluctantly, I admit—that the veneer is rather thicker than I thought."

"Are you intending to tell me that I may not be a total ignoramus?"

"I suppose I am. But don't get overconfident."

Janet laughed. "Yes, it's strange, isn't it? Perhaps you and I are similar people. We are best when warmed by the fire of an adversary."

"Yes. I think it must be so. Well now, to get back to my original point."

"Would you like a humbug?"

"What? Oh, thank you, yes." He reached into the bag she offered and popped the candy in his mouth then gestured for her to proceed down the path with him. "Here, let me take your rucksack. It looks rather heavy."

"Oh now, that's not necessary. I'm perfectly able—well, to tell you the truth it does dig into my left shoulder a bit." She took it off and handed it over to him.

Taplow hoisted the rucksack onto his back in one easy motion. "I've some padding material in my saddlebag. I'll attach it to the straps when we're ready to mount up again, if you'll allow me. Now, it seems to me that the real point of that verse—allegorical or not—is that men and women are different and that each has been fitted for different purposes and to act in different spheres."

She fell in beside him and absently pulled a leaf off an alder bush that lined the path. She began to dissent loudly as they made their way toward the others.

18.

Soldier's Leap is a craggy series of granite outcroppings, weathered and deeply fractured by cracks and crevasses, that form a narrow gorge through which the River Garry flows. They picked their way across the rocks to the very edge where the river boiled and roared some fifteen feet below. Gordon recited the history of the place from his guidebook, raising his voice to be heard over the sounds of the river. At nearby Killicrankie, in the first Jacobite uprising of 1689, a smaller force of Highlanders loyal to the Stuart King James and commanded by James Graham of Claverhouse, Viscount Dundee, surprised and routed a larger force loyal to the new King William and led by General Hugh Mackay. At this spot on the river one of Mackay's retreating soldiers was cornered by fierce Jacobites out for blood. His only chance lay in getting across the river. At this point in the story, Gordon paused dramatically. They all looked at the eighteen-foot chasm that separated the rock outcroppings on either side of the river.

"Surely it's impossible to jump across that?" Maggie said.

"You'd have to be a mountain goat!" Charles said.

"Or a gazelle," Gordon said. "But fear is a great energizer, because that's exactly what he did. Jumped clear across and disappeared into the forest on the other side." Gordon closed the guidebook with a satisfying thump. "I wonder if he made his way back to his own lines. Perhaps he fought again with MacKay at Dunkeld a few weeks later, when the Jacobites finally succumbed to the superior numbers ranged against them."

"Well, I hope he went back to his croft or his village and took no further part in such foolishness," Ben said. "That's Scotland all over. Scot fighting against Scot and then writing glorious songs of victory to hide an ignominious defeat—a defeat, really, for all of Scotland." He shook his head.

"Oh, don't dash my boyhood dreams, Ben," Charles said. "My father sang 'Bonnie Dundee' while we were cutting hay. And my mother used to read Scott's *Old Mortality* to us by the firelight with the snow sifting down on winter evenings."

"Yes, you lot in North America are the worst offenders. But Charles, we've got to wean ourselves off this treacly romanticizing of the past," Ben said. "Every time we Scots try to penetrate the reality of what happened to us—like, for example, the way the so-called gentry of Scotland quietly took for themselves the lands that should have belonged to the people who worked to make the lands productive—every time we try to face that issue head on, we're suddenly mired in a sticky field of—of marmalade!"

"Well, I don't know about the gentry of Scotland, Riddoch," Taplow said, "but in England, those with education, means and breeding have over the course of centuries provided peaceful and profitable habitation to the countryside. Are you suggesting that the rabble would have done a better job? Look at France and you see the result—anarchy, degradation, and blood in the streets."

"So, you're saying that these fine people acquired their lands legally and through merit?"

"It was so in my family, Ben. And I have always been proud of that." Ben turned to see Violet. She had been standing a little apart from Ben and Taplow, a bystander to their argument. Now she joined them and fixed Ben with an intent look. "Storbrae has been ours since the fifteenth century. In our library I can show you the original parchment signed by King James II granting the lands of Storbrae to the first Robert Pitkeathly, who served the king with great honour."

"Oh aye, I've no doubt you can, Vi. But why was the land the king's to give away in the first place?"

"Because he took it," Taplow said. "He had the strength to take charge of it and he exercised that strength."

Ben was momentarily stunned by Taplow's genial approval of such predation. But then he rubbed his hands together. "Well, Mr. Taplow, at least we don't have to waste time with romantic notions of honour and service. It's a bit strange that a good Christian like yourself would champion overweening power as the basis for decisions about land tenure."

"On the contrary. I acknowledge that we live in a fallen world full of cruelty and barbarity," Taplow said. "And we must look to Christ for redemption. I merely pointed out that there is tendency for the strong to take by force what the weak cannot defend. We rightly condemn this, yet some backhanded benefits accrue from it. Human society cannot thrive amid chaos. I've no doubt that Miss Pitkeathly's family have more than earned their title through sound administration stoutly reinforced. Would you not agree, Miss Pitkeathly?"

"I...I don't know, Mr. Taplow. I don't like your first premise, but I do know that I have dedicated my life to the well-being of my estate and everyone whose livelihood depends on it."

"That is good of you," Ben said. "But don't you see, Vi? Your tenants have no means to control their own lives. They have to come to you, cap in hand, to beg for considerations that should be theirs by right."

"That does not happen on my estate. I make most of the decisions now since my father is...is otherwise engaged, and my tenants know that they can approach me freely, and that I will listen to any proposal that will result in our mutual benefit."

"Look, I've no doubt you and your family are very superior examples in what is an unjust and demeaning system. Your existence allows other people to think that all we need is more people like you and things will come out right. But nothing will come out right until we pull down the whole rotting structure and start over with the right foundation."

"Pull it down!" Violet said. "I never heard—" She stopped, and looked across the gorge for a few moments, and then back at Ben. The annoyance on her face gave way to a wistful sadness. She shook her head. "If this is how you truly feel, Ben, then you don't understand me. And I suppose I don't understand you either. I'm not sure that there's a way to bridge the gap. However much we might want to be friends, it will always be there." She turned and began to walk away down the path.

"But wait, Vi! I mean surely there's room for argument! I don't—" Ben took his cap off and scratched his head as he watched her walk away. "Charles, she's taking it rather personally, isn't she? I mean, we were having a stimulating exchange and all of a sudden she took it all the wrong way."

Charles took his arm and steered him back toward the place by the rocks where the rest of the group was standing. "Looks like these things matter a great deal to Violet. Best to be careful how you talk about them with her."

"I was just trying to explain my point of view. Was I a little too——?"

"Maybe a little, yes."

"The thing is, Vi's a grand girl, isn't she?"

"Yes, she is."

"Of course, her politics are rubbish, but I think that's something to work on."

"Come on, you two," Janet said. "I want to take some photographs of you all by the Leap."

Janet had set up her camera and took a series of photographs of the Leap itself and of the members of the party in various bucolic poses along the rocks. Charles obliged by taking up an exaggerated coiled-spring attitude, ready to leap across the gap himself while Maggie pressed the back of her wrist to her forehead in the time-honoured tradition of melodrama.

There was unanimous relief that they would not need to return to the Loch Tummel road via the tortuous route they had taken to get to Soldier's Leap. Instead they rejoined the Perth–Inverness road at Killiecrankie Station and then took that road south to Bridge of Garry. Here they crossed the Garry again and headed westward on the Loch Tummel road. They were conscious of the fact that the detour to Soldier's Leap had taken more time than they had anticipated. It was now early evening. But the sun was still shining and a slight breeze had come up moderating the heat. Although their maps and guides said that the road ahead was hilly and winding, they were confident of covering the six miles between Bridge of Garry and the Loch Tummel Inn by sunset.

This confidence took a bit of a beating once they had been underway for about half an hour. The road was, indeed, hilly but also soft in places. There were points where rain had come rushing down the hillsides and almost completely washed the road away. Dismounting and pushing the bicycles through these washouts was the only safe alternative. They expected to have to walk up many of the hills, but the problems with the surface were so numerous—areas of loose stones alternating with deep ruts that threatened to trap their wheels—that it was also necessary to walk down some of the slopes. The effort required was sweat inducing. Maggie complained to Charles that she was in danger of turning into a grease spot. So when they heard a loud curse from Gordon on one of the few level stretches and looked back to see him dismounted and looking at his back wheel, they were not completely unhappy to have to stop and wait for him to fix his flat tire.

"Now then," Janet said looking at her watch. "That's unfortunate, but it can't be helped. Have you a puncture kit, Mr. Pollack?"

"Yes, indeed, though I was hoping not to have to use it."

"I'll give you a hand, Gordon," Ben said. "I'm a bit of an expert."

"Good of you, Ben. Thanks, but," he said turning to the others, "it's going to take us a while to get it sorted."

"Well, while you two do that perhaps the rest of us will take a break for tea," Janet said. "It seems a while since lunch and we'll be dining late at the inn at this rate."

They found a nice level spot off the road, got out the cakes purchased at Soldier's Leap, and some cheese, bread and sausages. These and water from their canteens and before long, they were all stretched out on the ground, heads pillowed on jackets and with newspapers or scarves shielding their faces from the evening sun. Annie took food and water to Gordon and Ben who gratefully mopped their faces with the wet towel that accompanied the food. She stayed with them, chatting, while they ate.

Charles, who was stretched out beside Maggie slightly apart from the others, was tracing the outline of her nose with a long stem of grass.

She giggled. "Tickles. Stop."

"Hmmm." He sat up, looking at the top of the hill on the other side of the road. "Did you see that?"

She pulled herself up on one elbow. "What?"

"Up there. On the crest of the hill. I saw something flash. There it is again."

"Yes." She sat up, shaded her eyes and stared at the hilltop. "I think there's a man up there."

"Yes. A man on a horse. And the flash is…hmmm."

"The flash is what?"

"A mirror or—no. More likely field glasses. Yes."

"Perhaps he's a bird watcher."

"Maybe. But if I was a betting man, I'd say he's watching us."

"Watching us? But we're not doing anything in particular that's watchable, are we? Oh. Hmmm."

"Yes, hmmm." He strained to see more clearly. "He has sort of a military bearing. Doesn't look much like a tourist. And he has ropes hanging from his saddle. Oh. Oh."

"Heavens. Do you think it's—?"

"I've seen him before."

"It's him, isn't it?"

"Shh. Keep your voice down. And stop looking his way. I can't be sure. But if it is him, I think I have seen him before."

"Yes. At the Black Spout."

"Yes, there. But before that, too."

"Where?"

"Back at Burntisland. Remember at the tea shop you asked me to raise your saddle. I went outside to do that and there was a man hanging around our bicycles. I hardly noticed him at the time. But now I'm pretty sure it was the same man we saw with Annie at the Black Spout this morning."

19.

In the time it had taken Charles to turn and relate that fact to Maggie, the man on the hill had disappeared from view. When they looked back at the hilltop, they saw only the lacy bracken outlined against the bright sky and the two rowan trees that had formed a frame for the man and his horse.

"Outside the tea shop?" Maggie said. "What was he doing there?"

"I don't know. He just seemed to be standing near our bicycles. When I started walking toward him, he turned and walked away."

"Oh, my goodness, Charles. Has he been spying on us?"

"Shh." He dropped his voice to a conspiratorial whisper. "Well, I think he was at least looking at us. But seeing him twice in three days doesn't necessarily mean anything."

"Three times."

"What?"

"Three times if you saw him in Burntisland."

"Yes, I suppose that's right. It seems somewhat beyond coincidental."

"And if it's the same man we saw at the Black Spout, he

has a more than casual interest in Annie."

"Hmmm. Yes, that's the troubling thing."

"What should we do? Contact the police?"

"Other than acting in a rather objectionable fashion to Annie and training his field glasses on us, he hasn't actually done anything."

"Yet…" When he didn't immediately reply, she said, "I wish we could talk to Andrew."

Charles looked at her, turned and dragged his jacket toward him. He pulled something out of the inside pocket.

"What are you doing?"

"Looking at a railway timetable."

"Let me see, too." Their heads almost touched as they tried to make out the tiny print.

"The quickest way would be to come via Perth and get off at Struan. Then he'd have to hire someone to take him to Kinloch Rannoch, I suppose." Charles said. "There are four trains tomorrow. If there's a post office near the Loch Tummel Inn, we could telegraph him from there tomorrow morning. With any luck, he could be at Kinloch Rannoch to meet us tomorrow evening."

"Should we tell anyone else?"

"I don't see how we can do that without betraying Annie's secret." He reached for her hand. "We must get her to confide in us. She knows you better than me. Do you think you could get her to open up?"

She looked over at Annie, who was still seated on the ground beside Gordon and Ben, quietly taking in their conversation. "I will try. But she seems so adamant. It may not work."

"You may have to tell her what we've seen. I don't want to frighten her, but she needs to know the seriousness of the situation."

She gave him a brave little smile and squeezed his hand. "I'll need to pick a time when there's just the two of us. Perhaps at the inn after we're settled for the night."

"Good. If you're half as good at prying secrets out of her as you are at getting them out of me, you'll do fine."

"We'll need to be watching, without looking as if we're watching."

"Yes. And we'll have to be careful not to do anything else that the others will find suspicious."

Gordon and Ben had fixed the puncture and reinstalled the tire. They packed up and took to the road again. It wasn't any easier going, but they were refreshed from their break and the weather had begun to cool a little. Janet had looked a little anxiously at her watch. It was close to seven-thirty.

"Well, never mind, it can't be helped," she said. "With luck we should still be able to reach the inn a little after sunset.

Past Bonskeid House, they descended into a little glen at the bottom of which they found a rustic wooden bridge across Fincastle Burn. Once across the bridge they found a T junction and as was often the case in the Highlands, there was no signage since all the locals knew their roads well and had no need of instruction. They took the turn to the right, which seemed to be the main road. After the turn there was a level stretch as they made their way through a shallow valley with a burn running along on the north side and green fields stretching gently away up the hillsides.

It was such a beautiful evening and the road so agreeable after what they had been through that they relaxed their pace and, feeling that the Loch Tummel Inn could not be far away, ambled along riding abreast by twos and threes and chatting happily. Charles had initially been riding toward the back of the group with Maggie and had been keeping a watchful eye as inconspicuously as possible on the hills and roadway junctions ahead. He could feel the temptation to relax into the beauty of the evening. He realized that he'd been whistling "The Road to the Isles" and stopped abruptly. *No. Need to pay attention. There's something going on here and we don't know what we're facing.*

Ben was ahead of them and trailing Violet, who was not encouraging him to catch up to her. Charles couldn't help smiling to himself. Nor could he help hoping that Ben was exactly who he appeared to be and that Andrew would confirm this. Almost immediately that warm thought was cancelled. *What if Ben's charm is just some kind of mask? Blast!* Ben had stopped suddenly, and Charles had to swerve around him and skid to a halt.

It was Gordon who had signalled the group to stop for a moment. He pulled out his ordnance survey map. "See here." He pointed to the map. "We've gone about two miles from the bridge over Fincastle Burn. We should be just about at Queen's View by now. We should be able to see Loch Tummel to the west, and the Tummel right to the south of us. But I don't see any river at all where the Tummel ought to be and there's no loch either."

Janet and Annie looked around and then at each other. "I think we must have taken a wrong turning," Annie said.

"But where?" Taplow said. "There were no turns in the road except at that bridge."

"It had to have been there," Ben said. "Yes. Look." He pointed to the map. "We should have turned to the left after we crossed the bridge."

"Och, I should have known," Gordon said. "I should have known. The road here isn't as winding and hilly as the guidebook said it should be. We've wasted over an hour going in the wrong direction.

"Now don't fret, everyone." It was Janet at her most

confident and commanding. "It's obvious now that we're not going to be able to get to the inn tonight." There were murmurs of worried assent. She held up her hand. "The sun is setting now, we've not brought bicycle lamps, and we've no way of knowing how long it will take us over these roads. Here's what I propose. It's a lovely night and I think it won't be terribly cold. Let's put our heads together and find a good place to sleep for the night. There will be enough light to allow us to set up camp. Annie and I have slept out many a night in the desert and I think this place will be a good deal more salubrious."

There was agreement all around the circle and even excitement at the thought of a night in the open. Charles and Ben were dispatched to look at the burn, which they could hear was only a short distance from the road, and get water for tea. The others walked their bikes off the road and through a meadow toward a bluff of trees lining the course of the burn.

"We should set up camp at the edge of the trees," Janet said. "We'll catch the breeze there and still have some shelter from the trees. The midges will not be so troublesome there as they will be closer to the burn. Now, firewood, everyone. We need kindling as well as larger branches. As much as you can possibly find, for we may have to keep the fire going all night."

"I've brought along two lengths of fishing line and a small fly kit, Mrs. Thorburn," Gordon said. "There may well be brown trout in the burn. It won't be an ideal fishing rig, but I can cut two poles and string the line on them, if someone will help me fish."

"I was rather good at fishing when I was a girl," Annie said, her sudden brightness underlining how withdrawn she had seemed all day. "Remember, Janet? Violet could see to the tea while I help Mr. Pollack make up the poles."

"Yes, I remember well the hours I spent with my line in the water," Janet said. "Not a single bite, and you were hauling them in like billy-o." She shook her head smiling. "Go along then, you two, and I hope for the sake of all of us that Annie hasn't lost her touch."

Gordon looked as if he had swallowed a beam of sunshine. "If we're going to fish together, Miss Gairdner, I wish you'd call me, 'Gordon.'"

"All right—Gordon. I used to use ribbed hare's ear flies. What have you got in your kit?"

"Aye, those are good, but I think I have a silver and a cinnamon sedge that will be better for this time in the evening."

They walked off, deep into a discussion of floaters and lures, toward an alder bush that had some promising looking suckers.

Out in the meadow at their selected campsite the rest of the group started to build a fire pit with smooth stones that they brought up from the stream bed. They decreed separate sleeping areas for the ladies and the gentlemen on either side of the fire pit. Taplow, Charles and Ben went scrounging for deadfall while there was still light enough to see it. Maggie was dispatched to gather bracken fronds to cushion the ground where they were going to sleep. Janet and Violet set about making tea and setting out the food left over from their afternoon tea. Before long the firewood scroungers were back and dragging a real find—a large half-rotting limb from a birch tree, covered with lichen. As well, Ben and Taplow bore armfuls of deadfall and dried branches of fir for kindling. Soon a blazing fire sprang up that was, if anything, too hot for the still warm evening.

Perhaps it was the fun of dealing with an unexpected

challenge or maybe the pleasing return to childhood pursuits in all their various tasks or then again just the fact that the weather was, for once, cooperating so beautifully. Whatever it was, Charles could feel a quiet thrum of happiness pulsing through their small group.

"Did I just hear a whoop?" Violet said.

"Yes, I heard it, too," Ben said. "It came from the burn."

"Aha!" Janet said in triumph. "Does anyone have any idea how to cook a trout without a frying pan?"

"Who says we don't have a frying pan?" Ben said, walking over to his bicycle. He produced, from his saddlebag, a small frying pan—dented, encrusted with grease and clearly not recent issue—but a frying pan nonetheless. Cheers all around.

20.

Annie and Gordon had cast and trolled heroically by the side of the burn while fighting off clouds of midges. Their efforts were rewarded by a catch of one decent sized brown trout and another small one. Two such fish were not really enough to split among a party of eight, but with their other food there was enough to satisfy them and the small morsel of trout extended to each of them on an improvised plate of beech leaves was made even more delicious by the fact that it had been won by their own labour. Supper now over, they were not quite ready to sleep and remained talking by the fire. Charles picked up a piece of fir and began to whittle.

Ben was convinced that there was a way of making torches using some dry vines and green alder stalks. He was winding the vines around the tops of the two stalks and was dousing the vines with the sperm oil he kept for his bicycle. Violet, a somewhat unwilling participant, had been commandeered to hold the stalks while he performed this procedure. Taplow was quizzing Janet insistently about the content of the sisters' latest manuscript fragment while they broke splinters off the birch log to feed the fire.

Maggie announced that she wanted to wash her shoes and riding spats down at the burn. She got one of the precious candles brought by the sisters and asked Annie to come with her to hold the candle high for better light. They lit the candle and made their way down the small bank to the water's edge. Maggie knelt down and began washing a heavy crust of mud off her spats.

"Annie," she said, "about what happened this morning."

The candle swayed and caused shadows to dance along the hazel bushes and bracken lining the stream bed. "Please, Maggie. Let's not go into it. I'd rather not talk about it just now."

"But…you see, we—Charles and I—we can help you. We know we can. Whatever it is, you shouldn't feel that you have to deal with it all alone." She stood up so that she was now on the same level as Annie.

Annie's face was heavily shadowed in the candlelight. "You don't know how much I would value your help—and Janet's." She gave an anguished look up the bank to where they could hear the low hum of Taplow's voice punctuated by the sharp, clear interjection of Janet's alto. Annie turned her face back. "But you see, it's up to me."

"Annie, if you are being threatened in any way by that man, surely it's a matter for the police."

"No! The police—trials, newspapers! Don't you see? The publicity that would naturally follow such a course would ruin everything Janet and I have been trying to build up. No. I must find a way. I must find a way."

Maggie hesitated and then plunged in. "But, Annie, you act as if whatever it is only affects you and that man. But in a way, we're all involved. We saw something today."

"What? What do you mean?"

Maggie looked up the bank and lowered her voice. "While we were having tea and waiting for Ben and Gordon to fix the tire…we looked up at the top of the hill—I don't think he realized that we saw him."

"Oh Lord. Please. What man? Who was it?" She was almost whimpering.

"The same man we saw you with this morning. Of course, we can't be absolutely sure, but it looked like him. And he seemed to be…well, watching us."

Annie put her hand to her mouth but made no sound.

Maggie continued, keeping her voice very steady. "So, you see, whatever this man is doing, he isn't doing it just to you now. It potentially affects all of us."

Annie continued to be quiet and then said, almost under her breath. "I must think."

"Annie? Are you there?" It was Janet calling from the top of the bank. "Wasn't there something you wanted to discuss? Better now or I shall fall asleep mid-conversation."

"Just coming!" Annie called up. "We've just finished."

Maggie kicked an innocent cobble into the stream in frustration and swatted a low lying branch with her wet spats as she watched Annie make her way up the bank with the candle.

"Hold it steady now. Hold it away from you," Ben said, striking a match. They had moved about twenty yards away from the campfire out into the open meadow closer to the road.

"This is mad, Ben," Violet said. "It's going to smell twice as bad when you light it."

Indeed, the smell of sperm oil had replaced the pleasanter scents of the forest and burn. Ben was undeterred and the lit match revealed an expression on his face somewhere between rapt eight-year-old and mad scientist. "If nothing else," he said, "the midges will be overcome by the fumes."

The torch in Violet's hand exploded into odiferous flame.

Ben lit his own torch off hers.

"Come on!" he said. "We have to perform a ritual midge dance in order to complete the spell!" At this he took off in long loping steps in a circle, yelling and whooping and jumping, the torch blazing, sizzling and crackling as he dragged it through the air. Violet hesitated as she waved her own torch around, then could no longer resist the lure of fire, darkness and young blood. She danced and spun in a circle, laughing, and then chased Ben. He turned around and chased her as she screamed in delight.

The torches exhausted the oil and fizzled out pretty quickly. Ben and Violet were left in heavy darkness in the middle of the meadow, straining for breath, still laughing between gasps. They could barely see each other but as their breath returned neither showed any inclination to return to the fire. It seemed to occur to each of them at the same time that they could see the others, who were sitting by the fire, but the others would not be able to see them. He set his torch quietly on the ground and without a word came closer to Violet and then closer still. She didn't move away but let her own torch slip from her hand. Now he was only inches away. They rested against each other, erupting in giggles again, while drawing more tightly together. The first kiss was tentative, exploratory. He drew back to see her reaction, but she reached up and pulled him back again. This kiss was not at all tentative. Then, with some difficulty, she broke away from him and with a brief squeeze of her hand on his, turned and walked back toward the fire.

Ben took his time walking after her and ran into Charles in the dark.

"Charles. You startled me!"

"Sorry. I was just having a bit of a look around before turning in."

"I don't think we'll be bothered by wild animals—apart from the midges."

"No, not animals. That's right. But I think we should keep up the fire as long as the wood lasts. And keep a bit of an eye out."

"Oh, of course. Are you—? Is there something going on?"

"No. No. Gordon says there may be tinkers around, that's all."

"Tinkers? There's too much loose talk about them. They're usually quite harmless." He caught Charles by the arm. "You've seen something, haven't you? Is it about Vi?"

Charles chose to ignore the question, but put a reassuring hand on Ben's shoulder. "I just think it would be good, Ben, if we—you and I—tended the fire and slept with one eye open."

"Of course. Yes. We'll take the fire tending in turns until we run out of fuel. And maybe in the morning you'll tell me what you've seen."

21.

Neither the ritual midge dance nor the gauze hoods Janet and Annie had brought along entirely warded off the insects, which were not bothered by a slight breeze and did not stop their assault until about two in the morning. The group had settled down to sleep, men on one side of the fire pit and women on the other, on beds of bracken fronds and with their waterproofs as covers. The gauze hoods, which covered their heads and were tucked into their collars, prevented the midges from attacking the ears, neck and face but it seemed the midges had an uncanny ability to penetrate to other zones that were not so well protected. Charles and Ben kept the fire up until three o'clock. The others slipped in and out of sleep, cursing and slapping at midges and changing position to ease their muscles, aching from the hardness of the ground.

Annie was restless. Each time Charles fed the fire, she seemed to be awake. The sisters had had a lengthy conversation before bedding down. Aided by one lonely candle, they had walked along the bank of the stream until they had found a clearing in the woods far enough away from the fire pit for privacy. The sounds of their voices were quite audible though the words were not. Charles had noticed that, unusually, Annie had done most of the talking and that her voice had seemed by turns importunate and exasperated.

The sky was light at five-thirty and the sun broke above the hillside to the east of their campsite by six-thirty. The fine weather seemed to be holding and so did the feeling of magic that had sustained them the night before, more muted now but still vibrant. Best of all, the wind had risen to the ideal speed: stiff enough to blow the midges away but not so high as to seriously affect their riding. They roused themselves and slowly built up the fire again with newly scrounged scraps of wood. Using water from the small kettles, they took turns washing by the side of the burn. There were complaints of aches and stiffness and some were nursing midge bites, but after tea, bread and cheese and the refreshing chill of the stream water, most found themselves none the worse for their night in the open. It had taken some time to organize the washing, the fire and breakfast, making everyone eager to be on their way, to get back to the turnoff at Fincastle bridge and take the correct road toward Kinloch Rannoch and Dunnlinton, Mr. Dibbage's hunting lodge. Janet's plan was to head for the Loch Tummel Inn, explain their absence, have a proper breakfast, get a change of clothing from the steamer trunk which, it was to be hoped, had arrived at the inn though they had not, arrange for the trunk to be sent on and then push on themselves to Dunnlinton.

It was eight o'clock by the time they walked their bicycles across the meadow and onto the road. Gordon pulled out his map and said to Janet, "There's a ruined castle about a quarter mile beyond the turnoff. It's not right on the road, but there is a nice path. There's a sixteenth-century bas-relief statue in the courtyard, of a fellow named William, Baron Wemyss. Look, he's in full armour. The book says not to miss it if you're in the vicinity."

"Oh, yes. I've heard of it."

Gordon handed the book to her.

"Look, Annie. Isn't Baron William a fine sight! And here's the layout of the castle. There's a tower, too, but the book says, 'Be careful while climbing the stairs.'" Janet looked up from the book, her eyes sparkling. "Look, everyone, I know we want to get to the inn," she said. "But would it be in order if we took a short look at this castle? It's called Castle Allean and it dates from the fifteenth century. Think of that. The path in is only about a quarter mile, and I'm rather itching to photograph a ruin or two."

They were intent on the comforts waiting for them at the Loch Tummel Inn, but a brief side trip to a ruined castle seemed allowable and they were all happy to indulge Janet in this small thing. They returned to the turnoff at the wooden bridge over Fincastle Burn and this time headed south down the right road bound for Loch Tummel and Kinloch Rannoch. The road was no less winding and hilly than before but a day of fine weather had dried the surface so that at least they had no mud to contend with. After about twenty minutes, they found the path leading to Castle Allean taking off from the Loch Tummel road and leading up the forested hillside. The path was narrow, but smooth enough that they could ride up as long as they stayed in single file. On the way they encountered a flock of sheep grazing in a meadow visible from the path and stopped for several minutes so that Annie and Gordon could inspect a stand of starry saxifrage and carefully press a specimen into Gordon's book. The path led to a level terrace in the hillside where what had been a smallish stone tower house stood watch over the valley of the Tummel. The tower house was a style of fort peculiar to Scotland; a high but narrow rectangular stone building whose walls were virtually impregnable. There was nothing left of its roof and almost nothing left of its walls. Ramparts had been built around the tower house, creating a courtyard, but the ramparts too had crumbled away except for one round tower, and its associated parapets, jutting into the sky to a height of about forty feet.

Annie, who was less charmed by the romance of decaying stonework, walked through the meadow outside the ramparts with her eyes cast downward looking at the grasses. "I wonder if we might find some mountain pansies here?" she said to Gordon, who was walking beside her.

"Are they native to this part of the world?" He took the small wildflower guide that she held out to him, her eyes still scanning the ground. He flipped to the index, found the appropriate page and began reading the entry to her as they walked out of earshot of Charles and Maggie.

"Those two are like peas in a pod," Maggie said.

"Yes. Nice to see her taken out of herself a bit," Charles said. He led her away from the rest of them who were spreading out each in their own fashion around the site.

"I gather you weren't able to persuade her to tell you anything more last night?"

"No. I'm afraid not," she said in a low voice, absently fingering her engagement ring. "I had to tell her what we saw—and when I did, I felt as if she might just open up a little, but then Janet called her away and that was that."

"The sooner we can telegraph Andrew the better, I think. And if Annie would only let us, we could talk to Gordon about the whole mess. I'll bet that he could give us some legal advice. Do you suppose he knows that something's up?"

"I wouldn't be surprised if he senses something. He's been very attentive the last two days, as if he wants to protect her."

The promised sculpture of William, Baron Wemyss, did

not disappoint. In the middle of the courtyard there was a column about eight feet high bearing the full-height figure in weathered bas-relief, the details of his armour still quite distinct. His face was entirely obscured by his helmet, which only made the whole effect more riveting. He faced the round tower and Janet was busy setting up her camera on its tripod at the base of the tower, where she could get the best view of the sculpture. Just as Charles was smiling to see her intense concentration on adjusting the brass dials of the camera, something caused him to look up at the top of the tower. Some rock dust sifting down—then some pebbles.

"Look out! Janet!" He ran toward her and from the corner of his vision saw that Taplow and Ben were doing the same. Janet looked up from her viewfinder and only had time to fall sideways. A craggy stone the size of a large loaf of bread landed with a huge thud about seven feet away from where she had been standing, embedding itself in the peaty soil that had accumulated within the shell of the ruin. Grass and mud blasted outward from the collision point spattering the camera, tripod and its owner, who was splayed on the ground when Charles reached her.

"Are you all right!" he said, helping her to her feet.

"Yes, thank goodness. Oh! My camera!" She began rubbing the mud off the bellows and the burnished wooden box. "No. It's all right, I think. Just a little dirt."

"Janet! Oh, my lord!" Annie ran up and swept her sister into a fiercely protective embrace.

"I'm fine, dear," Janet said, scarcely able to get words out, her sister was hugging her so tightly. "Really. There's no need for alarm. Don't be so worried." She gently patted Annie's back and gradually emerged from her encirclement.

"You could have been killed," Annie said, stricken and pale.

"No, dear. Look. Even if I hadn't taken evasive action,

the stone wouldn't have struck me. It landed a good eight feet away."

Annie looked at the stone but did not seem fully reassured.

"That was extremely lucky," Taplow said, beginning to help her clean off the camera. By this time all of them had gathered around her in an anxious circle.

"Providence has spared me, Mr. Taplow. You will not be rid of me so easily." It was a game riposte but said without her usual brio. She had said comforting things to her sister, but the incident had plainly shaken her.

"*Deo gratias*," Taplow said. "Come, let's sit down." He looked a bit surprised at her meekly letting him lead her over to a level section of the wall. She sat down.

"Whew!" she said. "My fondness for ruins has been a little tempered, I admit." She began pinning up wisps of hair that had escaped the bun under her hat. "What do you suppose the odds are that a stone, fixed in its place since the fifteenth century, should decide to come loose at this particular moment?"

"Pretty slim, I would think. It's—" Charles stopped, thought, then immediately started running toward the foot of the round tower. Ben followed a few strides behind. They found within the base of the tower a set of worn spiral stairs winding upward. They started up the stairs, grasping the rough stone of the walls for support. Some of the treads had crumbled away and these slowed down progress, having to be carefully stepped over. They emerged at the top of the stairs onto the remains of a parapet. Ben looked down into the middle of the ruin and found the others looking up at him, shielding their eyes. Charles had walked as far out onto the parapet as he dared go, to the point where the rest of it had crumbled and fallen away.

"Here's where it came from," Charles said. Ben walked

carefully along the parapet to where Charles was standing. They both looked at the vacant place on top of the wall where the stone had been.

"Look," Charles said. "See here? Those marks look fresh. They're not weathered."

"Yes. A knife or—a chisel, maybe. Or, no—maybe the claw end of a hammer—used like a lever."

They crouched down and examined the marks closely, running their hands over them, observing fresh-looking rock dust on the parapet beneath the place where the stone had been and the mortar around the stone that was only partly deteriorated and powdered. They stood up and looked at each other.

"That stone wouldn't have fallen on its own. It would have lasted another century probably," Ben said.

Charles went quiet, staring at the place where the stone had been. Finally, he said, "That's right. Someone loosened it, then pushed or dropped it." He looked toward the stairway. "But how did he get down without our seeing him?"

"I don't know. But we were all concerned about Janet. We were seeing to her and not looking anywhere else. He could have gone down the stairs and out while we had our backs turned."

"But you saw those stairs. Nobody could have gone down them that fast. Too much of a risk of tripping. And what if one of us had looked around and caught sight of him."

Ben shook his head in perplexity. "Perhaps he spread his black wings and flew up in the air to join his ungodly companions. Or maybe he's a spider." He ran his hand over the stones of the parapet, eyes narrowed. "You know, there's only one other way down. It's not impossible. He'd need the right equipment."

"What? What are you thinking?"

Ben crouched down again and ran his forefinger along the marks, light grey against the darker grey of the wall. He stood up, turned around, stood on tiptoe and bent his upper body over the outside wall of the parapet.

"Hang onto my knees, would you?" Ben said.

Charles was puzzled but did as he was asked and encircled Ben's legs, preventing him from falling over the wall. "Ben, for goodness sake, be careful there."

Ben was squinting along the outside of the wall. "If he didn't take the stairs, it's the only way. But I don't see…wait. There! Look here, Charles!"

They changed places and Charles assumed, with a little trepidation, the same bent-over position as Ben, looking in the direction Ben had been pointing. At first he had no idea what he was looking for but then he saw them. Three metal rings, like eyes, protruding out of the wall about two feet below the top of the parapet.

"What are those?"

"They're called pitons. Used in mountain climbing."

The blood was now pounding in Charles's ears so he raised his torso and slid back down the wall to a standing position.

"Mountain climbing? Good Lord. Surely you don't mean—?"

"I did a fair bit of climbing myself in the summers while I was at university. Never did this particular thing, but I've heard of it being done if you're coming down a rock face that has no hand and footholds at all."

"Are you telling me he went down the outside of the wall—what?—on a rope?"

"Yes, exactly." Ben peered over the wall again and stood for a moment thinking intently. "Right. Let's see….He took his axe—probably used that to loosen the stone, too—and pounded the pitons into the wall nice and tight. Then he would have threaded his rope through them just as you thread a needle and let the two ends trail down to the ground. Then he wound the ropes once around his body so that he could feed them out in a controlled way. He would have gloves on, for a better grip and so the ropes wouldn't burn his hands. If he had experience and good arm strength, he could lower himself to the ground quite quickly."

"And the rope?"

"He probably just pulled it down after him and off he went into the forest."

"Leaving the what-cha-ma-call-its."

"Leaving the pitons. It's a risky business. The pitons might not have borne his weight. I suppose that's why he used three. And he had to leave them in place. I suppose he just hoped no one would notice them."

"Or maybe, at this point, he doesn't particularly care."

"But why would he pick us to bother? Was he just waiting for the next group of tourists to scare? Just out for a prank?"

"No. This wasn't a random attack any more than the cutting of Violet's bicycle chain." Charles started to pace along the parapet, thinking out loud. "Here's how he could have done it. He knew there was a very good chance we'd come to Castle Allean. It's in all the guidebooks. The sculpture of Baron William faces the tower, so he knew that Janet would set up her camera near the base of the tower. All he had to do was get here before us, set his pitons in place, loosen the stone and wait. He wanted to show how strong and clever he is. Another turn of the screw."

"Another turn? Charles, look, you'd better tell me what this is all about. I'm all over confused. And what's all this about Janet? Why would someone want to hurt her? If you know what's going on, tell me!"

Charles was fighting an internal battle with his

conscience. "I—I gave my word that I would say nothing of this. But now, I think—that is, I greatly hope that God has a practical cast of mind." He bit his lip. "I think that things have reached a stage where for the good of everyone, I must break my promise. I can only hope that in time Annie, and God, who knows all human hearts, will forgive me."

"Annie? Why Annie? Shouldn't we be talking about Vi? Or Janet?"

"No. If I'm right, both the accidents were meant for the sisters and none of this has anything to do with Violet."

"Well," Ben said, but the look of confusion did not leave his face. "Well, I'm glad, for Vi's sake. But I'm no less in the dark than before."

"I'll explain more fully soon. But first we'd better go down and join the others."

"They'll want to know what we found."

"Yes. But hold off for a while. I need to speak to Annie alone. And then I think we'll need a council of war."

Ben smiled at the thought. "That's the spirit, Charles. Nothing like a minister for a good battle." He turned and started carefully down the stairs.

22.

Setter worked his way down a narrow Glasgow street just off the Govan Road. He was cautious where he stepped and where he placed his cane because the street was slick with the latest rain and strewn with garbage and a curious combination of grit and grease that seemed to have been carried down on the wind from the neighbouring steelworks. He had asked directions from several people and since his informants sounded as if they were talking with large wads of rubber in their mouths, he could only hope that he was actually headed for the offices of the *Worker's Clarion Call*. He felt uneasy altogether about Charles's telegram. Whatever could be happening on that bicycle tour that would cause Charles to ask for his help in making these inquiries?

On rounding a corner, he found himself on the narrowest of streets where he could almost stand in the middle and touch the buildings on both sides with outstretched arms. He asked again for directions at the bar of a quiet public house and was told that he should ask at the coffee house at the end of the close. He made his way down the narrow alley to a nondescript building that announced itself as the "Glasgow

Trade Unions Social Club." When he stepped inside, it took a while for his eyes to adjust to the subdued lighting. Five or six men with weathered faces sat at the scarred and scraped wooden tables and nursed large earthenware mugs. A thin man with lank grey hair in need of a cut stood at a bulletin board conning help wanted advertisements with a scrap of paper and a stub of pencil in his hands while another in heavy canvas overalls stood reading a paper next to a cabinet with the day's newspapers suspended from bamboo rods. A young man in shirt and suspenders stood behind a counter operating the crank of a coffee grinder. Behind him two round metal tanks, apparently full of boiling water, burped occasional clouds of steam from their valves.

Setter threaded his way through the tables and presented himself at the counter.

"What's your pleasure, sir?"

"Oh, ah, tea, please. A cup of tea."

"Right you are. I'll just make some fresh." The young man went about preparing the tea all the while taking short glances at Setter. "I see you're not from round here?"

"No. No, that's right," Setter said. "I'm from Canada. From Winnipeg, in the northwest."

"It's thruppence and that'll need to steep for a sec. Canada? Well, you're far from home." As he took a rag and began wiping the counter, he seemed to be trying to place Setter, to find some familiar context for him. It was a process with which Setter was familiar. He took after his mother mostly, in looks and skin colour, so the overall impression was native Indian. But he had blue eyes and chestnut-coloured, wavy hair. People knew that he looked different, but they didn't quite know which box to put him in.

"You know," the young man said, "I read all of R. M. Ballantyne's books when I was a bairn. All of 'em that I could get from the lending library. Trappers and fur traders. A life of adventure. Frenchmen and wild Indians." He paused and cocked his head. "Oh. Now. You wouldn't be...?"

"A wild Indian?" Setter laughed. "No, but I am a somewhat tamed half-breed."

"Strewth. You're the first I've met! Have you had a life of adventure then?"

"I don't know. I suppose I have, if you consider a policeman's life exciting."

"Ah, a policeman. Yes, I see. I didn't think you were a working man."

Setter was surprised to see the zest for thrilling exploits instantly snuffed out of the lad's eyes. "Well now, don't be worried," he said. "I'm not here on a case. Actually, I'm on sick leave." He tapped his cane on the floor. "Thought I'd see something of the old country while my leg mends."

"I see. Right. Well, that's a relief. We've had bad experiences with policeman, y'see. Your lot are quite suspicious of what we do here. Don't want the working man to know too much or gather too freely. They'd prefer us to be ignorant and do what we're told."

"Well, um. Hem!" Setter looked around the room. "Seems like a reasonable place to me. I don't see anything here that would contravene any laws we have at home."

"Perhaps things are freer in Canada. But something tells me you didn't just happen in for a cup of tea." He was looking Setter over in a wary fashion.

"Right you are. Very observant of you. Actually, I'm looking for the offices of the *Worker's Clarion Call*. It's a newspaper, I think. And up the way they said to ask here."

"Oh aye, ye've come to the right place for that, all right. The *Clarion's* offices are upstairs. Take that set of stairs over there and it's to your right as you get to the top. You can take your tea up if you like."

"Thanks very much. I'll do that."

After Setter had climbed the stairs he saw a door to the right at the end of a narrow, dark corridor with chipped and cracked wainscoting that smelled of something he didn't want to think too much about. When he came to the door, he had to light a match in order to make out the sign. It read, "*The Worker's Clarion Call—A Voice for the Working Man.*" Setter knocked and a muffled voice from within said something that sounded like, "Come in."

When he walked through the door, he saw a ramshackle desk made up of wooden shipping crates, covered with stacks of paper and books. Behind the desk was the same young man who had just served him tea.

"Well I'll be—" Setter said. "You mean, you're—"

"James Hervey. Editor of the *Clarion*. Also, publisher, typesetter, copy boy and janitor."

"Well, you might have said!"

"Sorry. My little joke. Ye've got to turn your hand to a lot of different things round here. I cover the counter downstairs sometimes when Lankin has to take his wife to the doctor, which, unfortunately, is a frequent occurrence."

"You're obviously a very busy man. Your staff is not large?"

"No, not at all large. There's myself and Riddoch, who does most of the writing and news gathering. My sister helps out on her half-day off, and we have volunteers who deliver the paper. The place runs on a diet of tea, enthusiasm and outrage. Somehow, though sometimes I don't know how, we get an issue out every fortnight."

"Just yourself and this fellow Riddoch, then. That's impressive. Have you known him long?"

"Oh, aye. We were scholarship boys together at

Hutcheson's. Many's the time we had to stand back to back in some fight in the schoolyard. Ben's a good man to have on your side."

"But he's never been in any trouble then? Any trouble with the police, say?"

"No, no. Not unless you count being hauled off for speechifying on the street during the steelworks strike last year. Wait. What are you trying to pull here? You told me you weren't here on official business!"

"I'm not. I'm just trying to get some information for a friend. A friend who has met Mr. Riddoch."

Hervey sprang up from his chair, knocking some papers to the floor. "Tell your friend to mind his own business and I'll tell you the same. I'd never have said anything at all if I'd known you'd come here to spy on us."

"Look, I'm sorry not to have been more straightforward with you."

"You bloody well lied to me!"

"I didn't. I was somewhat sparing with the truth. My friend is an honest man with no ill intentions toward Mr. Riddoch. He asked me to find out if Riddoch works for your paper and you've told me he does. If you vouch for him, that's fine with me."

Hervey continued to stare daggers for a moment, then sank back into his chair with a sigh. "I'd vouch for Ben Riddoch any day of the week. But you...you are a disappointment. When I first saw you, I was hoping you'd come to buy an advert in the paper. God knows we could use the money."

"Oh. Well, you know, life is not exactly rosy for policemen. Not in Winnipeg anyway. No, indeed. Low wages, long hours, poor working conditions. For example, I'm on sick leave without any pay. I have to fund it myself with my savings, and no guarantee that I'll get my old job back when my leg heals. So, perhaps I could use a subscription to your paper."

Hervey laughed. "Well, you've accomplished something significant. I never thought I'd develop a sense of fellow feeling with a policeman. I'll gladly sell you a subscription, if you're willing to pay the extra postage. Your name again?"

"Setter. Detective Sergeant Andrew Setter."

23.

Annie had said nothing for about three minutes. When Charles had asked to speak to her alone, she had agreed immediately. She seemed, somehow, beyond distress, beyond the panicked concern for Janet she had shown after the stone had fallen. She had arrived at a bleak but peaceable shore. They were sitting in the ruins of what had been, perhaps, a kitchen once, located off the ruined great hall of the tower house.

"I think the man we saw at the Black Spout is trying to frighten you, Annie. He's been shadowing us, observing us since we left Edinburgh, hasn't he?"

She said nothing, but slowly nodded her head.

"And he's directed his activities not at you, for that would be less effective. No, not at *you*, but at Janet. You'd do anything to spare Janet pain, and he knows that." She did not respond, so he continued. "The bicycle accident wasn't meant for Violet at all, was it?"

Annie shook her head.

"It was meant for Janet. He was clever, but he couldn't have known that Janet and Violet would exchange bicycles that day. The broken chain was risky. Still, he probably didn't think that it would fail on such a long, steep, hill. Maybe he intended at the most a slight injury, not to kill her."

No response.

"And the fact that the victim was Violet worked in his favour anyway since you were almost as upset by that as if it had been Janet. Then there's the matter of the falling stone. That was meant to—what should we say—turn up the heat. The stone was easier to control. He dropped it close enough to give you—and Janet—a good scare. He probably wanted to show you that he had the power to harm you and yours at any time if he so chose."

Pain flashed across Annie's face and she looked away.

"Now. Can you tell me what he wants from you?"

"Yes. It's the manuscript. The one we bought from him in Cairo last year."

"Then this man is—"

"Radulescu. Joachim Radulescu, the dealer who was at our house the night you came to dinner. How I wish now that we'd accepted his offer and sold the manuscript back to him. Then we would have been shot of him. I'd an idea of what his game might be, but Janet has been adamant that we should stick to our original plan to publish our facsimile edition and then donate the manuscript to New College."

"He must want that manuscript very badly to try to extort it out of you this way."

"Yes, I've been wondering about that myself. It must have to do with the monetary value. For he's surely not interested in its value for biblical study. Perhaps he has some unwitting, prospective buyer in mind who will buy it at a much higher price than we paid for it originally.

"The price he was offering was a fair one?"

"Oh, a respectable one. More than we paid for it, so we wouldn't have been out of pocket."

"But why would you not go straight to the police when this all began? This is surely criminal harassment."

She got up off the ledge she had been sitting on and walked over to a large chamber built into the wall that might once have been an oven. "There's something else, you see. Something that he knows about me. He's been holding it over my head. He warned me that if I ever go to the police, he would publicize it widely in just the circles where Janet and I have been trying to build a reputation." She turned to face him. "All of our work over the last ten years would be discounted, ourselves disgraced, and the way for women scholars coming up behind us would be harder than ever."

"I see. That's why you were trying so hard to persuade Janet to sell."

"Yes. But you know Janet. She's not very persuadable." The thought brought a fleeting smile to her face.

"Well, you can see that we'll have to go to the police now, can't you?"

"No! No, Charles. He was very angry that we went to the police after Violet's bicycle accident. He thought I should have found some way to stop that. He said that if the police involvement went any further, he would carry out his plan. And he's quite capable of doing it."

"But, Annie, you can't let him get away with what he's doing. It's not just you and Janet any more. Now we're all involved, and we're all in danger to a certain extent from him. He's reckless. We've seen that. And at the very least, we have to tell the others what is going on, though we needn't touch on the—er—the blackmail."

It was the first time that word had been used and its mere sound seemed to crush her. Finally, she said, "Janet knows that something's wrong. She'll perforce be relieved to exchange bewilderment for at least partial clarity. But with

Mr. Taplow, it's like baring one's underbelly to a lion. And—and then there's…" Her voice trailed off.

"Annie, do you remember Psalm 91? 'Surely he shall deliver thee from the snare of the fowler'?"

"Yes, it's one of my favourites."

"For years I thought that the 'fowler' was just a metaphorical reference to Satan and his cunning traps for us. But the meaning of the passage expands the more you think about it. This fowler does not just set traps for us out in the world; he makes us set snares for ourselves—within our minds. It often helps me to understand that, if I've gotten myself into a tangle, with God's help I can also find the way to untangle myself. Maybe that thought will help you, too."

"Perhaps. I will try to take that to heart, Charles."

It was a palming off reply; he hadn't reached her. "Well, that's enough for now," he said. "Let's call for Janet to join us."

Janet was not satisfied with partial clarity. At first, she was preoccupied with the news that the two accidents that had befallen the party were not accidents at all and that Radulescu was behind it all, a person whose oily charm she had often found amusing. Never had she thought him dangerous. But soon the obvious question occurred to her.

"But, Annie, if you had told me this in the first place, we could have gone to the police together. This is Scotland and a woman need not be subject to thuggish treatment without resort to law! Why did you not tell me immediately?"

"Because, Janet…it was—" she stopped, and took a deep breath. "He knows something about me, Janet. Something that happened long ago, that I thought would stay in the past. But our moments of weakness find us out, do they not?"

"Something? But Annie, we have shared everything since you were born—our work, everything. I would be a fool to say that I know all there is to know about you, but I do know your great strength and your goodness. Whatever could it be that you so fear it being disclosed?"

"I—I wish I could tell you. I have tried to work myself up to it many times. But I have so relied on your having a good opinion of me."

"You need never fear losing it! Never! Come, dear. Lance the wound and all will be well."

"I cannot. Isn't it enough that I will have to resort to public confession?" She waved her hand to indicate the assembly waiting for them in the ruins of the great hall.

Janet's expression softened. She put her arm around her sister. "Well, never mind for now, pet. This is enough to be going on with. You'll tell me when you're ready and now—" She looked over at Charles, who nodded. "Now we'll tell the others what they need to know and make a plan."

The others were sitting along the ruined wall of the great hall as if they were lining up for the dentist. They had not been totally surprised to hear from Ben that the stone had not fallen of its own accord but they were dumbfounded at the perpetrator's Prisoner of Zenda–like escape and unnerved at whatever further revelations might be coming. When they learned the name of the man and that he had been responsible not only for Violet's accident but for a campaign of intimidation directed at Annie, they reacted each in their individual ways. Maggie had been waiting impatiently for the trio to address the group, and had been hard put to fend off the questions of the others while they were waiting. Gordon looked stricken but never took his eyes off Annie. Violet was, for an instant, relieved that she was not the target of Radulescu's malice, then appalled at herself for Annie's sake. Taplow was quiet and unreadable except for a few incisive questions. Ben was pleased to have a few more pieces of the puzzle, and a little embarrassed at having attributed criminal intent to Dwight Cavers. The subject of blackmail was not mentioned, either by Annie or by Charles, but the fact that Annie had let matters get this far without involving the police or telling her sister began to raise questions.

"I've had dealings with Radulescu myself," Taplow said. "He's far from a gentleman and definitely without scruples. I wouldn't put it past him to use any means of persuasion. But why have you let him do it, Miss Gairdner?"

The question hung there until Charles stepped in. "We all need to know what is going on for the good of the tour, but let's not press Annie any further now."

Annie got up from the place where she had been sitting on the ruined wall and walked out to face the others. "No, Charles," she said. "It's right that they should know everything. Mr. Taplow, the fact of the matter is that Mr. Radulescu knows something about me, a thing about my past, and he's using it to…" She closed her eyes and swallowed. "To blackmail me. That is why I did not want to involve the police and why I have, unfairly, put you all at risk as well."

The group was stunned into silence.

"I just want to say to everyone that I'm sorry you have been dragged into this," Annie continued. "It's hardly what you imagined when you signed on at Maclaren's. I'm sorry for the whole business."

"But, Annie, you're acting as if all this is your fault and that is simply wrong," Gordon said. "The fault is all on this— this Raduwanski or Radamiski, or whoever the damn fellow is." He got up and walked to her side, facing the rest. "We are all your friends. Some of us are new friends but no less firm for that. I have no interest in what this Raduselski has against you. It can have no adverse effect on my regard for you." He turned to her. "I'm sure the others here would say the same.

We'll all stand by you and face this fellow down together."

As Gordon looked at Annie and then at his shoes, the others murmured approval. Annie rewarded Gordon with a shy smile.

"That's the spirit, Gordon," Maggie said.

"All for one and one for all, is it?" Taplow said. "Bravely put, Pollack, but I think we had better have something more to throw at this fellow than our collective might."

"I do dislike agreeing with Mr. Taplow," Janet said, "but I think we had best telegraph to the Perth police once we get to Kinloch Rannoch. And let's make a plan for increased vigilance between here and there."

24.

They were a quiet, preoccupied group as they cycled back down the narrow path. At every crack of a branch or sudden bird call or rustling in the undergrowth, they jumped. Once they regained the road to Kinloch Rannoch, they formed up in twos. Seeing that Gordon had taken the place beside Annie, Janet pulled in behind them and Taplow glided up beside her. Charles had asked, a bit self-consciously, whether anyone had brought along a weapon of any description but, of course, nobody had. Taplow suggested, by way of lightening the mood, that they might arm themselves with the bread knife and the cheese parer but that hardly got a rise out of Janet and he sank back in his saddle to think his own thoughts.

Though he had a hard time convincing himself, using his best logic, Charles thought it unlikely that Radulescu would try anything else that day. He would wait for Annie and Janet to stew a little and come to a decision. If he expected Janet to capitulate and sell, he was barking up the wrong tree there— though he could see the attraction of just selling the manuscript and ending the whole matter. But even if Annie were to tell Janet whatever the dire secret was that Radulescu held over her, he suspected Janet would still be for going to the police and risking that Radulescu would either not have time to spread his vile spoor around or that even if he did, the ensuing storm of public attention could be weathered.

Annie was so rattled at the thought of the police becoming involved. What if the thing—whatever it was—was something that would result in Annie herself going to prison? This was a disturbing thought and, in fact, he found it impossible to believe that Annie could ever be capable of knowingly committing a crime. But for the first time, it occurred to him that she might have something to fear from police involvement, something other than the risk of disclosure from Radulescu. He began to chew his lip. It would be so much easier to know what to do if only Annie would open that final door. As long as she remained silent, Radulescu was holding all the cards. Radulescu was here now, somewhere out there, watching them, calculating his next move. And for the time being they were thrown back on their own resources.

He began to wonder, quite against his natural instinct, whether there was a way to, essentially, trap Radulescu, truss him up and hand him to the police in one handy package. That would deprive him of his ability to spread whatever information it was he had on Annie. If it were simply an embarrassing incident from Annie's past or the like, Radulescu's arrest would provide ample grounds for people to discount whatever he said. As a general rule, Charles was a strong supporter of both God's laws and man's. But he was also conscious of the fact that they were not one and the same, and if he had to choose, he knew which would claim his allegiance.

The weather seemed to be closely following the mood of the touring party. By the time they stopped to take in the

Queen's View, a magnificent high rock outcropping that afforded a view across the valley of the Tummel and down the length of Loch Tummel to the west, mist was hanging on the hills opposite, obscuring the top half of the brooding triangle that was Schiehallion. The dampness began to slowly penetrate their clothes. They were all relieved when, underway again toward the Loch Tummel Inn, Janet declared herself to be more susceptible to the damp, having spent the night outdoors, and broke out her waterproof earlier than expected. Within minutes the rest of the party were all wrapped in their capes.

They arrived at the Loch Tummel Inn in time for lunch. The innkeeper took pity on them after hearing about the reason for their failure to show up as planned the night before. For a fee, haggled over by Janet, he allowed them to temporarily use the rooms that had been set aside for them since the new guests had not yet arrived. They washed, changed their clothes and had a huge lunch in the dining room. There being no post office and, consequently, no telegraph service at the inn, Charles and Maggie were eager to push on to Kinloch Rannoch. After seeing their steamer trunk onto the post office wagon, bound ultimately for Dunnlinton Lodge, Harald Dibbage's house, they mounted up again at three-thirty. Fortunately, although there was still a heavy mist, it had not deteriorated into driving rain as they had feared.

The road between the Loch Tummel Inn and Kinloch Rannoch twisted around and combined with steep hills, which were now slippery, the going was slow. Often they had to walk their bicycles both up and down the slick, rutted hills. When they finally got to Kinloch Rannoch late in the afternoon, they were exhausted and unsure if they could manage the extra two miles to Dibbage's lodge. Janet declared a break for tea and Charles and Maggie just got to the post office before it closed for the night. They were composing a telegram to Setter when the elderly postmistress, who was also the telegrapher, said, "Lauchlan? Are you by any chance Mr. Charles Lauchlan? That is, the Reverend Mr. Charles Lauchlan?"

"Yes, I'm Lauchlan. Why do you ask?"

"There's a Chinaman who's been calling around, asking for you. I couldn't make out why he sounded like an American, being a Chinaman, and he hasnae got a pigtail. So perhaps he's been abroad for a long while."

"A Chinaman? I don't— What was he asking about?"

"He wanted to know if you'd already been through this way. I told him not to my knowledge. But it's not everyone who comes to the post office when they stay here in the village."

"Do you know where this Chinaman is now?"

"Aye, he'll be having his tea at the hotel just now."

"Thank you. Can you send that right away?"

"Yes. Surely. I'll just send it off and then close up."

As they walked their bicycles away from the small, whitewashed cottage that housed the post office, Maggie said, "Who do you suppose this man is?"

"I don't know, but I am curious. How would he know that I was going to be here? We're going to have tea and scones at the hotel anyway. Let's see if he's there."

They made their way over to the Craiganour Hotel, a large, rambling two-storey, grey stone building with many gables overlooking Loch Rannoch. They found a barn around the back of the hotel where they could park their bicycles out of the mist. When they entered the large dining room, not yet very populated, since it was too early for the main dinner crowd, the others were ranged around a table. Charles waved to them but scanned the rest of the room, looking for a Chinaman without success. What he did find was a man sitting with his back to them. There was something familiar about the hunched attitude and the carefully folded newspaper by his plate, situated in reading distance but not in splotching distance. A cane lay carefully hooked onto the back of his chair.

Charles let out a whoop of recognition, "Hah hah! He must be a blasted mind-reader!" He grabbed Maggie's hand and pulled her toward the quiet table where the man was sitting.

Setter jumped his chair backward with surprise when he saw them, pulled himself up to a standing position and the two men participated in the hand-shaking and back-thumping of men who are genuinely glad to see each other.

"I suppose I should search your person in order to find your opium stash," Charles said.

"What?" Setter said.

"At the post office they're wondering if you're from Hang Chow or Tai Pei."

"Oh, yes." He looked both amused and annoyed. "The postmistress. I did try to explain that I'm from Canada, but I couldn't shake her firm conviction that I'm a Chinaman. Not even my blue eyes dissuaded her. So, I just bid her farewell in my best Bungee. She was thrilled, thinking it to be Cantonese, I suppose."

"Well, never mind, Andrew," Maggie said. "The ability to go incognito as a Chinaman might be an advantage here."

Setter turned to Maggie, blushed, and shook her hand vigorously. "Miss Skene—so nice to see you again. But you two look a bit damp around the edges."

"For heaven's sake, Andrew, call me 'Maggie.' We've just been over the worst road of the trip. More walking of the bicycle than riding. We're half-dead."

"Well, sit down, for goodness sakes, and have some supper with me."

"Wonderful," Charles said. "But for us it had better be tea and scones. We've still got two miles to go to Mr. Dibbage's house, where we're expected for dinner."

The kitchen was mercifully quick with the tea and scones and with Setter's trout, turnips and potatoes. With the first cup of milky tea inside them, Charles and Maggie were restored enough to wonder what had magically brought Setter their way before they had even summoned him.

"I suppose it was that telegram, really. You said not to worry, but I knew you wouldn't have sent it if there had not been some pressing reason for the information. Then there was no letter to follow when one had been promised this morning. And I suppose I was a bit bored all by myself and curious about what was happening to the two of you. After I left the *Worker's Clarion* office in Glasgow this morning, I took the West Highland line train to Rannoch Station. And here I am."

"The *Worker's Clarion*?" Charles looked over at the other table and lowered his voice. "Were you able to find out about Ben Riddoch?"

"Yes. The editor confirmed to me that he works for the paper. Said he was a decent fellow and I'm inclined to believe him. After years in police work, you get a feeling for these things."

"See? I told you so," Maggie said and stuffed a piece of scone in her mouth.

"I'm relieved. But how did you know where to find us? You couldn't have gotten our telegram," Charles said, "We just sent it half an hour ago."

"I expected you to be here already, according to what it said at Maclaren's. Before I went across to Glasgow, I dropped in at Maclaren's Travel Itineraries and persuaded the girl at the counter to let me have a look see at your itinerary. They're pretty free and easy. She said two other gentlemen had asked to see the same itinerary last week on separate occasions."

"A foreign gentleman?" Charles paused mid-scone.

"She didn't say. She said one was some kind of professor. He was one of the men whose tour was cancelled. She said he'd asked to be put on Mrs. Thorburn's tour. Said he knew her and she'd be happy to have him."

"Oh, so that would be Taplow," Charles said.

"She must have misunderstood, though," said Maggie. "I remember Mr. Taplow saying that he didn't know Janet was leading our tour until the last moment."

"Yes," Charles said. "I heard him say that, too."

"Oh, well, funny…I might have misheard her," Setter said. "But what's all this about? You said you sent me a telegram?" He poured himself a cup of tea and waited to be informed.

Charles laid out the whole story of the trip: Violet's accident; the threatening man with Annie who turned out to be Radulescu, the antiquities dealer; the stone falling near Janet; Radulescu's blackmailing of Annie and threatening more of the same unless the sisters sold their manuscript to him.

"But surely this is a matter for the police." Setter was incredulous. "Uttering threats. Attempted assault. Blackmail. This man has to be stopped."

"Shhh! Keep your voice down." Maggie shot a worried look at the other table. "That's what we think, too. And the police are working on the assault on Violet. But Annie is so very reluctant to tell them about the attack on Janet and the blackmail, we're a bit stumped as to what to do."

"But there's no choice in the matter, surely," Setter said. "That's the only way to prevent the man from doing any more harm. The constabulary must be allowed to do its work."

"But, you see, Annie will not tell us what it is that Radulescu is holding over her head. I'm afraid she may not cooperate with the police," Charles said. "We have tried every which way to get her to tell us. Even Janet can't pry it out of her. She can't bear the thought that something in her past will lead to the undoing of everything the sisters have worked for. And—frankly—we can't soothe her by telling her that he wouldn't likely spread that news around, because he's clearly a man without a conscience."

"That would, I think, be an argument for overriding Miss Gairdner's concerns—for her own good—and involving the police as soon as possible," Setter said.

"I'm not suggesting avoiding police involvement altogether, Andrew," Charles said. "After all, you're a policeman."

"Oh, no. Not on your life." Setter held up his hands, palms forward. "I have no jurisdiction here. I wouldn't tolerate it in my patch—some wandering policeman sticking his nose in where it doesn't belong—so I won't do the same in their bailiwick either."

"Look, it's time we need, Andrew," Maggie said. "Just a little time to persuade Annie to come around on her own. It will be so much better for her if she would, don't you see?"

"Look, I can see that you want to make things easier for Miss Gairdner," Setter said. "And all things being equal, so would I. But you're also opening her and her sister to danger the longer you wait."

Charles had to admit the truth in that argument. He sat back in his chair and sighed. "You're right, of course. But what can the police really do at this point? We can't prove that Radulescu took a hacksaw to Janet's bicycle chain. And we'll have a devil of a time proving he dropped that stone near Janet. We've got some evidence, but nobody actually saw him doing anything. And as to the threats he made in person to Annie, if she won't cooperate, we've no proof there either except that

Maggie and I got some vague impression of threatening behaviour from a man who had his back turned to us most of the time and was seventy-five feet away in the distance. With a half-decent lawyer, he could easily walk out of court a free man."

Setter sat back in his chair. "Well…it's far from an airtight case, as you say." He began to rub the thigh of his bad leg. "But you realize what you're saying, though, Charles?"

"What do you mean?"

"You're suggesting that, in the absence of Miss Gairdner seeing sense, we wait for Radulescu to do something more, something that *will* stand up in court."

"Hmm," Charles said. "Yes. I suppose that is the implication." He looked at Maggie, who sighed and nodded. "You're right, of course, Andrew. Janet and Annie simply can't be exposed to that risk—or the rest of the party."

"But, Andrew, we could use your knowledge of policing and the law," Maggie said. "Why not come with us to Dibbage's? We'd feel a lot more confident with you there."

"I can't do that! Invite myself to a house party! Mr. Dibbage will shut the door in my face the moment he sees me. And in this case, I wouldn't blame him."

"No, he won't. There are about a hundred rooms in his house, so the sisters say. It's huge. He's made pots of money in textiles and I'm sure he wouldn't begrudge you a room once he knows that we need your expertise."

"Oh, come on, Charles, you can't tell me that he's used to putting up the likes of me. Let's be realistic."

"Why anticipate difficulty, Andrew. He may just welcome you in a spirit of international cooperation—and show you his priceless collection of Chinese porcelain."

Setter saw the glint of mischief in Charles's eye and threw his hands up in the air, exasperated. "Now, don't you start with that."

Whether he was worn down by their arguments, or intrigued at the scent of an interesting case, or in need of company, or a combination of all three, Setter relented, and went off to find a local man with a horse and cart to convey him to Dibbage's later that evening.

25.

They were relieved to find that the road now ran parallel to the shore and was as flat and serene as Loch Rannoch itself. Since the sun had finally emerged from the mist and was burning the residue of it away, the last two miles to Dibbage's would be a much easier ride than the preceding eleven miles. Charles sought out Janet and Annie as they cycled along and broached the subject of Setter staying with them at Dibbage's house.

"Och, I'm sure Harald won't mind," Janet said. "He's a dear friend of ours, isn't he, Annie? And he'll see the value in having Sergeant Setter with us."

"We'll have to fully inform Mr. Dibbage about what has been happening, of course," Charles said.

Annie winced noticeably at that, and Janet briefly squeezed her sister's elbow.

Janet and Annie directed the group to turn right into a lane flanked by an orderly parade of basswood trees. At the end of this lane, Dunnlinton Lodge, Harald Dibbage's Highland retreat, came into view, all crenellated parapets and outcroppings of rounded turrets, in the most exuberant Scottish baronial style.

"Strewth," Ben said. "It looks like a giant wedding cake."

"Yes," Janet said. "Harald is a Yorkshireman but he made all his money in Scotland and there's no one more zealous than a convert, as they say. It is a little—em—overdone. But it's very nice and comfortable inside. And Harald has it fitted out with the latest conveniences." Ben sighed at that, as he contemplated another night in the open.

When they got to the front door, Janet and Annie dismounted, had Violet and Maggie hold their bicycles, and rang the mechanical doorbell. A footman answered, called back into the house for reinforcements, and presently Harald Dibbage himself emerged onto the terrace. Bald, except for a fringe of white hair, Dibbage was already dressed for dinner in evening clothes. He looked genuinely glad to see everyone and bustled around directing the servants to do this and that, straining to hear Janet's introductions of the party, and giving hearty handshakes. The whole teeming mass slowly filed into the house all talking at once. Ben started to walk his bicycle away from the house, waving at his former companions, but Janet caught Harald's arm and said something to him and Dibbage motioned to Ben to come back.

"Mr. Riddoch, is it? Come along in, lad. Have a drink with us at least before you go off. Come on along, now."

Ben didn't need much persuasion. He turned his bicycle around and in no time a servant had taken it from him and rolled it away, following the other bicycles that were being wheeled around to the back of the house.

They were all gradually ushered into a large drawing room furnished with surprising taste, given the exterior of the house. They sank into comfortable wing chairs and sofas, grateful for the fire in the huge fireplace with its massive, elaborately carved walnut mantelpiece. Servants began handing around glasses of sherry.

"Now, what I suggest is that we have a bit of a drink and let the servants get your rooms organized. My housekeeper, Mrs. Fairclough, says your trunk arrived in good order a few hours ago. So, you'll be able to change for dinner, which will take place in…"

He turned to his butler, Williams, who said, "Approximately one hour, sir."

"Excellent," Dibbage said. "I've another guest, a business colleague who arrived yesterday, unexpectedly. He's been out shooting today and will join us for dinner, too. When we've finished our sherry, Mrs. Fairclough and the footmen will see that you get to your rooms and that you have all that you need."

There was a clatter in the hallway outside the drawing room and the door swung open to reveal a lean, tall man, in his mid-forties, dressed in tweed plus-fours and jacket with a leather patch at the shoulder. He smiled at the assembled crowd as if he had just walked on stage.

"Ah, there you are. This is Mr. Dwight Cavers, everyone. Come in, Cavers. Janet, will you do the introductions?"

26.

Charles watched, trying to control his surprise, as Janet took Cavers around, making introductions to the ladies in the party first. She came to Violet last.

"Miss Pitkeathly and I are already acquainted," Cavers said, taking Violet's hand. "How nice to see you again, Miss Pitkeathly. You left London so suddenly. I didn't have a chance to say goodbye."

"Yes, em, I'm sorry. A pleasure to see you again, Mr. Cavers," Violet said, her voice flat. "And quite a surprise, too. *Maman* said you were going to the Hart-Menzies' hunting lodge this weekend?"

"Yes, that's right," Cavers said. "But I needed to discuss a business matter with Mr. Dibbage first. A last-minute thing as it happened. I'll go along to the Hart-Menzies tomorrow evening."

The introductions turned to the men next. Ben watched with his brows drawn together and the edges of his mouth pulled down, seemingly unaware that several pairs of eyes were trained on him. Cavers was introduced first to Gordon and to Charles.

"And this is Mr. Ben Riddoch, Mr. Cavers," Janet said. "Ben is a journalist we met on the way who has been accompanying us and been very helpful to us."

"How do you do, Mr. Riddoch," Cavers said, taking in Ben's considerably road-weathered appearance. "Are you with the *Herald*, by any chance?"

Ben fixed his eyes on Cavers. "No, Mr. Cavers." The "Mr." seemed to stick in his throat and then he winced as Cavers gave a determined shake to his bad hand. "*The Worker's Clarion Call*. You've heard of it?"

Harald's eyes opened very wide. Charles tried not to smile.

"Er, no. I can't say that I have," Cavers said. "But any paper that encourages workers to pitch in and work hard is welcome as far as I'm concerned."

"Oh, we do that, all right," Ben said, with just a hint of flint behind his smile. "We urge our readers to pitch in and work hard for their own rights and those of their unions."

"Weeell," Janet said, noting the look of undisguised annoyance that crossed Cavers's face. She took him by the elbow and steered him away from Ben. "I'm awfully keen, Mr. Cavers, to know about your shipping concerns. Annie and I are very fond of travel, aren't we, Annie? And you being Canadian, I'm sure you'll have much to talk about with Mr. Lauchlan and Miss Skene."

Cavers was not fooled completely by this diversionary tactic. As Janet kept up her barrage of conversation, he eyed Ben suspiciously from across the room. For his part, Ben spoke when spoken to, but otherwise kept his eyes on Violet. In short order they finished their sherry, and Mrs. Fairclough reappeared with a clipboard in her hand, ready to see the guests to their rooms.

Ben stood up and crossed the room to Harald. "Thank you so much for your hospitality, Mr. Dibbage. I hope you won't mind if I call you, Harald. It's an idiosyncrasy of mine."

"Not at all…Ben. I grew up in a coal-mining family. We were plain folk and I try never to forget where I came from."

"You've been very kind, Harald, but I'll be going now." Ben looked around at the group. "I'll be off to Skye tomorrow."

He began to bid them all goodbye in turn, starting with Janet and Annie. He murmured his thanks and shook their hands.

"I sincerely hope that all will be well with you, Annie. I wish there was more I could do to help."

Annie blinked rapidly, said nothing, but gripped Ben's hand in both of hers.

"Goodbye, Ben. And good luck. You've a fine future ahead of you," Janet said.

He turned to Taplow. "Yes, best of luck, Riddoch," Taplow said. "You've a good mind. I've no doubt you will ultimately stumble upon a firmer set of values."

Ben laughed and shook Taplow's hand heartily.

By now, Janet and Annie were looking quite distressed. Janet seemed to be trying to get Harald's attention.

Charles noticed that Ben's limp, which had not been much in evidence since the previous day, had grown suddenly worse, and that the injured hand, with which that morning Ben had peeled an apple, was now held close to Ben's belt in a gesture of protection. *Ah*, Charles said to himself. *I see what the game is. Pour it on, Ben. And bat those innocent brown eyes of yours some more. You're almost there.*

"Gordon?" Ben said, turning to Gordon and extending his hand. "Very nice sharing the road with you."

"All the best, Ben. Truly," Gordon said. "I've enjoyed our conversations."

Janet had worked her way over to Harald and had whispered something in his ear. Looking at her, he nodded.

Now Ben had come to Violet. He shook her hand and held it.

"Well, goodbye, Vi." He looked as if there was something more he wanted to say, but nothing more came out.

Violet looked pale. "Yes. Goodbye, Ben."

They were still holding hands when Harald said, "Look here, Ben. We can't have you sleeping rough tonight. The weather's closing in again and your wounds haven't healed yet." He turned to Mrs. Fairclough. "Put Mr. Riddoch in the east wing, next door to Mr. Lauchlan. Oh, and look for that suit of Mr. Michael's—the one he doesn't fit into anymore since he took up rugby. The size should be about right."

Mrs. Fairclough barely suppressed a look that questioned the sanity of her employer, but the others chimed in all at once, "Yes, Ben, stay here...too wet to be out of doors... plenty of room...could use your support...shame to break up the group now after all we've been through."

"Well," Ben said, "if you're sure it's not too much trouble, Harald. Such wonderful hospitality. It really is very kind of you." The limpid brown eyes were once again working overtime.

27.

During the hour when the rest were changing for dinner, Setter arrived at the house, steeling himself to be shouldered out the door the moment he entered. True to form, the greeting by the footman at the door was chilly. He was told to go around to the servant's entrance and wait while footman consulted butler, and butler consulted master. Presently the door at the servant's entrance was thrown open and Harald Dibbage himself, missing only the tiniest beat when he saw Setter, greeted him warmly and took him by the elbow.

"Sorry you've been made to wait here, Sergeant. I didn't have time to properly inform the servants to expect your arrival. Please accept my apologies." In short order, Harald sent Setter off with the footman in search of his assigned room.

After an hour of settling in their rooms, washing the stains of the road away, and raiding the contents of their steamer trunk for more suitable clothing, the group was introduced to Setter. They were then led into Harald's immense dining room, which, to no one's surprise, was decorated in the requisite tartan, stag's heads, and oddments of armour and ancient weaponry. Harald had clearly had his own way in this room. If I were decorating a stage set for *Redgauntlet*, Charles said to himself, I could not do better than this.

They were still milling around the table, finding the place cards with their names on them, when the door to the dining room opened and Ben walked in. Standing irresolute in the doorway, he was, for more than a moment, the centre of attention. Washed, shaved, hair tamed and pomaded, he was dressed in a well-cut dark sack suit with waistcoat and necktie. The celluloid collar of his spotless white shirt embraced his tanned neck as if it had been made specifically for him.

"Sorry I'm late, everyone. I'm not used to someone else dressing me. Em, that is…well, you know what I mean."

"Ben, how handsome you look!" Janet said. "It's quite a transformation."

Ben blushed and did a pirouette to give the company the full effect. "Yes, but I expect, come the chimes of midnight, Janet, Cinderella will revert."

"May I show you to your place, sir?" Williams indicated a place next to Violet. As Ben sat down, he noted that Cavers was resplendent in formal evening dress and had been placed on the other side of Violet.

Dinner progressed very pleasantly, with Dibbage insisting that everyone call him "Harald", Ben and Cavers trying, in turn, to monopolize Violet's attention, and Setter hesitating before each course in order to see what piece of cutlery Janet selected before he did the same. The dinner was excellent and, in spite of having already eaten at the hotel, Setter tucked into it with almost the same enthusiasm as the rest. Then the ladies, led by Janet, retired to the drawing room but were soon joined by the men.

As the coffee was served, Harald said, "Now, I couldn't

help overhearing what Ben said to Annie before dinner. The men were tight-lipped over their port when I asked if something was wrong. Sergeant Setter's here. And you're all behaving as if you've been through some sort of trial. If my dear Ada was still with us, she would have winkled it out before now. But I'll just have to be direct. Something's going on, isn't it? So, come, Janet, tell me what it is. You know I won't rest until I find it out."

There was a sobering silence. The evening had been so pleasant, their welcome to Harald's house so warm that Radulescu, though not forgotten, had seemed to exist only far off, as if he were a clockwork figure that had stopped for the moment and needed their attention to be set in motion again.

Finally, Janet, who had been fingering the pearls at her neck, drew a deep breath and began. "You're right, of course, Harald." She looked over at Annie. "We've been waiting for the appropriate moment to broach the subject and I suppose this is it. I'm sure you'll help us to deal with it. You've always been such a tower of strength."

Janet laid out the tale of Radulescu's threatening gestures toward Annie, of the two incidents involving Violet and herself, and of Radulescu's clear intention to ratchet up the pressure on Annie to force the sisters to sell their manuscript to him.

"But this is outrageous!" Harald said. "Let me alone with this blasted fellow, and I'll soon show him what's what."

"You'd have to get in line, Harald," Cavers said. "I'd like a good crack at him myself." He gave Violet a glance of proprietary concern.

Harald thought for a moment. "But that's no good, is it, Dwight. A fellow like that doesn't learn anything from a beating. He licks his wounds and then comes back at you. No. He has to be stopped for good and all, and the only way to do that effectively is to turn the matter over to the police. Isn't that so, Sergeant Setter?"

"That it is, Mr. Dibbage. As I understand it, because of the nature of the offence to Miss Pitkeathly, the County Police had to deal with that matter. I assume that would be the case again for the incident with the stone at the castle. But, frankly, the offence that would be the easiest to arrest and convict on would be the matter of the blackmail. But— um—I believe Miss Gairdner would be required to press charges in that case."

"What? The blackmail? Annie?" Harald looked at Annie, then at Janet.

"Yes, Harald." Annie said, putting down her coffee cup and straightening her back. "You might as well know. Everyone else does. Mr. Radulescu has been threatening to publicize a piece of information about me. From my past. If it were revealed, all of our academic work of the past several years would be fatally discredited."

"But—but I have known both of you for over twenty years, and never have I heard one hint of—"

"I know, Harald—and thank you for your faith in me," Annie said. "But, regrettably, that is, one does not always live up to one's own ideals. Funny." For a moment she paused and seemed lost in a memory. "Someone else said that to me once."

"But wait a moment," Harald said. "You say that the police are involved over Violet's accident?"

"Yes," Annie said. "He was enraged about that."

"He would be," Harald said. "All of you now know about what he's been doing? And some of you have actually seen him spying on you?"

"Yes."

"And now Dwight and I know, too."

"Yes, Harald," Janet said. "We felt it was only fair, since you might get caught up in all this anyway."

"Well, if the police are already involved and the circle of people who know what he's trying to do is widening, and he's been sighted spying on you, wouldn't your average rat want to scuttle back under the floorboards? Why would he keep coming if he knows we're going to call in the police to investigate further?"

"Hmm. It's a good point, Harald," Charles said. "And if he were an ordinary, timorous rat, he might have slunk away, as you say. But, now that I think about it, he hasn't actually spoken to Annie since before the castle incident. So, I don't think he could know for certain whether Annie has told us anything. He threatened her with exposure and warned her not to tell anyone else. He also told her to discourage any further police involvement. For all he knows, she's obeyed to the letter."

"Yes," Janet said, "that's right. He doesn't know—or can't be absolutely sure—that Annie has had the good sense to confide in us to the extent she has."

"If he had come out of the shadows, we could have confronted him, but he hasn't. So we can't be confident that we're shot of him, Harald." Gordon looked at Annie with concern. "We have to assume that he's still following us."

"I see," Harald said. "Then he may very well be watching now, somewhere out there."

The others acknowledged the truth of this with various nods of assent and muttered agreement.

"I'm afraid so, sir—um, Harald," Setter said. "I don't suppose you're on the telephone?"

"Unfortunately not, Sergeant. We've hopes of a line up this way, but it'll be a few years yet. There's the telegraph in Kinloch Rannoch. I'm afraid we'll have to wait until morning at this rate before we can get into the village to alert the local constable."

"And he'll have to telegraph Inspector Storrs in Perth," Charles said. "How long do you think it will take Storrs to send someone here to investigate?"

"Could be mid to late afternoon tomorrow," Harald said.

"Then we must use the resources here to protect the ladies in the meanwhile," Setter said. "For instance, it would be best if all the entrances to the house could be guarded during the night. I would propose myself to organize a watch for you if you could provide me with some men, Harald."

"Of course, Sergeant," Harald said. "There're the two footmen, and I'll have Williams call in Finlay and his boy from the stables. And we can get some of the shepherds to pitch in if need be."

Setter went off with Williams to organize the watch and the company, left to finish their coffee, began stifling yawns.

Ben leaned over to Charles and said, "Don't you think we should mount a watch on the ladies' doors, Charles?"

Charles thought about it for a moment. "Bravely proposed, Sir Galahad. But you and I have had exactly two hours sleep in the last twenty-four, and we've been through the roughest ride of the whole trip today. Gordon and Taplow are only slightly fresher. Exactly how long do you think we could manage to stay awake?"

"But I've just had three cups of excellent coffee."

"Which will perhaps keep you awake fifteen more minutes than you would otherwise manage. Leave it to Setter. He knows what he's doing."

"Lauchlan's right, Riddoch," Cavers said. "After all, you're pretty banged-up and Lauchlan looks like he might not even make it upstairs. I'm in the same hallway as the ladies. I'll keep an eye out."

"Oh, surely that won't be necessary. We're hardly school-girls, any of us," Violet said. "Janet and Annie caught a thief by themselves in the desert." She drew herself up in her chair and looked steadily at Cavers. "And I took Miss Skarsgaard's practical calisthenics course last year, which arms one to deal with things like untoward gentlemen."

"Oh, I don't think this fellow Radulescu falls into the category of a drunkard who annoys women in the park, Miss Pitkeathly," Cavers said. "You'd be no match for him."

"I wouldn't sell Vi short, Dwight," Ben said, with a sly smile. "She might completely bowl him over quite by accident."

"Ben," Violet said, "for heaven's sakes, this is serious." But she smiled and her colour deepened.

28.

Harald and Setter were the first to emerge for breakfast the next morning and chatted companionably while tucking into their eggs, bacon, and kippered herring. The others slipped into the dining room gradually. Both Janet and Annie looked a bit embarrassed and confessed that they had been slow to leave the comfort of their beds. The previous days' ride and the underlying tension caused by Radulescu had taken more of a toll than any of them had been prepared to acknowledge.

Setter appeared no worse for the night of vigilance. In fact, he seemed more relaxed than he had the night before, having slipped comfortably back into the policeman's role from which his injury had barred him for several months. It seemed logical that he should be the one to go to the village and deal with the local constable and so, with breakfast finished, Setter and the stableboy set out for Kinloch Rannoch in a cart drawn by a sturdy little Highland pony.

Once these steps had been taken, there was a general sense of relief and a realization that nothing much more could be done for the moment, either to protect Annie or to counter her tormentor. They spent the morning getting caught up with the newspapers, arranging for their riding clothes to be laundered, writing letters, and generally enjoying having nothing more pressing to do for the moment. Cavers announced that he would be delaying his departure for the Hart-Menzies estate, saying that he wanted to stay and help with plans to protect Annie and Janet. On hearing this, Ben lowered his newspaper and gave Cavers a look through narrowed eyes.

Over lunch they talked about what to do in the face of any new threat posed by Radulescu. The day was fine and they didn't want to spend it cowering in the house. That would feel like capitulation to Radulescu's bullying tactics. It was decided that no one should venture out alone and that the female members of the party should be accompanied when outside by at least one man.

Placing his napkin carefully in its ring, Harald said, "The rain's holding off and there's plenty to see and do. I'm for a bit of fly-fishing on the river, myself. Would anyone like to join me? I can provide waders, creels, and rods. The whole rig-out."

Gordon's eyes lit up. "That sounds wonderful, Harald. I'd like that. Annie, why don't you come along. It'll do you good."

"Oh, thank you, Gordon, and Harald," Annie said. "It does sound nice, but I'm not really feeling up to it. I think I'll just go to my room and read, if you don't mind. No, really—I'll be fine. You go ahead and enjoy yourselves, and I'll see you at dinner."

The others had ideas of their own. Charles and Maggie hinted strongly that they would like to go off by themselves and announced that they would walk along the lakeshore.

"Well, it says in Gordon's guidebook that there's a fine walk up along the hills to the north of here, about five miles in all, there and back," Ben said, looking directly at Violet. "Would anyone care to join me?"

"That sounds bracing. It'll be a change to walk uphill without a bicycle," Violet said. "Janet, won't you come with us?"

Janet had to calculate the need for chaperoning that had just been thrown her way and her concern for Annie. "Well, I don't know. I don't want to leave—"

"Nonsense, dear," Annie said. "I'll be fine here in the house. There are plenty of people about and the servants have been told to be on their guard. Off you go." She made shooing gestures at them all and she seemed, Charles thought, in spite of her supposed indisposition, to be more at ease than she had been for several days.

"I've some letters to write," Taplow said, "so I can help cover the home front."

Janet smiled at Taplow with relief and agreed to join the hill walkers.

"I wouldn't mind a good walk, myself," Cavers said to Ben. "Mind if I join you?"

"Wouldn't you rather be out shooting innocent grouse, Dwight?" Ben said.

"No, I wouldn't, Riddoch." Cavers halted, mid-thought. "You seem remarkably recovered since yesterday?"

"Ah, well, yes," Ben said. "I think there must be something in the air up here that promotes healing." He rubbed his hands together. "Very well, then. Let's set out in, shall we say, twenty minutes?"

Setter jumped down from the cart, using his good leg to take his full weight and flinching slightly as the other touched down. Kinloch Rannoch was comparatively bustling for there was an open market on Saturday mornings during the summer, and enough tourists nosing among the stalls to make the small village seem much bigger than its real size. He was relieved to be on his own again. Though Harald's hospitality had been genuine, he had felt the odd man out as usual. He could laugh at Williams's and Mrs. Fairclough's discreetly concealed consternation at having a wild Indian to see to, but he got sick of that pretty quickly.

He asked someone who seemed to be a local where the constabulary was, and was told to look for a low cottage with a blue door at the eastern end of the small High Street. He found the place easily and entered, dipping his head under the top of the low door frame. There was a wooden counter running the length of the small room and a desk behind it. Setter saw a silver bell on the counter, which he reached out to ring, but then noticed a small sign, somewhat dog-eared, propped up on a wooden stand by the bell.

CONSTABLE UNAVOIDABLY CALLED AWAY ON A POLICE MATTER.
ENQUIRE AT THE POST OFFICE.

Damn, Setter said to himself. *Another few rounds with the postmistress.* But to his relief, today the post office was manned by a young lad of about sixteen wearing a rough tweed suit one size too big for him, and heavy brogues. In short order the young man informed Setter that Constable McKechnie had been called out to the Bonnaird Estate, near the Falls of Garry, where the laird had complained of someone stealing his lambs. He wouldn't likely be back till after sundown.

"Damn, again," Setter said.

"I'm sorry, sir. We've just got the one, y'see. Just the one constable for all of Rannoch."

"No, no. I understand," Setter said. "Sorry, I wasn't swearing at you. It's just frustrating, that's all." He thought for a moment of telegraphing Inspector Storrs himself. *No, I wouldn't appreciate it if the tables were turned. Best to go through the proper channels if I want to get on their good side.*

He told the lad that he could be found at the hotel, where he would be staying overnight and asked him to tell the constable to contact him when he returned to the village, no matter how late. This arranged, he put his hat back on and turned toward the door.

"You're not a Chinaman at all, are you?" the boy said and when Setter turned back to look at him, he added. "Em…if you don't mind my asking."

"No. No, I'm not," Setter said and was about to say something rude, until he looked at the boy and realized from his intense expression, that he was genuinely curious. "I'm a half-breed from Red River, in Canada. One of the country-born of the northwest. A whole world away from here."

"Oh, aye! I've read *The Great Lone Land* three times. I'd like fine to see it."

"Maybe you will someday." Setter tipped his hat in farewell.

29.

The two parties of walkers set off from the terrace and waved to each other as they separated, Charles and Maggie to follow a trail to Rannoch Station on the Highland Railway line to the west; and Ben, Violet, Janet and Cavers to the north to thread their way among the low, sheep-covered hills to the north of the house. The weather was that Scottish form of inconclusive: overcast, but with occasional, promising glimpses of blue.

Charles and Maggie had just reached the path they were looking to follow when Maggie stopped abruptly. "Blast. I've just realized I'm wearing the wrong hat if it rains. This one will turn into a sodden mess. You wait here, and I'll just run back to the house and get the other."

Charles chose a tree to sit under, took out his penknife and began to look for a piece of wood to whittle away at while he waited.

Maggie half-trotted, half-walked back to the house. After she'd fetched the correct hat from her room, she walked by Annie's door, which was slightly ajar. She peeked around the door to satisfy herself that all was well: no one there. *She must be downstairs after all*, Maggie thought. Nothing to be alarmed about, really. She went down the massive main staircase and into the drawing room on the main floor. A quick look around all the nooks and crannies of the room showed that it was empty. Across the hall in the library, she found Taplow sitting at the large library table with his small address book, pen, inkwell, and writing paper neatly laid out on the green leather tabletop.

"Have you seen Annie?"

Taplow looked up from his work. "Not since luncheon. Isn't she in her room?"

"No. But I suppose she might be taking a bath. I'll just check."

She took the stairs upward quicker and went to the lavatory door closest to Annie's room. The door was shut, but the sounds of bathing, which she knew would be so much amplified by the high ceiling of the room, were absent. All was quiet.

"Annie? Annie, are you in there? Annie, it's Maggie. I just want to come in for a moment." But when she tried the door, it was locked.

"Are you all right, Annie?"

No answer. No sound. Maggie paced in front of the door, trying to think whether to be concerned. She ran back to Annie's room. Still no one there. Her eye was caught by something white on the pillow of the carefully made-up bed. She crossed the room and found that it was an envelope. She picked it up. It was addressed to Janet. In an instant she was down the hall and running down the stairs.

"Williams! Williams! Somebody! I need help with the door upstairs."

Taplow came running out of the library just as Williams appeared from the basement, dressed in an apron and silver-cleaning gloves. Maggie grabbed the sleeve of Taplow's jacket and began towing him toward the stairs.

"Quickly! You too, Williams. We have to get the door of the lavatory open. No time—I'll explain when we get there. Hurry!"

They took the stairs two and three at a time, Williams and Taplow trailing Maggie. When they got to the lavatory door, Maggie said, "She's in there and she's locked the door. I found a letter she wrote to Janet in her room. We'll have to force the door open somehow." She hurled herself against the door, but Taplow elbowed her aside.

"Williams, perhaps with the two of us?"

"Right, sir. When you're ready."

The two men began to bash their shoulders against the door in unison. On the third attempt they suddenly fell inward and sprawled on the lavatory floor. Maggie found Annie behind the now open door, gripping the handle as if it was all that was keeping her standing. She had on a dressing gown and her left arm was wrapped in a blood-soaked towel. She let go of the door handle and walked unsteadily to the bathtub, which was full of water. Maggie caught sight of an open straight razor on the floor, staining the white tiles red. Annie sank down onto the side of the bathtub.

Maggie dropped to her knees beside Annie. She felt for Annie's other arm, ran her own hand along it until she got to the wrist. There was no cut.

"Williams, fetch a doctor, please," Maggie said, standing up and grabbing a towel off the rack. "Mr. Taplow, do you know how to make a tourniquet?"

"I think so, but it may not be necessary. I'll try putting pressure on the wound. You keep her warm."

Maggie wrapped the towel around Annie.

"Annie?" Maggie said. "You're all right, now. You're going to be all right."

Taplow rooted through the linen cupboard, found some hand towels, and fashioned them into a thick pad, which he pressed carefully with increasing pressure against the blood-soaked towel around Annie's wrist. Together, Maggie and Taplow gently raised her forearm until the wrist was higher than her heart and held it there.

"Do you think you can walk, Annie?" Maggie said.

"I think so." It was the barest whisper and the first thing Annie had said.

Later, after Annie had been put to bed with the help of one of the maids and Mrs. Fairclough had bandaged her wrist, Maggie sat on the edge of the bed and held Annie's good hand.

"You should sleep now, Annie. The doctor will be arriving soon. I'll sit with you until he gets here."

"I didn't cut the second one."

"The second? Oh, of course. Thank goodness you didn't. Rest now."

"But—it's important. I came to a decision, and I didn't cut the second one."

"Shhh. We can talk about this later. Janet should be coming back from the walk soon."

"No. Not later. I want to talk to you before Janet comes."

"Before Janet? Why?"

"Because I need a bit of a rehearsal…before I talk to Janet."

"I see. All right, Annie. I'll listen."

"I did it because I was ashamed—and afraid. I was afraid the strain…I was afraid of being that way again, of losing control of my mind. All the signs were there: my thoughts racing, sleep not coming. Just the way it happened in Switzerland."

"In Switzerland? Annie? What was it? What happened in Switzerland?"

"It was as if I fell into a dark hole and I couldn't get out of that hole. I didn't know who I was, or where I was. It was horrible!"

"Do you mean—was it a nervous collapse?"

"I mean, I went mad, Maggie. I was completely lost. And if I have to be that way again, it will bring such shame on our family. I'm sure there must have been something I did to bring it on, something wrong, a weakness in my character, or some sin that I have committed all unaware and God—"

"No, Annie! No. Don't punish yourself this way." Tears ran down Annie's face and she turned away her head.

"Annie, listen to me. Some of the most forward-thinking research into the mind has been done by Professor James, and by other doctors whose lectures I attended at Tübingen. They say that diseases of the mind are just like those of the body. In time, perhaps we will know why they happen to certain people and how to prevent them from happening. You were no more responsible for your episode of neurasthenia than—than Ben was responsible for his dislocated finger."

"But I felt certain it must be my own lack of...of something necessary, of strength to resist it. Why could I not prevent it from taking hold of me?"

"I'm not a doctor. Dear knows, and if I knew that, I would be the toast of— But wait a moment. Annie, is this what Mr. Radulescu is holding over you? Did he know something of your breakdown?"

Annie sighed. "Yes, he was there in the hotel in Switzerland, for the hiking and climbing. We were slightly acquainted. I had made a friend there. Someone, a man, that I thought would be more than a friend." Annie gripped Maggie's hand

and looked searchingly at her. "I was deeply in love with this man, but I found that he was simply courting me to while away his time, as an amusing aside on his grand tour before he returned to his home in Boston."

"Oh, Annie. I'm so sorry."

"When he left, I fell down that dark hole. Down and down and I couldn't get out. I'm told that I had to be carried out of the hotel, raving." She paused and dropped her voice so low that Maggie had to strain to hear her. "So deep in that hole that I have no memory of it."

"And—and Radulescu?"

"He must have seen me in that state, and remembered me when we bought that manuscript from him last year in Cairo. I was terrified that he would say something to Janet. He didn't, but he had it in reserve when he decided that our manuscript was more valuable than he'd originally thought."

"But how were you able to keep this from Janet?"

"She had just married Merton and gone to live in England. That's why I was in Switzerland, at a bit of a loose end. And, I suppose, hoping for a romance of my own after a few disappointments in that department."

"But if you were so ill?"

"I recovered, thank God, and thanks to the clinic I was taken to near Geneva. It took six months, but I came back to myself. While I was there, Merton fell ill and died. Janet needed me and I came home. It helped me a great deal to be needed by someone. After that, I—well, I tried to tell her so many times, but I was so ashamed, the words just wouldn't come."

"And now that you've told me?"

"That's why I wanted to tell you: that's why I didn't cut my other wrist. I decided that I wouldn't let Radulescu do that to me. Strange that all the dread I felt, all the fear of slipping into that state of mania, became quite still at that moment. I decided that nothing could be worse than the feeling of being shamed to death by him. So, I tried to stop the blood myself. Then when you called at the door, I remember thinking very clearly that perhaps if I could tell you, then the next time wouldn't be so hard. I called out that I was going to open the door, but I don't think Mr. Taplow and Williams heard me through all that commotion."

"Oh, Annie!" Maggie gently put her arms around Annie. "You've done it! You've come through."

30.

Dinner that evening was a strangely merry affair. Annie was still in her room and under orders from the doctor, who had arrived from Kinloch Rannoch late in the afternoon. She was to rest for two days. He said he would look in on her the next day to change the dressing and after that, if there was no infection, she should be able to care for the wound herself, with the aid of her sister.

It was clear from Janet's attitude at dinner that Annie had told her about the episode of neurasthenia, and that Janet had been so relieved to know the source of her sister's pain that she was almost giddy. She had told the others that the dreaded secret was now out in the open, but had not given any further explanation. Maggie could tell that the others were highly curious in spite of themselves, as she would have been in their place, but she remained close-lipped. She knew that Annie was still in a vulnerable state of mind and her sense of privacy had to be respected. If Annie wanted to tell the others she would do it in her own good time.

"Think of it!" Janet said, sipping her coffee in the drawing room. "I do sincerely believe that, as Christ said, 'Ye shall know the truth and the truth shall make you free.' Now that horrible man has no hold over us. Annie has told me all there is to know and we need not be afraid of the consequences."

"I am happy for you, Mrs. Thorburn," Taplow said. "Men like Radulescu sicken everything they touch."

"That is so, Mr. Taplow," Janet said. "But I haven't thanked you for all you did for Annie. I am extremely grateful."

Taplow said nothing, but inclined his head to her.

"Of course," Janet said. "This means that we shall live to fight you another day."

"I shall look forward to that," Taplow said quietly. "May you, and I, have strength for the battle."

"But presumably, Radulescu is still out there somewhere," Charles said. "He still thinks he has the upper hand over Annie, so is plotting to get your manuscript even now."

"Aye," Harald said. "We still need to be on our guard against him. It's unfortunate that we're not further along with the police. Sergeant Setter's note said the constable would not be back until—" Harald looked at his watch. "—until about now. Even if Constable McKechnie rousts Miss Grant out of her bed to send a telegram to the County Police in Perth, they won't be able to get here until tomorrow afternoon at the earliest. And, of course, tomorrow is the Sabbath."

"Well, I for one will be sleeping more soundly tonight than I have for several nights," Janet said.

"I'm glad, my dear," Harald said. "But keep your door locked just the same. Now, where has Gordon got to? I promised to teach him how to tie a Black Pennell fly."

"He's just slipped up to Annie's room. He promised to read to her."

The others had gone to bed. Violet was preparing to do the same and was searching the shelves in the library. Harald had quite a good section on animal husbandry and she was auditioning one fat volume as her bedtime reading material. She was so engrossed that she did not hear Cavers enter the room and quietly close the door to the hallway.

"I see we had the same idea, Miss Pitkeathly," Cavers said.

"Oh!" Violet started. "Mr. Cavers. Lord! You must be very good at shooting. You've mastered the quiet approach."

"I'm sorry to startle you. Please forgive me," Cavers said and crossed to where she was standing. "But, it's funny, ever since we met, I've had no luck at keeping you in close enough range to really talk to you. May we talk now?"

"Em…well." Violet looked around and saw that the door had been closed. "I suppose so. But it is quite late."

"I'm afraid I'm not much good at romantic speeches, Violet. I know that young ladies are supposed to tease their beaus and deliberately appear to be indifferent to them. It's supposed to test our mettle, make us more ardent. Well, I am more ardent, so there's no need for this pretense."

"Mr. Cavers, I do not indulge in those kinds of parlour games. I'm not feigning anything."

"Look, I'm not the kind of man to beat around the bush. I am offering you marriage, Violet. I am worth substantially more than a million pounds, and my business is going nowhere but up. But never mind that. I am offering you myself. I can be a good husband to you and a good father to our children. I've waited a long time for the right person." Cavers gripped Violet's hands and pulled her toward him. "It's you, Violet." He took a deep breath. "Now, will you do me the honour, the inestimable—"

"Don't! Mr. Cavers! Please listen to me before you say anything more," Violet said, straining to free her hands. "I have done nothing to encourage this. Would you mind letting me go? I have never given the slightest intimation to you that

I welcomed your attentions. Really, this is most vexing. Let me go!"

Cavers released her hands with a bewildered look. "What the—? Well, what were you doing at all those balls and dinners in London, then, if you're not looking for a match?"

"I'm not interested in marrying *you*, Mr. Cavers. I haven't rejected the entire male species."

The light dawned for Cavers. "I'll be damned. There's someone else, isn't there? Don't tell me Riddoch got in before me! Damn his hide! That's what comes of letting women bicycle all over the countryside!"

"If that is an example of your attitudes, then I am doubly right to reject you!"

"It can't be Riddoch, Violet! Are you telling me that you prefer that—that slogan-spouting layabout to me? Riddoch will spend his whole life undermining his betters while you support him. He's a blasted gadfly of so little substance, it's a wonder he doesn't float entirely away!"

"Ben actually listens to me and appears to care what I say, instead of talking past me, as you do. You haven't once said that you wanted to get to know me better, or that you cared about me as anything more than an heir-producing machine and a provider of lands of convenience."

There was a rustle of papers behind them.

"Well, I certainly liked the sound of that, Vi." The voice came from somewhere behind a large bookcase. "I thought 'heir-producing machine' was particularly good. Although, Dwight, the gadfly phrase was also extremely clever. Really, I wouldn't have thought it of you."

"Ben!"

"Riddoch, what the hell? Have you been here all this time! Damnation! I've had about enough—"

"Steady on, Dwight. Look, I apologize to both of you. I

didn't intend to eavesdrop, but I was over on the other side of the room reading Harald's rather excellent selection of newspapers. Then the two of you started to yammer and I couldn't escape."

Cavers said, "Ha!" jerked his head toward the ceiling and put his hands on his hips.

Ben put his little notebook and pen in his pocket and walked slowly toward them. "Vi's right though, Dwight. You never once said that you love her, or that you'd put her first before everything else. She's a wonderful girl, in spite of her upbringing and—"

"My upbringing? Thank you, Ben Riddoch, for your condescension," Violet said. "My *upbringing* didn't seem to matter to you while we were on the road. Or did you regard me as a challenge?"

"No, Vi. What I'm trying to tell you is—"

"You were going to go off to the Isles, doubtless to romance some other innocent girl. Then Mr. Cavers appeared and suddenly the chase was exciting again. Apparently, you're not as scornful of competition as you pretend to be."

"No, Vi, no. You've got the wrong idea. I stayed because I care for you and because Dwight here was likely to barrel ahead. And I wasn't sure what his game was."

"Oh, come on!" Cavers said. "As if you had no game of your own!"

Ben turned to Cavers. "Look, you're the one who—"

"He's right, though, isn't he?" Violet said. "After all, I'd be quite the feather in your cap, wouldn't I? You could tell all your socialist friends in Glasgow how easy it was to seduce the witless female proprietor of one of those estates you say my family stole from its rightful owners."

"Oh, I think you're too kind to him, Violet," Cavers said. "He's more than a seducer. Take away all the political blather and you'll find a man who lusts after your money just as much as any chinless wonder with an overdraft at his club."

Ben grabbed Cavers' lapels, shook him, and pulled him forward so that Cavers' face was uncomfortably close to his own. "No. Do you hear me?" He gave Cavers a shake. "That is an insult to Vi and I won't have it. Do you think she could care for a man like that? Do you?"

"Stop it, both of you! Ben! Let go of him. Please!"

Ben let go, wincing as the material of Cavers' tailcoat caught on his injured finger, but Cavers stood his ground.

"Please! Back away, Dwight. Ben, put your hands down."

The near-combatants held each other's gaze for a long moment, then both took a slow step backward, breathing heavily.

"No more of this tonight. I mean it. No more!" she said, and exhaled in relief as they remained apart. "Thank you. Now, I'm going to bed and I hope you will do the same." She looked from one to the other with a sad expression, reached for her book and left the room.

The two men stared at the closed door for a moment. Ben tugged his waistcoat back into position. "She's got the wrong idea about me, Dwight. And so have you. But I have one advantage that you don't have."

"What's that?"

"The fact is I've got nothing to offer her of a material nature and I don't need anything of a material nature from her."

"I doubt that but, anyway, how could that possibly be an advantage?"

"All I have to prove to her is that we could have a life together. Because I offer only myself and I want in return only the unencumbered Vi. That's all."

31.

Charles made his way through the crowded courtyard of the castle as quickly as he could without actually knocking people down. It seemed to be a fair day of some sort, and hawkers and animals were bent on getting in his way. Didn't they know he had to hurry? It seemed as if he'd been looking for her forever and no one he met knew where she was, or they didn't care and tried to waylay him on some pretext or other. He finally reached the far side of the courtyard and found the entrance to a spiral staircase. He dashed upward, taking the stairs two at a time with the oil from the torches lighting the stairway acrid in his nostrils. Then all of a sudden he was in a ballroom with dancers laughing and beckoning him to join in some kind of "Eightsome Reel." He was caught in the middle of their circle and didn't want to be impolite, so he tried a few high cuts, which seemed to impress the dancers and they yelled their encouragement. He had always considered himself a good dancer, so he showed off a few more of his best steps. He really seemed to be dancing well and the music was intoxicating. He looked up at the stage and saw a man dressed as a clown beating time on a large drum. Then a terrible feeling, anxiety mixed with confusion, flooded back. Why had he been diverted by this silly dancing? He had to find her and there was no time to lose. He had to. Now, what was that noise? The clown banging on the drum was calling his name. *Not now, for goodness sake. Don't you see I've got to—hmmm?* For some reason he had a pillow covering his head. He shoved the pillow to one side and through bleary eyes turned his head and caught sight of lace curtains billowing out from a window.

It wasn't drumming after all. More like knocking, not loud but at persistent intervals.

"Mr. Lauchlan? Mr. Lauchlan, I'm sorry to disturb you. Sir? I need a word, sir."

Charles came fully awake with a start. "Yes. Yes, hold on a moment. I'm coming." He threw the bedclothes back and swung his feet to the floor in one quick movement. After rolling to his feet and fighting the sudden dizzying sensation, he grabbed a towel, wrapped it around his waist and shoved his hair back from his eyes. When he opened the door, he found Williams, who looked relieved at being able to stop the infernal racket.

"Oh, Thank goodness, sir. You're awake. So sorry to disturb."

"Williams? What—is something wrong?"

"Well, sir, something has—em—come up and we could use your assistance. I wonder, would you be kind enough to dress and meet Mr. Dibbage in the dining room?"

"Well, yes, of course. But what's happened?"

"Mr. Dibbage will inform you fully, sir, of what we know at present."

"At present? Right, well…I'll be down directly. What time is it?"

"Just gone six-thirty, sir."

When Charles walked through the door of the dining room, Harald and several other men were clustered around the buffet table eating what looked like rolls filled with bacon and drinking coffee. One of the footmen, with livery buttoned haphazardly and a shirt-tail hanging down, bustled in and out of the kitchen, placing dishes and filling coffee cups. They were all dressed for outdoors and looked in fact as if they had already been out in the weather. Charles recognized the one wearing leather gaiters as Harald's estate manager.

"Ah, Charles. Bit of a surprise wakening, I'm afraid. Sorry to drag you out of bed earlier than normal."

"That's all right, Harald. Good morning, gentlemen." They all murmured a welcome around full mouths. "What's happened? Is everything all right?"

"I'm glad to say that all under my roof and on the estate are well. But Dekker here woke me an hour ago with some sobering news."

Charles picked up a coffee cup from the buffet. "What about?"

Dekker, the estate manager, picked up the thread. "One of my men was walking out early to look for a ewe that went missing last night. When he was walking past the weir that we operate on the burn, he saw something caught there. At first, he thought it might be the ewe but...well, it turned out to be a body."

"A body? Good Lord! Was it—?"

"Dead. Yes," Harald said. "It appears that the poor fellow drowned in the burn."

"Have you identified who it is?"

"Not as yet. He's certainly not from around here. I fear it's some traveller walking in the hills who lost his way and fell into the water during the night. No telling where he might have fallen in upstream."

"Poor man," Charles said. "He died all alone then, with no one to help him."

"It appears so. I didn't know what to do for the best. I presume Constable McKechnie will be arriving with Sergeant Setter at some point, so we ought not to move him yet. But, I mean, it seems horrible just to leave him there by the side of the burn until then. I wondered, you know, if you could come out and say a bit of a prayer for him."

"Yes, yes of course."

At that moment, the door to the dining room opened and Taplow stepped into the room, giving them all a tentative look.

"Good morning, gentlemen. I heard stirrings and I wondered if I might be of help."

Harald told the story again, which Taplow received gravely, and within minutes they were all following a wooded path to the weir, which was located about a quarter mile from the house. Charles walked shoulder to shoulder with Taplow, but neither was very talkative, nor was Charles looking forward to what they would find at the end of this path. He had seen death up close many times, but had never seen a victim of drowning before. Taplow looked exactly the way Charles felt and, when Charles asked him, Taplow said that he had once had to help fish a body out of the Cam and that he had found the experience "rather unsettling."

The body, now covered by a horse blanket, had been hauled up from the place where it had been entangled and placed by the side of the impounded pool created by the weir. There were sounds of the river rushing both downstream and upstream from the pool, but here the water was quiet. Once they had all gathered round, Harald gently pulled the blanket away from the head and chest.

"I'll be damned!" Taplow said. He leaned in closer to the body.

"What?" Harald turned to him. "Do you know him?"

"It's Radulescu. It's the man we've all been guarding against!"

Six months, Constable Davie McKechnie had confided to Setter on the way out from Kinloch Rannoch. It had been only six months since he had joined the Perthshire County Police and become the sole constable in Kinloch Rannoch. He was all of twenty-one and green in every way, Setter observed as he and McKechnie knelt over the body of Joachim Radulescu.

Looking back to his own first collision with a dead body, Setter felt keenly for the lad. He whispered under his breath, "It helps not to look too closely at first. Focus on that rowan tree over across the way till you get your bearings. That's right, take a few deep breaths. Now, if this were Winnipeg, I would be asking these gentlemen for all the facts they might know about this man. But take your time getting up."

McKechnie said nothing, but nodded and swallowed. He and Setter got up slowly from their knees, McKechnie still looking at the rowan and Setter leaning heavily on his cane. Charles suggested that they have a prayer before the constable began his inquiries and the young man looked relieved.

As the small party of men removed their caps and bowed their heads Charles realized with a shock that none of his standard prayers for the dead would do for Radulescu, an attacker of the innocent and a blackmailer who, as far as Charles knew, had been completely unrepentant. After a moment's hesitation, he commended Radulescu's soul to the infinite mercy of God, using a quote from Psalm 51: "Wash me thoroughly from mine iniquity, and cleanse me from my sin." He felt like a hypocrite repeating these words when all he felt was contempt for Annie's tormentor.

After the collective "Amen," McKechnie took out his notebook and pencil and, clearing his throat, began the finicky procedure of taking statements, first from Geordie Henderson, the shepherd who had found the body, then from Dekker and Harald, and finally, from Taplow, who had to formally identify the deceased.

The constable announced, at the end of the statements, in a voice just a little louder than necessary, "As this appears to be a case of accidental death, I will now take charge of the body. And I will be calling in a superior officer and the procurator fiscal, who may wish to order a—em—a—"

"Postmortem?" Setter said.

"Yes, that's right, a postmortem examination."

"We'd best move him into a byre or an outbuilding," Dekker said.

"Ah, no. I'm afraid I cannae allow that, sir. It's best that we move him as little as possible until the inspector and the fiscal get a look at him." He took off his helmet and dried his forehead with a handkerchief while looking at the sky. "I just hope it isnae going to be a warm day."

"It's likely going to take some time for reinforcements to arrive, Constable," Setter said. "Perhaps there are provisions for these situations?"

The look of a desperate forest creature crept back into McKechnie's eyes. "Yes. Yes." He unbuttoned the top of his tunic and drew out of an inner pocket a small book with the title *Powers and Duties of the Police Constable* embossed in gold on the cover. After a couple of minutes of intense concentration on its pages, he snapped the volume shut and announced, "Em, in the absence of a superior officer, I will conduct an initial examination of the body and its clothing, and I will ask two of you to formally witness my search. Sergeant, if you wouldnae mind?"

"Certainly. Glad to be of service."

"I'll be happy to be the other witness," Charles said, forestalling Taplow, who had hovered uncertainly, seeming to argue with himself as to whether to volunteer.

McKechnie approached the body and knelt beside it again, the other two following. The young constable removed his helmet and set it carefully behind him. He laid his notebook close by and began his observations. Setter gave a series of prompts thinly disguised as questions: about body temperature, the extent of rigor mortis and the extent and location of lividity. McKechnie duly observed, commented, and wrote in his notebook.

"It seems odd that a relatively young, fit man would drown in such a small river," Charles said. "The current is strong, but nothing an experienced swimmer couldn't handle. There are plenty of rocks to grab and scrabble onto."

"Mebbe he fell in and hit his head," McKechnie said. Setter nodded and McKechnie looked closely at the head and tried gingerly to lift it, in order to see all the way around. "Hmph. Stiff. Hard to say without turning him over, but so far I can't see any sign of blood or broken skin, or any swelling."

"I wonder if there are broken bones," Setter said. "An injury like that would hamper him swimming to save himself. That and the cold might induce shock."

The constable cleared his throat. He had remained quite pale, but Setter sensed that he would be able to steady himself. McKechnie began running his hands along the arms and legs. "The stiffness makes it difficult, but I can't feel anything—no obvious broken bones."

McKechnie began to search methodically through Radulescu's clothing, turning out all his pockets and noting the contents in his notebook. There was no wallet, purse, money, or identification.

"He's been robbed then." Taplow's voice surprised them, since the others, not being involved in the search or the witnessing, had withdrawn from the body about ten feet and had begun to chat quietly. Taplow had remained close to the group huddled over the body and, though he had been pacing slowly to and fro, had evidently been following the examination closely.

"Aye. It seems that way," McKechnie said.

"I've heard that tinkers frequent these parts. Given a chance, they might indulge in thievery, and worse," Taplow said.

"Or he deliberately removed those things himself," Charles said. "Could it be suicide?"

"Ha!" Taplow said. "That's the last thing that would occur to a man like Radulescu. He could never deprive the world of his presence."

"Wait! Look at this." Until now, though he had been sorely tempted, Setter had prevented himself from touching the body, leaving that to McKechnie as was fitting. But now he ran his fingers over some dark marks on Radulescu's neck. "Can you loosen his tie and collar, Constable?"

McKechnie looked closely at Radulescu's throat just above his collar. "Is that not the lividity?"

"No, I don't think so. See, it isn't mottled. And the pattern is different." Setter motioned the constable to proceed. McKechnie loosened the knot of the necktie and with difficulty opened the top button of the soft-collared shirt.

"See, here," Setter said. "It looks like there's a mark where the tie knot has been pushed hard against his throat."

"So, it could be bruising, I suppose."

"I agree, Constable. I think it's bruising. Any notion what might have caused it?"

McKechnie looked intently at Radulescu's neck and a look of horror passed slowly over his face. "Strewth! The poor bugger's been throttled!" Incredulous, he looked up at Charles and Setter. "That is…that is, em…it appears as if the deceased has been strangled."

32.

"I simply can't believe it!" Janet said. "You're sure? I mean, that it is Radulescu?"

"Absolutely certain, Mrs. Thorburn," Taplow said. "As I told you before, I've had dealings with him on more than one occasion."

"But, strangled?" Violet's hand drifted up to her throat. "Who could have done that to him?"

"We won't—that is, the police—won't be able to address that matter until a doctor confirms the constable's finding of death by strangulation," Setter said. "Since the constable has to remain with the body, I've suggested that I go back to the village right away and telegraph this latest news to Inspector Storrs in Perth. He'll have to come along with somebody called the proc—the proc—"

"The procurator fiscal." Harald said.

"Something like our Crown attorney in Canada, as I understand it," Cavers said.

"Well, you'll have a deal of trouble convincing Miss Grant to open the post office and send a wire, Sergeant," Harald said. "It's the Sabbath and most folk hereabouts are rock firm in their intention to do no work on the Lord's Day. In fact, you'll have to wait for her at the church door and paint this as the direst emergency."

"Well, surely a probable murder should count as that?" Setter said.

Harald and Setter left the breakfast room to organize Setter's return trip to Kinloch Rannoch and left the company—with the exception of Annie, who was breakfasting on a tray in her room—trying to come to grips with the news that Annie's tormentor had been suddenly and violently silenced.

"I can hardly take it in," Gordon said. "Such a shock. But I can't really say that I'm sorry the blackguard is dead. I mean, Janet, at least he won't be able to do anything further to hurt you and Annie. But who could have done you such a macabre favour?"

"Yes," Janet said, a pained look on her face, "that was my first thought, and God forgive me for thinking it."

"Well," Taplow said, "excluding the possibility that Miss Gairdner rose from her bed of pain to do the deed, we can only speculate that he was set upon by thieves, perhaps tinkers. If he decided to fight them—and he was just rash enough to do it—they could have panicked and done more than they intended."

"I suppose so, Taplow," Ben said. "But aren't the police likely to think of an explanation closer at hand? I mean there are several of us here who, if the opportunity presented itself, would at least have thought about hastening him into the next world."

"For goodness sake, Ben!" Violet said. "You can't be suggesting that one of us did it?"

"No. I'll here and now proclaim my innocence, in spite of Dwight's dark looks over there, and my faith in all of you, but we have to be realistic. Police always look at motive, and no one in this room wished that bastard anything but ill. Excuse my language."

"I'm sure we can all account for our movements in a convincing manner," Maggie said. "For example, the four of you." She pointed to Janet, Violet, Ben and Cavers. "Presumably you were together all the time during your walk yesterday. You'd have hardly had an unwitnessed moment to commit a murder—of Radulescu, at any rate."

Charles couldn't quite stifle the lopsided smile that came to his lips in response to Maggie's probably unintentional teasing remark, and he saw more than one similar one around the room. It did rather lighten the mood, though not for everyone. Violet had blushed crimson, Cavers glowered and Ben's automatic smile seemed forced. Looking at them all, Charles was reminded of something Maggie had said on the way to the Black Spout. He and Maggie did have an unspoken—and perhaps unexamined—faith in these people, most of whom they had never met before this week. The necessity of pulling together against an outside threat had deflected any questions about each other. Radulescu's death was certainly timely from Janet and Annie's point of view. Charles was finding the questions that began forming up in his head rather uncomfortable.

They caught up to Setter in the stable yard, where he was helping a stable hand hitch a fresh pony to the cart in which he and McKechnie had ridden from Kinloch Rannoch.

"We've come to help you with the rig," Charles said.

"Kind of you, but there's no need. I can now follow the route to the village in my sleep."

"Well, we have an ulterior motive," Maggie said. "We need the benefit of your famous rational skills."

"How can I refuse when you put it like that," Setter said. He gave a nod to the stable hand. "Thanks very much, Gregor. I'll take it from here." The boy handed the tack to Setter, touched his cap to Maggie, and returned to the stable.

"It's like this." Charles took the bridle from Setter. "We can't think straight about this business. And you have to admit, it's more in your line."

"Well, hold on now. It's the Perth County Police whose job this is. I'm just a bystander." He put the horse collar around the pony's neck and began fastening the harness.

"Who do you think you're fooling, Andrew?" Maggie said. "Not yourself, I hope. You're in it up to your eyeballs and, what's more, you're enjoying every minute."

Setter laughed and grew a bit red about the ears. "All right. I suppose I am feeling rather in my element. But that doesn't change the jurisdictional facts. If I can be of help, I won't fail, but I've got to maintain a hands-off position unless asked."

"Well, we're asking," Charles said, slipping the bridle over the pony's head. "After you left, Ben raised the possibility that one of us could have been the murderer." He looked over at Maggie. "We hate to think of that being true, but we also can't get over the fact that Radulescu's death was incredibly convenient as far as Janet and Annie are concerned. Tell us we're wrong to be thinking this way."

"Well, actually, no one should be ruled out as a suspect without a thorough airing of the evidence. You know that as well as I do."

"But surely the ladies can be eliminated," Maggie said as she ran her hand down the pony's nose.

"Not necessarily. Women in the grip of strong feeling can have surprising strength," Setter said. "Look, don't get down in the mouth about this. It's likely that no one in your party is guilty. He could have been attacked by someone intending to rob him. I'm just saying that the circle has to be drawn wide at first. Then we look at motive and opportunity. That's the key to reducing the diameter of that circle till it holds just one person."

"I suppose we'll have to wait for Inspector Storrs and the procurator fiscal—and the doctor—to arrive before that whole process can start. Wait, I think we have to pull the cart forward a bit." Charles and Setter pulled on the shafts of the cart so that the pony was positioned properly between the shafts and began fastening the traces to the harness.

"There, that's good," Setter said. "Yes, it's unfortunate. The longer it takes for a doctor to examine the body, the harder it is to pinpoint time of death accurately, and so on."

"I suppose," Maggie said, "that if the murderer is still around here—in the house or on the grounds, say—he might reveal something through his behaviour. It's like Professor Planck says about atoms: no one has ever seen them, but we can be pretty sure they're there because of the way they behave. So, we ought to be on the lookout for strange doings."

Setter and Charles laughed. "I never knew physics had so much to say about murder investigations," Setter said. "But listen, you two, leave it to the police to investigate *strange doings*. This is a dangerous business and I would be much more comfortable while I'm gone if I knew the two of you were staying well out of it."

"Don't worry," Charles said. "We'll just keep our eyes open. I think we know where the boundary is."

Setter, unconvinced, gave them a look and shook his head. "I certainly hope that you do. Just remember what I said." He got up onto the seat of the pony cart with some difficulty, settled his cane in the footwell, shook the reins, and drove off down the lane.

33.

"Let's go for a walk," Charles said, his eyes following Setter's progress as he reached the end of the lane and turned the pony cart eastward toward Kinloch Rannoch.

"Yes, let's," she said, taking the hand he held out to her. "You may laugh all you want, but physics does have a lot to say about murder investigations, now that I think of it. You have to put emotions to the side and try to see what's in front of you in as objective a way as possible. Think what would have happened if Newton had not questioned the received wisdom of his age about how bodies with mass behave."

"I can't think of what." He batted his eyelashes fetchingly.

"You can't escape it that easily," she said, laughing and dancing out in front of him, backing down the path as he walked toward her. "We wouldn't have the law of universal gravitation, that's what."

She stopped suddenly to underline her point, causing him to bump into her. The warmth of her breath was on his face and also her scent, compounded of lilac water and something earthier. "If we're talking about irresistible forces, here's one that I think eluded poor Newton," he said, gently pushing her until her back rested against a tree trunk and kissing her.

For a short while they rested in each other's arms, taking comfort there because, in spite of their mutual effort to make light of it, the morning had been disturbing. Then more urgent feelings took over which they knew could only be indulged so far; a sweet and seductive game of pushing against that imperative.

When Maggie broke away, Charles took his cap off and fanned his face, casting his eyes upward. "When we are safely married, remind me to tell you about the effect on the male of prolonged temptation without the outlet of fulfillment." He sighed deeply.

She laughed and pressed her hands to her face with embarrassment. "I'm so sorry, my dear, dear Charles. To ask you to be patient just a while longer seems cruel, but I do have to ask it, for just a while longer."

He sighed again, nodded assent, and kissed her hand. "Maybe," he said, "we should leave biology and return to physics." They resumed their walk down the path. "I gather you think we should set our feelings aside and submit our little group to methodical scrutiny."

"Yes, exactly. Let's start with the people who had something obvious to gain by Radulescu's death."

"Annie and Janet."

"Yes. I'd put Gordon in that category too."

"Right. He had nothing personally to gain, but it's pretty obvious how he feels about Annie, even in the short time he's known her. He'd be very angry with Radulescu. But angry enough to kill him? I can't see it."

"No, I can't either. But we can't totally eliminate him from suspicion."

"Can we eliminate Annie by virtue of her weakened

condition and the wound to her wrist?" he said.

"Working on the law of probabilities, I think we can. Or at least put her at the bottom of the list, as being extremely unlikely."

"Janet then?"

"Not so easy to eliminate. She's very fit and you've seen how fiercely protective of Annie she is. But she's Free Church to the core. Can you imagine her breaking the Sixth Commandment?"

"No, but remember what Andrew said about the grip of emotion. I suppose she must stay on the list, on a level with Gordon." Charles saw a log along the side of the path and motioned her to sit down beside him.

"What about the others?" she said, lifting her skirt free of the mud of the trail as she sat down.

Harald was placed just below Janet and Gordon and above Annie on their probability list. He was clearly fond of both sisters, but he was also over sixty and seemed unlikely to be a physical match for Radulescu.

One by one they discounted Violet, Ben, and Taplow as having no strong or discernible motive to kill Radulescu. Cavers was even farther down the list, having never before met Annie, Janet, or Radulescu for that matter. They reviewed their list and felt that the exercise had been interesting, but that no great insight had been gained. Maggie looked at Charles who was pressing his lips together and narrowing his eyes.

"What is it?" she said.

"Taplow. Think about what it is that ties Radulescu, Annie, Janet, and Taplow together."

"Manuscripts?"

"Manuscripts. Exactly. The buying and selling of the same."

"But that's an association only. What motive could

Taplow possibly have for murdering Radulescu?"

Charles shook his head and sighed. "I don't know. But that's the point, isn't it? We don't really know anything about our new friends beyond the short frame of our acquaintance on the road. But Taplow…you pick up subtle whiffs of things from people, maybe things that are a little jarring or that don't add up."

"Such as?"

"Well, take for instance his sudden appearance on the tour. Of all the people in the world, what are the odds of the sisters' arch enemy turning up to join our bicycle tour?"

"It seemed very surprising at the time, but he didn't know that Janet was the tour leader."

"Yes, but I've been wondering about that. Remember when we first met Andrew at Kinloch Rannoch? He said that the girl at the counter at Maclaren's said that Taplow knew Janet was leading the tour, and yet he still wanted to join us."

"Yes, that's right. I'd forgotten. But does that really mean anything? He told a white lie to cover up…what? Maybe a desire to ferret out what the opposition is thinking? An opportunity to do that landed in his lap and he acted on it."

"Yes, but did it? Did it just land in his lap? You heard Taplow say he hadn't been further from Cambridge than Norfolk in years for his holiday. Suddenly he takes a notion to bicycle through the Highlands?"

"Are you suggesting he knew the sisters were planning this trip and he arranged things deliberately so that he could join their tour?"

"It wouldn't be that hard to do, would it? Setter was able to read our itinerary at Maclaren's easily. Let's see. Taplow comes up to Edinburgh looking for some way of finding out what the sisters are up to. He finds out somehow—from a servant at Greenhill Gardens, say—that the sisters are arranging a tour through Maclaren's. He sets up a bogus tour there too, then his fictitious tour mates cancel and he throws himself on the mercy of Maclaren's."

"But what about Gordon? He was supposedly on the same tour."

"Hmmm, yes," Charles said, "that's a problem. Ah, but you see, Maclaren's wouldn't know that Taplow's other tour mates were fictitious. Gordon didn't want to cycle alone—he told me so—and Maclaren's said there was room on Taplow's tour. Gordon's presence made Taplow's tour look more legitimate. They arrived at our tour as a pair, thus making Taplow's presence less singular and suspicious." He beamed in triumph.

"You have a very devious mind."

"Comes from years of foiling parishioners' plans to avoid the minister's visit."

"But, really. Even supposing that Taplow intended to join Janet's tour all along, that only suggests he wanted to get some sort of information out of the sisters. What does that have to do with Radulescu?"

"Well, all right. This is where my devious mind grinds to a halt. I have no idea, other than the fact that Taplow had previous dealings with Radulescu, presumably over acquiring manuscripts. You heard him say that he was trying to build the holdings of his college's collection."

They both thought about this for several minutes. Charles picked up a stick and drew lines and circles in the mud of the pathway. Maggie pulled a sprig of leaves off the tree next to the log and ran her fingertips along the veins of the leaves. But no further meaningful connections between Radulescu and Taplow materialized out of these musings.

"Well, we're not going to get any further sitting here," she said, standing up and tossing the sprig of leaves into the forest. "We need more information."

"Now, wait a minute. This isn't a game, darling girl, however much we may find it fascinating to speculate on these matters. Andrew's right. A man has been killed, the murderer might be close at hand, and the police are the ones best equipped to deal with it."

"I realize that. But poor Constable McKechnie is sitting up there all alone and it will be hours and hours before Inspector Storrs gets here. We're just being good citizens and observing what there is to observe."

Charles fixed her with a skeptical look. "All right. Let's agree, though. Observation and perhaps the odd discreet inquiry, and we leave the rest to the appropriate authorities."

"Agreed," she said and pulled him up off the log. "Now, the appropriate authority would probably appreciate some tea and a scone or two. It's awful to leave Constable McKechnie all by himself out there."

34.

When Charles and Maggie found him, McKechnie was sitting with his back against a tree trunk about ten feet from the body, now once again covered by the horse blanket. McKechnie quickly clapped his helmet back on as Charles and Maggie approached and simultaneously sprang to his feet. He looked both relieved and happy to see that they were on a mission of mercy. As the constable wolfed down the first of the scones, and held out his mug as Maggie poured the tea from the earthenware bottle, Charles asked the constable, as discreetly as he could, whether McKechnie had given any thought to taking statements from the rest of Harald's house guests. McKechnie replied, between huge swallows of tea, that Inspector Storrs would likely do so if the doctor's examination confirmed that Radulescu had indeed been strangled. But if McKechnie himself was entertaining any suspicions about the house guests, he was keeping them to himself.

Charles and Maggie left the bottle of tea and the remaining scones with the constable and made their way back to the house. When they walked into the drawing room, they found that the others had begun to gather there, anticipating lunch.

Against Janet's objections, Annie had made her way down-stairs on Gordon's arm. She was now sitting in an overstuffed armchair, pale, and with her bandaged arm in a sling.

"So good to see you up and about, Annie," Charles said. "But are you sure you're ready?"

"Quite sure," she said. "I was finally ready to face up to that man and his hateful provocations, but now, how strange not to have that burden anymore—and to be relieved of it by such violent means." She turned to Janet, who nodded in agreement. "This we did not expect and do not welcome. It makes one wonder what could be coming next."

It was a sentiment shared by them all. The unease of being in limbo while waiting for the inspector and procurator fiscal to arrive had kept them all close to the house, waiting for the next thing, whatever that might be.

"Setter estimated that Radulescu died sometime between four o'clock and midnight yesterday," Charles said, crossing the room to lean on the mantle. "Did anyone notice anything suspicious yesterday during that time? Did anyone hear anything?"

"The four of us were hillwalking until about five," Janet said.

"That's right," Violet said. "But I didn't notice anything untoward. Did you?"

She addressed Ben and Cavers. Ben shook his head. "We were pretty tired by the time we got back to the house. I had a bit of a lie down, then had a wash, and changed for dinner."

"If this is a subtle way of asking us about our move-ments yesterday, I did the same as Riddoch," Cavers said. "Washed, changed, came down for dinner. Drinks in the drawing room with everybody else. After dinner, I—um," he glanced over at Violet, "I got a book from the library and went to bed. The first thing I heard about the murder was this morning at breakfast."

Violet reported exactly the same list, as did Janet.

Charles rubbed his toe absently against the fender of the fireplace. "What about you, Harald, and Gordon? You were fishing in the river yesterday, weren't you?"

"Yes, that's right," Harald said, looking at Gordon, who nodded. "We were fishing the stretch of the river just before it reaches the loch, so we were downstream of the weir. Not bad fishing, as it happens. We both caught two fair-sized brown trout. Then just like the others: washed, dressed, and came down for dinner."

"Yes, the same for me as well," Gordon said. "I looked in on Annie after dinner and read a few pages of *Idylls of the King* to her. When she fell asleep, I took the book to bed with me. Then nothing till all this commotion greeted me at breakfast."

"What about Taplow?" Charles said.

"He helped us see to Annie, then went back downstairs once we started getting Annie to bed," Maggie said. "Then I didn't see him again until dinner."

"He wasn't downstairs when we arrived from our walk," Janet said.

"No, that's right," Violet said. "And he didn't turn up for drinks before dinner either."

"I suppose dinner was the next we saw of him," Ben said. "I felt like quite the toff sitting across from him in my suit, seeing as he was still in his plus fours and Norfolk jacket. Said he hadn't had time to change."

"That's right. I didn't think to ask him where he'd been," Maggie said, trying not to sound too concerned. "Did he mention it to any of you?"

"No," Ben said. "He seemed more interested in tucking in to Harald's excellent beef."

"Well, he probably just went out for a breath of air,"

Charles said. "Where is he, by the way?"

"I passed him on the stairs about an hour ago," Gordon said. "He was looking a bit drawn. Said he was going back to bed and not to wait lunch for him."

"Oh," Charles said. "Right, well, it was a nerve-wracking morning after all. He was the one who had to identify the body. He said he'd had to do something similar in Cambridge once. Must have brought back some bad memories."

The others returned to chatting among themselves and Charles and Maggie walked through the open French doors into the conservatory, ostensibly to admire Harald's orange tree. When they were out of earshot of the others, Maggie said, "There doesn't seem to be too much untoward about everyone's activities yesterday, thank goodness. Most of them were in sight of someone else most of the time, except when they were changing for dinner."

"And also after they went to bed, of course," Charles said. "But the servants were on watch again, so if anyone left the house after bedtime, they would have been seen."

"As for Mr. Taplow, we don't know where he was between about three o'clock, when he disappeared downstairs while Mrs. Fairclough and I were getting Annie settled into bed, and seven o'clock, when he turned up for dinner."

"He didn't have time to change for dinner, which suggests he was out at least for the latter part of that time," he said. "But let's not jump to any premature conclusions. There's probably a perfectly innocent explanation."

"No. Agreed," Maggie said. "But that time gap is the biggest unknown in our data."

"Yes," Charles said, rubbing his chin. "There's still time before lunch. I think I'll talk to the servants who were on watch last night."

"Good. I'll help. You take Finlay and that boy who sees

to the horses, the one with red hair. They're out back in the stables, I think. I'll take Frederick and that other footman—the one who polishes the boots every morning. They're probably in the scullery."

Charles was a bit concerned that she was throwing herself into these supposedly discreet inquiries with too much intensity. But he had to admit that she was rather good at getting information out of people in a pleasant, nonthreatening way. She moved toward the kitchen and he headed out the back door.

Finlay, who took care of Harald's horses, carriage and carts, was easy enough to find. He was in the tack room rubbing saddle soap into the lustrous surface of a brown leather saddle. He looked up from his work as Charles hesitated in the doorway and rapped on the door frame.

"Yes, sir? Can I help you with something?"

"Um, yes. Mr. Finlay, isn't it?"

"Yes, sir. That's right. Finlay will do."

"Well, uh, Finlay, as Sergeant Setter has been called away again, and, uh…in view of the unfortunate death of Mr. Radulescu, I thought I would ask you a few questions about how the watch went last night."

"Are you helping the sergeant then, sir?"

"Um, yes. In a way. I'm just gathering a little information for him while he's gone." Charles smiled winningly and hoped Finlay would not question that answer too closely. He forged ahead with a show of confidence. "Now then, I think you were guarding the north door?"

"Aye, that's it, sir. I was at the main north door and young Gregor—he's my stableboy—was guarding the servant's entrance at the other end of the house on the north side."

"I see. When did you take up your post there?"

"At ten o'clock, sir. That's when the sergeant told us to be there. I was there until this morning when Mr. Dekker came in and told me to find Mr. Williams and get him to wake the master."

"And during the night, were you able to stay awake? I would imagine it would be quite difficult."

"Aye, well, I had Cook make Gregor and mysel two flasks of coffee each. To tell you the truth, I'm that awauk still, I may not sleep the nicht either."

Charles laughed. "I appreciate your dedication, Finlay. And you saw nothing unusual during the night? No one from the house left by your door and no one came in?"

"That's right, sir. It was quiet. I didn't see a soul until Mr. Dekker came in from the estate house."

Charles thanked Finlay and asked where he might find Gregor, who had kept watch at the servant's entrance. Finlay directed Charles to the stalls where the horses, six in number and one pony, stood impassively as they followed him down the barn with their large, liquid eyes. In a stall at the end he found Gregor, the young man who had earlier helped Setter harness the other pony. The boy was bent over the hoof of a tall chestnut mare, cradling the hoof in his long leather apron and painting a bad-smelling ointment of some sort on the bottom of the upturned hoof.

"You're Gregor, I think?"

"Aye, sir. That's me."

Charles gave Gregor the same line he had fed to Finlay and fortunately, the boy accepted his story with no apparent questions. It turned out that Gregor had had the same kind of night as Finlay. Quiet. No one had gone in or out of the servants' entrance while he was on his watch.

Charles was about to take his leave when Gregor, putting the hoof down gently and straightening up, said, "The man that died, sir?"

"Yes?"

"Well, I wondered if he was the same man I spoke to yesterday. The man wasnae from here, and I heard that the dead man was a stranger, so I wondered."

"You spoke to a stranger yesterday?"

"Yes, sir. I was in the far paddock. It's up the hill quite a ways from the house. The man called me over to the fence. He gave me a piece of paper and asked me to deliver it to someone down in the house."

There was a strange prickling sensation at the back of Charles's neck. Without thinking, he raised his hand to the back of his collar. "Which man? One of the other guests?"

"Aye, sir. The tall gentleman. English. Talks like a toff."

"Taplow? Mr. Taplow?"

"Aye, sir. That's the name." Gregor looked a bit guilty. "The man up the paddock gave me a little money for my trouble. I hope I didnae do wrong?"

"No, no. Gregor. That's fine. Nothing to worry about." Charles asked a few more questions to get the situation clearly in his mind. A strange man, who was dressed like Radulescu, had given Gregor a note to give to Taplow. Gregor had delivered the note to Taplow in the library, at about four-thirty. Gregor had not read the note and had no idea what it contained, but he said that Taplow, having read the note, left the library and appeared to head for the back door of the house.

"Gregor, I'm going to ask you to come with me to see Constable McKechnie. I want you to tell him what you've just told me."

"All right, sir. But I'll have to ask Mr. Finlay. I'm not to leave the stable before I've done all the horses that need tending."

"That's fine, Gregor. I'll come with you to see Finlay. And Gregor?"

"Yes, sir?"

"Constable McKechnie will probably want to know if the man who gave you the note is the same one who was pulled from the weir this morning. Are you up to that?"

The boy swallowed. "I suppose I'll have to be, sir."

35.

Charles looked on as Constable McKechnie took Gregor's statement. Both were seated with their backs to the tree that had been McKechnie's backstop before. When Gregor had viewed the body, he had all but fainted, and the constable and Charles had lowered him down against the tree. McKechnie had dipped his handkerchief in the weir, wrung it out, and placed it on the back of the boy's neck.

The man who had given the note to Gregor had been Radulescu all right. And while the boy answered McKechnie's questions, Charles turned over in his mind just what the significance of this information might be. What had been in the note? Since Gregor had seen Taplow heading for the north door, the door that faced the hills to the rear of the house, it was most likely a summons of some sort. Either that or the information contained in the note made Taplow want to go out and find Radulescu. If Taplow had somehow met Radulescu up in the hills somewhere, that would have accounted for his lateness getting back for dinner. If Taplow had found Radulescu, he certainly hadn't let on to anyone that he had seen the man who, until this morning, had been acknowledged as a dangerous adversary by the whole tour group, including Taplow himself. Charles didn't like the implications of that at all.

"Constable, I'm going to leave Gregor in your capable hands. Will you be questioning Mr. Taplow further on this?"

"Aye, Mr. Lauchlan, but I've still got to wait here with the body. The rules are that the body must be in my constant custody. But would you be kind enough to tell Mr. Taplow that I would like to speak to him urgently?"

"Yes, of course. I'll go and get him for you."

Charles made his way down to the house and ran into Maggie in the hallway.

"There you are. I wondered where you'd got to. Apparently both footmen who were on watch, Frederick and Henry, saw nothing. The others have gone in to lunch. What is it? What's wrong?"

Charles had grabbed her arm and hurried her to an alcove under the stairs. In a hushed voice he told her quickly about Gregor's story.

"I've got to go and get Taplow and take him up to Constable McKechnie."

"What if he did meet Radulescu yesterday? He could just have been warning him to stay away from us. It doesn't mean he was the one who killed Radulescu."

"Right enough," Charles said. "We don't even know if Taplow did have a meeting with Radulescu. We don't really know what was in the note."

"But one thing is clear." She narrowed her eyes and looked at some indefinite point in the distance. "He got a note from Radulescu yesterday and he didn't tell anyone about it, least of all the constable when he identified the body this morning."

"Yes, that's about the size of it." Charles rubbed the back

of his neck. "Right. I'll go up and get Taplow. You go in to lunch, but I don't think we want to tell this latest bit of news to the assembly, at least not until the constable has had a chance to talk with Taplow."

"Promise me you'll be careful," she said as he waved her toward the dining room.

"I will. I'm just the escort at this point. Go on, I'll be there as soon as my duty is done."

She hesitated but he urged her on and, with a slight pout, she turned and headed toward the door of the dining room.

At the door to Taplow's room, Charles hesitated, took a deep breath and knocked on the door. "Taplow? Mr. Taplow? Sorry to disturb you. May I come in?"

No answer. Charles put his ear to the door. No sound of stirring. He knocked louder and called louder. Still no answer. *Hmmm. Well, in for a penny, in for a pound.* He turned the door-knob and entered. The drapes had been pulled closed and the room was in shadows. Taplow had gone back to bed and was huddled under the covers.

"Taplow? Look, sorry to have to wake you like this, but a situation has come up, and we need you."

There was no sound or movement from the figure curled into a defensive posture under the covers. Charles approached the bed, bent down and placed his hand gently on where he thought Taplow's shoulder might be. *What? Something's wrong here. What the*—? Charles patted his hand down at several points along the figure. Then he grabbed the top of the coverlet, blanket, and sheet, and flung them back from the figure in the bed. Cushions: cushions and a bolster from the sitting room next door.

Charles's knees collapsed and he sat down in a bedside chair with a thump. Then jumped up like a jack-in-the-box. "Blast, Taplow! For heaven's sake! Don't you see how this looks?"

The bolster on the bed gave no reply. *But then. Maybe you don't care about that now.* He thought back to Taplow that morning up by the weir: pale, hangdog, pacing slowly while Setter and the constable examined the body. Was this behaviour more than a display of nerves from a man who had seen this kind of sight before? And why was it Taplow, of all the other guests, who had roused himself to attend to the dead man found entangled in the weir gate?

All the whirligigs in Charles's brain were spinning. *How much of a head start has he had? It can't be more than an hour and a half.* A plan was crystalizing out of a fevered series of quick conclusions. *Setter's not back from the village. Inspector Storrs won't get here in time at this rate, and McKechnie has to stay with the body.*

There were gasps of disbelief around the dining room table from everyone except Maggie. One of their own guilty of murder? It could not be. Charles tried to deal with their shock as gently as he could, but he knew that speed was of the essence.

"The fact is, Taplow's left for whatever reason, and he didn't want his departure to be noticed till he was good and gone. Someone's got to follow him and, if possible, find out where he is, so that the police know where to look. We can do that if we think about the likeliest directions he could have taken."

"But, Charles, shouldn't we leave this to the police?" Gordon said.

"I'm not proposing that we try to capture Taplow, Gordon. As you say, that's a matter for the police. I'm only suggesting that we see where he's gone, if we can, before the trail gets cold."

"I'll wager he's headed to a railway station." It was Ben.

"Rannoch Station or Aberfeldy then," Cavers said.

"No, not Aberfeldy," Harald said. "Struan. It's half the

distance and it's on the main line.

"I know the road from here to Struan," Violet said. "I cycled it once when I was at school. There are some rough bits between here and Trinafour, but from there to Struan is easy by bike."

"Which is closer, Rannoch or Struan?" Charles asked Harald.

"Rannoch, by a couple of miles."

The plan was quickly finalized. The sisters and Gordon would stay with Harald at Dunnlinton, inform Constable McKechnie about Taplow's absence, and wait to brief Inspector Storrs and the procurator fiscal. Charles and Maggie would go to Rannoch Station. Cavers and Ben would take the road to Struan Station along with Violet, who would guide them. Harald offered his horses to the searchers but neither Maggie nor Ben had riding experience. Since the roads were now dry and in reasonably good condition, both parties opted for bicycles. The two groups were to keep in touch by telegraph from their respective train stations if possible, keeping in mind that it was the Sabbath, and no one was to actually make face-to-face contact with Taplow. Everyone frantically pulled together food, wet-weather clothing, and anything else they could think of for the road. They were all filled with intensity and purpose and Charles felt a little guilty at the feeling of excitement, the thrill of the chase, as he and Maggie waved off the trio headed to Struan and pedalled away from Dunnlinton on the road westward. His mood had been heightened a few notches by the discovery that Taplow's bicycle was missing from the outbuilding where their bikes had been stored.

The road from Dunnlinton Lodge to Rannoch Station on the West Highland Railway line skirted the north shore of Loch Rannoch and then headed due west, following the course of the River Gaur toward Rannoch Moor. Knowing that Taplow, if he had taken this route, was about two hours ahead of them, they set a pace that they could maintain just this side of breathing hard, though the sun and a whisper of a breeze coming off the moor tempted them to be lazy. The road made a gradual uphill climb, but it was gentle enough that the climb was not taxing. Although the dominant colour around Dunnlinton Lodge had been various hues of green tinting bluffs of trees on the hillsides stretching northward from the house, the further west they travelled by the Gaur, the more barren the landscape, with rougher contours to the hills and gullies gouged out of the rocky soil. Boulders sat atop the dry heathland, as if scattered by a giant hand throwing dice.

After an hour's riding, they came in sight of the railway line and a lonely group of buildings perched on a slight rise. As they came closer, they could see a small house and, down in the railway cutting, the small station and siding. They rode up the gravel drive and found there a garden by the house, lovingly reclaimed from its barren surroundings, in which a man could be seen tending what turned out to be potato plants. He was wearing the hard-peaked cap and navy-blue tunic of the West Highland Railway.

"Good afternoon, sir," Charles said as he dismounted his bicycle. "It's a beautiful day for gardening."

"Aye, so it is." He turned and looked in the direction of the house with a concerned expression on his face. "Elspeth doesnae like me to be hoeing and tending on the Sabbath, but earwigs pay no mind to the Lord's Day."

"Are you by any chance the station master?" Charles said.

"I am that. Donachie's the name. Are you wanting to book tickets?"

"No," Maggie said. "We're looking for a friend who

might have come this way. He may have boarded the train here."

The station master removed his hat and wiped his brow with a large handkerchief. "You'd be Americans, I suppose?"

"No, we're Canadians as it happens," Charles said. "Our friend is a tall gentleman, English. Riding a dark green bicycle. Probably wearing a light brown tweed suit with plus fours and a Norfolk jacket."

"Canada. Well now, we don't get many Canadians hereabouts." He cast his eyes over the bleak landscape. "Mind, we don't get that many from anywhere, but I've a nephew, my sister Peggie's lad, in a place called Saska—Saskata—"

"Saskatchewan?" Maggie said.

"No...no, that's not quite it."

"Saskatoon?" Charles said. "Look, we're really in rather a hurry—"

"Aye, that's it. Do you know him by any chance? Hamish is his name. Hamish Rankin?"

"I'm afraid not, Mr. Donachie. Look, did our friend board the train here?"

"Aye, well. Not being from here, you'll not know the schedule. People are going to miss trains if they don't know the schedule. That's what I told the gentleman that was here a few hours ago. There's only one train northbound and one train southbound on the Sabbath. Elspeth doesnae like it, but the mail has got to go through, Sabbath or no."

"Did you say a gentleman? Was he English?"

Donachie scratched his chin and thought. "I suppose he was."

Maggie repeated the description of Taplow. Donachie said that on balance the man he had talked to sounded like Taplow.

"He didn't board the train then?"

"No, no. He didnae seem to care which he caught, but since he missed the northbound by an hour and the southbound doesnae go through here till seven the nicht, he was out of luck."

"Mr. Donachie," Charles said, "think very carefully. Which way did the man head when he left here."

"Aye, well, he said he didnae want to go back the way he came and there's no other way from here except the path across the moor to the King's House. That's the way he decided to go, but I told him that path is too rough for a bicycle, so he left it with me and I put it in my garden shed. He said he'd send for it in a few days."

Charles and Maggie had a hurried consultation. Their initial plan had just been to get to the station and see if Taplow had got on a train. Now Charles proposed to take the path to King's House himself and try to find information about Taplow's next move from there. He instructed Maggie to go back to Dunnlinton, but she declined to be instructed and said she was going with him to King's House. Since the weather continued fine, he relented easily. They pulled out their map and Donachie found the trail across Rannoch Moor for them.

"Mind now," Donachie said. "You shouldn't take this path unless you're prepared for all weathers. That's what I told the other gentleman."

Maggie flipped through the pages of their guidebook while Charles looked at his watch. Just past two o'clock. "The King's House," he said, "is that a hotel?"

"Aye. That's right."

"Here's the description of the trail, Charles. It's thirteen miles from here to King's House. We can take our food and jackets in our rucksacks. Let's see, walking about three miles an hour…"

"Better make it two. And thirteen miles is quite a long walk, considering we're starting late."

"Right, fine, two miles an hour conservatively, that's between six and seven hours. At that rate we won't be getting to King's House until about nine, at sundown."

"Hmmm. I think maybe we shouldn't risk it."

"Nonsense! We have food and water and warm clothing, and look at the sun. If we don't go, we'll lose track of Mr. Taplow. The light lasts almost until ten. We'll be all right."

Charles shielded his eyes and looked at the horizon to the northwest, where the mountains rimming the Vale of Glencoe marked their destination. "I'm not sure. I suppose we can manage it. But we'll have no time for lollygagging."

Having left their bicycles with Mr. Donachie, they set out on the path toward Loch Laidon at the eastern edge of the moor. Rannoch Moor was an immense, shallow bowl scraped by glaciers out of a granite plateau some 1,000 feet above sea level. Into this bowl the streams from the surrounding mountains emptied and, without anywhere to go from there, formed scattered pools, lochans, and rich organic bogs dense with spongy peat mosses and rimmed with tough sedge grasses. Tussocks of heather on mushroom-shaped mounds dotted the treeless expanse in the dryer parts of the moor higher on the bowl's edges, and everywhere the air had the tang of altitude.

Charles had done some moor walking in his New College days and the metal of the compass case that warmed to his hand when he reached in his vest pocket gave him added reassurance that, in case the clouds lowered and the mist rolled in, they would be able to chart a course toward King's House in the Valley of Glencoe. Maggie was positively brimming with enthusiasm for the challenge and chirped like a little bird at the sheer breadth of the moor as they emerged from the forested path by Loch Laidon. She was delighted at the muted purple of the heather on its tussocks, the dry green of the sedge grasses edging into their autumn brown and the tea-coloured water in the pools.

"It's quite like the prairies in its way, isn't it?" she said. "You have to look closely at the smallest details to appreciate it. It's not obvious scenery like—oh, say—the lakes in Switzerland. You can't help but be bowled over by them. But here, and at home, you have to wait and watch and let the details find you."

"Fair enough, but could you speed up a bit while you're waiting to be found?" He looked at his watch. "We've got to make very good time if we're going to have any chance of catching up to Taplow. You can bet he's not letting the sphagnum grow under his feet."

She answered him by doubling her pace immediately and taking the lead on the path. They spent the next hour trying to outpace each other. The path angled away from Loch Laidon and headed westward in the direction of King's House and, every so often, they saw fresh footprints where the path was wet. Maggie swore that she had taken special note of Taplow's brogues and that she could see their outline in these footprints. Charles thought it was certainly possible; the trail was clearly not heavily used, and if Taplow was ahead of them by a few hours, the prints could well be his. They took fresh energy from this thought and increased their pace.

After another mile the trail became intermittent, punctuated with boggier patches out of which the mounds of heather emerged like islands. Through these wet patches, they had to jump from one mound to another to keep their feet dry. But, by the map and the compass direction, Charles was confident they were still on course and, though the path was not obvious, they kept picking it up again with little difficulty. The sun had disappeared behind a solid bank of clouds and without it the breeze that had seemed so refreshing caused them to pull on their jackets.

They had been walking now for three hours. Hunger and leg fatigue could no longer be held at bay by nervous energy. Maggie's slackening pace and his own reminded them that they had only had a chance to eat some sausage rolls and tea, gulped quickly while they packed their gear. There was a ruined shepherd's hut marked on their map. When they found it, they made noises of relief, staggered inside the ruined foundation and spread their waterproofs down on the floor. If there had once been a roof to the hut it was long gone but the remaining walls, though crumbling, enclosed a space about ten feet by eight feet, and offered some shelter from the wind.

"Whoof!" Charles sank down to a sitting position and let the air out of his lungs as he leaned his back against the stone wall of the foundation. "This is challenging work. I wonder if Taplow stopped to eat."

"That's just what I was thinking. Surely he must have." Though she was tired, Maggie was wandering about the mud floor with her eyes cast down.

"Come and sit down, for heaven's sake. I'll get out the bread and cheese."

"In a minute. Just wait. There!" She picked up something from the floor. "Proof!" She brought the item over to him holding it between thumb and forefinger.

"What is it?"

"A piece of cheese rind. I'll wager it matches the cheese we have in our rucksacks. And it's fresh, not dried up and wizened."

Charles took the rind from her and looked at it. "Could be off that immense round of Arran cheddar we saw in the kitchen when Mrs. Dewar was making up our lunch packets."

They tucked into the large pieces of cheese and sliced bread that smelled wonderfully of yeast, determined to take no more time to eat and rest than strictly necessary. The food was doubly welcome because there was no question now; the weather had deteriorated. They blessed Mrs. Dewar for the bracing flask of raspberry cordial. Looking at the mist already hiding the top of Buachaille Etive Mòr, the mountain called "The Herdsman of Etive," that guarded the eastern end of the valley of Glencoe. Charles suggested they save half the tea for later. After sitting quietly with their eyes closed for a quarter of an hour and willing themselves to store up energy, they set out over the moor again.

The terrain was wetter here and in places they were forced to pick their way around bogs, hopping from mound to mound, or finding a ribbon of sedge that offered dryer footing. It had begun to rain lightly and as they were walking directly into the wind, it was harder to see the terrain underfoot while blinking away the rain. They slogged on, each choosing a slightly different route and more focused now on the inward struggle than on outward communication. As he was planning a path across a particularly large bog, Charles realized that it had been some time since they had seen anything like a path. He was sighting with his compass and trying to shield his map from the wind and rain.

"We've lost the path again," he said. "We need to angle over that direction."

"Oh no! No!"

"Don't worry. It's just over——"

She cut him off with another wail. She was about ten feet to his right, only she seemed shorter than her usual willowy stature. He half-stumbled, half-splashed over to her and found that she had sunk knee-deep into a pool of foul-smelling muck.

"It looked like it was solid but I sank in, and now I'm stuck," she said. "And if I move, I just get stucker."

"Hand me your rucksack and I'll pull you out."

He planted his feet wide apart on what seemed to be the soundest ground, took her hands and pulled, and pulled again. She was in above her knees now. *No good. Don't panic. She's frightened. Got to calm down.*

"All right. Let's just take some time to breathe. Just be still."

"I'm going to sink—"

"No, you're not. It's just mud, and I won't let go of you. Take a few breaths. That's good. Now. All we have to do is concentrate on freeing one leg at a time, moving slowly and deliberately. That's right, pull, pull, pull with steady pressure. Steady…steady."

Charles was leaning back, legs and feet planted as firmly as he could, holding her hands to steady her while she pulled her right leg upward. They worked away at this with no visible progress.

"It's not working, Charles.

"No, keep going. It will—"

"Oh, wait. Yes, it's moving. I can feel it!"

As her right leg appeared at the surface of the mud, miraculously with the shoe still on, he pulled her toward him so that she was lying more or less horizontal on the surface, her left leg still deep in the mud.

"Good! Excellent!" He was gasping with the effort now. "All right, extend your right leg along the top of the mud. That's it; more like a swimming position. That's better."

Now that she was in this swimming position, he slithered down so that he was lying on the firm ground at right angles to her. From there he could pull her gradually, inch by inch, up the sloping edge of the mire pool and inch by inch her left leg followed, along with the rest of her. Now she could grab hold of a clump of sedge with one hand and help him by pulling and wriggling while he pulled her by one arm and the waistband of her skirt. After five minutes of constant effort, she was free. They lay in a mixture of peat water and sodden moss, wet through now but at least on solid ground. They struggled to an upright position, staggered toward a boulder big enough and dry enough to hold them both and sank down on it holding each other tightly.

"Whatever would I do without you?" she said.

"Darling girl," he said and hugged her tighter. "Don't thank me. I got you into this mess in the first place, remember? I should have insisted you go back to Dunnlinton. Sheer stupidity."

"That's nonsense and I don't want to hear any more of it!"

He was surprised at the vehemence in her voice.

"We're a team now," she said. "Where you go, I go. And the place we're going now is to King's House as fast as we can. Get up and take a compass reading. I'm going to take off my skirt." She stood up and started undoing the buttons at her waistband.

"Wha—what?"

"Don't worry, I'm going to put it on again. But if I don't get the mud off it and wring it out, it will be like a lead weight around my legs. Come, dear. We've got to move quickly now to keep warm."

In an instant, he realized how right she was. He took out his watch. Six o'clock and they'd just lost about fifteen minutes of walking time while freeing her from the mud hole. Charles looked at the map while she stripped the mud off her skirt, squeezed the water out of it and did the same to her petticoat. She pulled a pair of gloves from her rucksack and put them on, the only dry garments she now possessed.

He calculated that King's House and safety was still about five miles away. *Now it's a race*, he thought. *A race against the cold and the oncoming darkness. No choice, though. We can't turn back. Our only hope is to just push on, hard as we can.* He forced himself to look carefully at the map and the guidebook.

"I think the going will get easier a little way ahead," he said, not really sure if it was true. "See—here. If we can get to Black Corries Lodge—about two more miles—then the book says the trail widens into a cart track and it will be easier to follow."

She squinted at the map. "Yes, I see. Even if it gets a little dark we should still be able to follow the trail to the hotel from there."

"That's my girl." He kissed her and helped her on with her rucksack. Mercifully the rain had eased off a little, but they wore their waterproofs still, more as a shelter from the wind than the rain. Everything they could do to keep their spirits up, they did. They decided a cadence and marched in tempo to it. They suggested songs to each other with a pleasing tempo and sang them, not out loud but under their breath and then in their heads to save energy. Music-hall songs. Nursery songs. Patriotic songs about maple leaves and the Queen and home. Then hymns, not the lugubrious ones, but the fighting ones: "Will Your Anchor Hold" and "A Mighty Fortress." All the while the cold was trying to rob them of strength. They were in the middle of a desperate inner version of "Onward Christian Soldiers" when Charles spotted something off in the distance, something white.

"That's it!" He said, pointing. "That has to be the Black Corries Lodge!"

As cold and tired and bedraggled as she was, she gave a little hop and jumped into his arms and they twirled around. It was, indeed, the solid, plain, whitewashed house used by the nearby Strathcona Estate as a way station for stalkers hunting on the moor. When they came closer and knocked on the door, no one came and no lights were visible through the windows, but its mere presence and the fact that it stood sentinel to the promised wide, well-travelled cart trail to King's House was enough to cheer them. They celebrated by drinking the last of the raspberry cordial and bolting the remaining cheese and bread hungrily.

They set off down the cart track, its outline easy to discern even though the light was fading. The footing was easy—beautifully smooth and dry compared to what they had been through. In another mile they could see what must surely be smoke from the chimney of the King's House Hotel, though the building itself was hidden in a fold of the Valley of Glencoe. It could not come too soon. Maggie had started shivering uncontrollably a few miles back and Charles had begun to feel rather detached and sleepy himself. He fought the urge to just lie down in the road and give in to sleep. Pulling the rucksack off Maggie's back, he slung it over his own and put a supporting arm around her waist.

"Only a little further. We're almost there."

She hadn't the strength to reply, but did her best to smile through chattering teeth. They entered a kind of slowed-down dreamtime. In what could have been an eternity or just a few minutes, they staggered through the front door of the hotel. He couldn't tell who was supporting whom by then, and he wasn't taking in his surroundings too well. There was a bustling and a commotion. A woman with a proprietorial air looked aghast at them and immediately said, "Och, look at the sight of you! Poor wee girl! Come along with me, pet." There was something about a hot bath and Maggie went off with the lady supporting her. Charles felt suddenly bereft and wasn't too sure that he could remain standing.

A booming voice. "Think of you out on the moor and soaked through in that wind, sir! And look at the state of you. You're lucky to be alive, man!" Charles was vaguely aware of being led by the arm to the hotel desk.

He was leaning on the desk not knowing what to do but considering falling down, when a glass of tawny-coloured liquid appeared.

The same booming voice emanated from a beefy-looking fellow with unfashionable sidewhiskers. "Now then, sir. Get this down you. I never knew a dram to fail in warming a man."

Charles drank the liquid fire and the man was right. The shock of it made him gasp but otherwise he could not imagine a more wonderful sensation. He drained the glass.

"Let's get you up to your room and I'll draw you a bath, too. We've got just the one room left, but I'm sure you and your wife will be comfortable. Poor soul! She looked half-dead, but I'm sure she'll come round after the bath."

The man took his arm and supported him up a set of stairs and along an endless hallway and into a lavatory with a large bathtub of amazing whiteness. The innkeeper lit the flame under a boiler affair and, saying that the bath would be ready in jig time, disappeared out the door again. In this half-dream state, Charles worked at getting his clothes off while the bath water was heating. His fingers would hardly work to undo the buttons and fasteners, but by the time he had struggled out of his clammy singlet and drawers the bath was heated, drawn, and ready. Sinking into it was a more heavenly experience than the whisky and he decided that he might just stay in it forever. But then there was a loud knock at the lavatory door and the innkeeper bustled in.

"Best not to fall asleep in the bath, sir," he said. A wise man. A very wise man. Bundled up in towels and a flannel sheet, Charles was led to a room. Once inside he thanked the man, threw the towels and sheet on a chair and just had time to notice that Maggie was already there in the bed, sound asleep, before he crawled under the covers and with a welcoming sigh, allowed oblivion to claim him.

36.

The wait was interminable. Setter sat with Constable McKechnie on a settee facing the fireplace making what passed for small talk among policemen and, like the rest assembled there, nursing a glass of whisky. He had already regaled Inspector Storrs and Mr. Nicol Baillie, the procurator fiscal, with stories of the time he had accompanied two murderers from the Pembina Hills to trial in Winnipeg and had run into a bear en route. Storrs and Baillie stood with their backs to the fire in the drawing room at Dunnlinton Lodge. They were still trying to get warm after their rain-lashed ride from Struan Station by pony cart. They had been met at the station by Violet, Cavers, and Ben, and been filled in on Taplow's surprising absence and the two search parties that had set out to track him. Only Baillie's assertion of the full force of the law had been sufficient to persuade the local blacksmith at Struan to hitch up and drive his pony cart on the Sabbath. Violet had accompanied them back to Dunnlinton on the cart, while Cavers and Ben toiled along behind on their bicycles. Exhausted, the Struan trio had already retired for the night, and so had Annie.

Harald, Gordon, and Janet sat quietly at the other end of the drawing room, alternately reading and chatting. They had all been waiting for about two hours, while Dr. Lawler conducted a rough and ready postmortem on Radulescu's body in a room hastily set up for the purpose in the basement near the scullery. It was now almost midnight.

Setter was slowly taking the measure of Storrs and had decided he liked the man. While it was clear that Storrs did not approve of civilians behaving like near-vigilantes, he allowed that the remoteness of Kinloch Rannoch sometimes called for departures from accepted practice. Setter considered that in like circumstances, he would have felt the same way. The man respected the rule book but was not hidebound by it. That was good. Also, Storrs had betrayed no discomfort when he arrived at Dunnlinton and found that the policeman he had been communicating with by telegram was Canadian, and a half-breed at that. He was, at the very least, surprised, but he hid it well and Setter appreciated the effort. And Storrs had so far not harped on the fact that Setter was considerably outside his jurisdiction, but rather had encouraged him to continue to sit in on discussions of the case.

About the procurator fiscal, Setter was less sure, since Baillie was some sort of lawyer and therefore outside the constabulary fraternity. He was glad there were no procurators fiscal to deal with in Canada. Imagine a Crown Attorney being able to direct a murder investigation! The thought of how Inspector Crossin at home would have felt about that almost made Setter guffaw, which would have been quite inappropriate.

Finally Dr. Lawler appeared, still in a blood-spattered apron. "Well, gentlemen, on balance, I agree with Constable McKechnie's finding of strangulation. It's unfortunate that so much time has elapsed since he was found or I would be able to tell you more."

Lawler took up the only vacant spot in front of the fire and detailed his findings. Strangulation, probably with bare hands rather than a ligature. There was no water to speak of in the lungs, suggesting that Radulescu was already dead when he entered the water, and that the body had not been in the water long enough for the lungs to fill. Evidence of scratches and lesions on Radulescu's fingers indicated he had struggled with his assailant, but there was no visible presence of blood or tissue under the fingernails, nor of fibre from clothing that might help to identify the assailant. Time of death hard to determine precisely, but probably sometime between four p.m. and eight p.m. the previous day. He'd taken samples from stomach contents and other samples for analysis at the laboratory in Edinburgh and he would be able to say more once these results were available.

Setter was relieved not to be in limbo anymore. It was now official; they were embarked on a murder investigation. Well, "they" did not officially include him, but near as.

"Gentlemen—and lady," Baillie said. "Thank you for your patience. Because of the weather and the darkness, there's little else we can do tonight. But tomorrow Inspector Storrs will have more questions for you and I must get back to Perth as quickly as possible with the body to file the appropriate documents. Mr. Dibbage, I must ask to impose upon your hospitality. We four need a place to sleep for tonight." He indicated Storrs, McKechnie, Dr. Lawler, and himself.

"Already in hand, Mr. Baillie." Harald said, reaching out to pull the cord that summoned Williams. "We've rather a full house, but if you don't mind doubling up, I'll have Williams and Mrs. Fairclough see you to your rooms."

"About the others?" Storrs said. "Mr. Lauchlan and Miss Skene is it? Were you expecting them back tonight?"

Harald looked at Janet, who looked at Gordon. "Well,

they left in such a hurry," Janet said. "We thought they would be back by now if there was no sign of Mr. Taplow at Rannoch Station."

"Yes, perhaps that means that they're following a lead of some sort," Gordon said. "If there was no sign of him at Struan, doesn't that make it more likely he boarded the train at Rannoch?"

Inspector Storrs gave an uncomfortable twitch of his moustache. "Hmm," he said. "Well, I rather hope that they are safely stowed at some inn or hotel for the night and have made no effort to make actual contact with Taplow. The last thing we need is to have to mount a search for the searchers." He turned to follow Baillie and the constable, but turned back at the door to the hallway. "Oh, yes. I'll want to ask you all some further questions tomorrow morning. If you don't mind, Mr. Dibbage, I'll commandeer the library after breakfast."

Harald nodded assent.

"Excellent. We'll begin at eight o'clock, sharp. Constable McKechnie will let you know when you're wanted."

37.

Storrs sat at the large mahogany writing desk in the library and began looking through the statements that he and McKechnie had taken from the members of the household. McKechnie sat in a chair slightly to one the side of Storrs. To his satisfaction, Setter sat on the other side of Storrs, having been invited to do so by the inspector.

"Now then, Mrs. Thorburn, it would seem that the connection between you and your sister and this Radulescu was the buying and selling of antique manuscripts. Is that right?"

"Yes, Inspector. We bought a manuscript fragment from him last year, and it seems he was quite desperate to buy it back from us. That was why he was trying so hard to—em—persuade Annie to sell."

"And this also would seem to be the one connection we know of between Radulescu and Mr. Taplow?"

"So it would seem, Inspector."

"Can you think of any reason why Taplow would go out to make some sort of contact with this Radulescu in secret?"

"I've been wracking my brains, Inspector," she said.

"Having got to know Mr. Taplow a little bit in the last few days, I can only think that it had something to do with manuscripts—but apart from that, I'm at a loss."

"Is it possible, Mrs. Thorburn, that Mr. Taplow went out to meet Radulescu in some misguided effort to prevent him from troubling your sister further?"

"And perhaps things got out of hand?" It was Annie. "We have given that some consideration, Inspector. Judging from our short acquaintance, Mr. Taplow is very much wrapped up in his own affairs. He has devoted all of his energies to scholarship, and made it clear that he deplores our views on biblical matters and our venturing into the academic world. I doubt that he would put himself at risk for the likes of us."

"Oh, don't misunderstand, Inspector. He is witty and surprisingly good company." Janet said, blushing a little. "Really, we liked him much more than we expected to. But I think…" She cast a rueful glance at Annie. "I think it is much more likely that whatever it was that caused him to meet Radulescu—if that is indeed what happened—had more to do with his own interests than with ours."

"McKechnie, you've searched Mr. Taplow's room?" Storrs said.

"Aye, sir. From stem to stern. He left nothing of a personal nature behind."

"So, there's nothing there to help us discover if he had any other reason to harm Mr. Radulescu, and therefore nothing to tie him to the murder scene, other than the fact that he received a note from Radulescu."

"And the fact that he's run off, sir."

Storrs leaned back in his chair and rubbed the back of his neck. "Yes, but run off to where? He could be headed anywhere from Argyll to Aberdeen at this rate. We've still heard nothing from Lauchlan?"

"No, sir. But you know how few telegraph offices there are in this part of the world."

"Is there any more persuasive argument for the complete extension of the telephone into the Highlands?" He took off his pince-nez and rubbed his eyes. "Well, Mr. Baillie will have ordered a high alert for all the police across the country. What about work on other fronts? It's damnable luck that our principal suspect is far from his own territory—oh, excuse me, ladies. Ordinarily we would have searched Taplow's home by now. Where would that be again?"

"Presumably in Cambridge, Inspector," Janet said. "Probably in his college."

"A jurisdictional nightmare." Storrs muttered, almost to himself. "We'll have to request the Cambridge Police to get a warrant. And they'll have to search for us. How they'll know what they're looking for, I don't know. If it comes down to matters relating to these…these old manuscripts—they won't even know what they're looking at."

Setter cleared his throat. "If you'll permit me, Inspector, I have a suggestion that might deal with these problems."

"Yes?"

"Yes, well, at home we have provisions for appointing special constables to undertake certain duties of a temporary nature."

"Yes, go on."

"Well, these ladies know a great deal about Mr. Taplow's work and could be of singular assistance in the search of his things."

"Sergeant, I appreciate your advice, but are you seriously suggesting that we swear in Mrs. Thorburn and Miss Gairdner as special constables?"

Setter laughed. "No, indeed sir." He looked over at Janet and Annie. "Though I think they might make admirable ones. No, I'm suggesting you swear me in, get me a warrant to search Taplow's home and then I can escort the ladies to Cambridge as special advisers to the Perth County Police."

Storrs snorted and sat back in his chair in disbelief. "Really, Sergeant. I never heard such a ridiculous suggestion in all my life."

"Ridiculous? Maybe," Setter said. "But I would say it's just ridiculous enough to work. Look, sir, you need a man on the scene in Cambridge. I'm your man since I'm already familiar with the case. You need expert advice to interpret what will be found in Taplow's home." He pointed expansively to Janet and Annie. "These ladies are his rivals in knowledge of ancient biblical manuscripts."

"Look here, special constables in Scotland are used for crowd control during riots and that sort of thing. And anyway, these ladies don't want to be caught up in a police investigation. That's too rough for such douce bodies."

"Actually, Inspector," Janet said, "we are not as douce as all that. We have slept many a night under the stars in the Sinai Desert. The wilds of Cambridge University hold no terrors for us. Were we called upon, we would consider it our civic duty to assist the Perthshire Police in their inquiries."

Storrs continued to shake his head in mock wonderment.

"Em, excuse me, sir."

"What is it, Constable?"

"Well, sir, I've just been going over the manual. See, here: the section on special constables?" McKechnie handed over the small, well-worn volume to the inspector. "In there it says special constables can be used for crowd control and guarding armaments depots, right enough. But there's nothing saying they have to be limited to those activities. It seems to me that...well..." He flagged under the older man's intense gaze. "Well, sir, it seems to me that you and Mr. Baillie could

~254~

use your own discretion in the matter."

Storrs looked at the manual, following the appropriate section with his finger. He looked at Setter. He looked at the sisters and then stared off into the distance. "Right!" he said suddenly and slammed the book shut. "McKechnie, you've missed your calling. It's the law for you, my lad!" He clapped the constable on the back. "Very well. Sergeant, and ladies, pack your bags, if you please. I can hardly wait till I see Baillie's face when I tell him. Come along. We've not a moment to lose!"

38.

Maggie lay on her side and ran her hand down the smooth contour of his back. She hesitated and then continued on, tentatively, over the muscular swell of his buttocks. He stirred and turned over on his side to face her, smiling sleepily. But the world was starting to impinge on the golden bubble they had been inhabiting for the last several hours. They wanted to stay in that blessed state, but it would not do. Reality could no longer be ignored: neither of them had corrected the innkeeper's assumption that they were married. Having failed at this duty, Charles ought to have slept on the floor. But Charles had not slept on the floor. They should, then, have slept with a sword between them like Tristan and Isolde or, at the very least, divided the sheets into separate, chaste cocoons. But there had been nothing between them except the electricity of skin on skin. Once they had awakened to that state in the pre-dawn hours, nothing—no sword, no appeal to respectability or what people would think, no biblical admonitions, no thoughts of the possible ramifications nine months away—could stop the sweaty, urgent completion of what had been held back for so long.

Worse still, they compounded the error by a slower, more languorous exploration of these blissful new fields, where there were no blockades or restricted zones and certainly no regrets or shame. They had almost died on the moor and none of those other things mattered—except to the world outside themselves and now that had to be faced.

Maggie turned over so that they were lying comfortably with her back to his front, spoon fashion. "Can Canadians get married in a Scottish registry office?"

"I don't know. I suppose so."

"Well, that won't do, anyway. I would want Father to marry us, and Aunt Jessie to be there. What about getting married at home on Balmoral Street the Saturday before Thanksgiving?"

"Hallelujah!" This was somewhat muffled due to the fact that he was nuzzling the back of her neck. "I'll be the thankfullest man in the Dominion."

"Good. We can telegraph Father and Aunt Jessie today. Oh, and your father too. You know, when you do that I find it hard to think."

"Mmm. Thinking is overrated."

"We should get dressed."

"Can't. No clothes."

"Oh. That's right. Mrs. Everett took them away to launder and dry last night. At least I vaguely recall that. But, Charles?" She reached around to poke him in the ribs.

"What?"

"We need to find out if Mr. Taplow stayed here last night. What if he saw us and cleared out?"

With a jolt, Charles realized that he had not given one thought to Taplow and his whereabouts since their troubles began on the moor. Of course, it was possible, even likely, that Taplow had registered at the King's House before them.

To his knowledge, there were no other places to stay between King's House and Ballachulish. They had been in no fit state to deal with any of that last night. He reached over to his watch on the night table. Just past seven o'clock and the sun was up. If Taplow had been here, he might well be gone already.

There was a knock at the door. It was a maid with their clothes. They dressed hurriedly, self-consciousness lending speed to the task. Maggie turned her engagement ring around so that it looked like a wedding band and they composed their faces in the way they supposed all married couples wore who were about to breakfast together.

Charles had just written, "Mr. and Mrs. Hartley Breck, Plum Coulee, Manitoba, Canada" in the hotel register. His first idea had been to write, "Mr. and Mrs. Ferdinand Armbruster" but Maggie had overruled that.

"Very good—eh—Mr. Breck," Mr. Everett, the innkeeper said. "I've no doubt you slept well. Breakfast is served in the dining room, just there at the end of the hall."

"Thank you. You're very kind. Say, may I ask you…?"

"Yes?"

"Well, we met a man when we were travelling a few days ago. I never did catch his name. He dropped something on the trail and I would like to return it to him." Charles went on to give a description of Taplow and asked if by any chance he had stayed the night at King's House.

"Aye, I believe I know the gentleman you mean. He arrived several hours before you. Requested a tray in his room and we never saw him again until this morning." Everett ran his finger down the entries in the register. "Here it is. Mr. Burgon is his name."

Charles tried not to show the jolt of excitement that ran

through him. "I—is he here, then?"

"Just left about a half hour ago, sir. That's a shame. He asked about the way to the trailhead for the Devil's Staircase—that's the path that goes to Kinlochleven and Fort William.

"Did he mention where he was headed? Kinlochleven or Fort William?"

"He did not. But he did ask for a copy of the sailing schedule for the *Gondolier*. That's the steamship that goes up the Caledonian Canal to Inverness, so I would say he was making for Fort William."

Charles sat on his immediate reaction, which was to grab Maggie and head for the door. He had to think. Was there any way to catch up to Taplow?

"Is there a faster way to get to Fort William?"

"Yes indeed, sir. If you take the postal cart from here to Ballachulish, you can take the coach to Fort William. That's what I told the other gentleman, but he insisted that he would enjoy the walk. I hope he does for it's over 25 miles."

"Are you going to eat that piece of bacon?"

"Yes. Do you want some more?" Charles said through a mouth full of eggs.

"Yes, frankly, I do. I know it will be the third plate of bacon we've been through, but we haven't really had a decent meal since breakfast at Dunnlinton yesterday. And who knows when we'll eat again."

Charles's was still feeling quite smug about this morning's bit of detection. By taking advantage of postal cart and coach travel they could enjoy a leisurely breakfast at King's House and still arrive in Fort William before Taplow. Moreover, while waiting for the coach to leave North Ballachulish for Fort William, they would be able to go to the post office there and send telegrams to Dunnlinton and to the police in Perth, telling them that it seemed likely that Taplow was headed to Fort William and, if so, he would reach there at about nine in the evening. All things being equal, Charles and Maggie would reach Fort William about five p.m. By that time the Fort William police would be on the lookout for Taplow and the whole matter might be resolved by the end of the day.

They rode to Ballachulish, jouncing along on the bare wooden benches of the small postal cart, crossed Loch Leven on the ferry that plied between Ballachulish and North Ballachulish, dispatched the required telegrams in North Ballachulish—including one to Maggie's father in Winnipeg and Charles's father in Kingston—and took the coach to Fort William in a sort of golden haze. What had happened between them, so wonderful and so potentially problematic, reordered everything ahead. Gone were thoughts of lazy sightseeing and further exploration of the old country. Their minds ran on to finishing the bicycle tour, returning to Edinburgh, and speedily booking steamship tickets on the fastest boat back to Canada and home.

At the police station in Fort William they were expected, and were ushered into a small office in the back by a grey-haired constable named Doig, whose tunic buttons strained to close over his ample belly. After a brief pause, they were joined by a youngish officer who identified himself as Inspector Ferris of the Fort William district, Inverness-shire police. They gave the inspector a detailed physical description of Taplow and what he was wearing when last seen that added some details to the description furnished by telegram from Inspector Storrs.

Later, after they had reluctantly registered at separate hotels for the night—he at the Waverley, she up the street at the

Caledonian—and had dined together at the latter, they walked aimlessly but not unpleasantly up and down the High Street of the town. There was still some light in the sky at ten, and Ben Nevis was still visible as it towered over the town. They were too keyed up to settle and, besides, Inspector Ferris had asked them to be prepared to identify Taplow if his sergeant and constable, who had been dispatched in plain clothes to watch everyone travelling through the last section of the Devil's Staircase trail, successfully apprehended their suspect.

As they walked along looking idly in the shop windows, Charles and Maggie didn't talk much, only remarked on this or that detail, brushed hands occasionally, and smiled at each other. For the rest, they were thinking their own thoughts.

Charles had to admit that he would miss the excitement of the chase. And there was something else, too. He found himself wishing that he could at least talk to Taplow. At first, he had been unwilling to believe that Taplow was the murderer. Surely there was some mistake. But Taplow's continued flight undermined that hope. Then there was the shock of that false name in the hotel register. Charles had to force himself to confront the reality of Taplow's guilt. What terrible force could move the hands of such a seemingly civilized man, a scholar, to all outward appearances an ardent Christian? A man not so very different from himself. He thought of those hands fastened around Radulescu's neck, digging into the flesh, squeezing. *No. It would be best not to think about that. Best to blot that picture right out.*

These thoughts were interrupted by the sound of brogue-clad steps behind them and laboured breathing.

"Mr. Lauchlan. Wait, please! Mr. Lauchlan." It was Constable Doig.

"What is it, Constable?" Maggie said.

Doig struggled to catch his breath and pulled out a large

white handkerchief to mop his brow. "Whew! We've got him! That is, we've got three suspects in the net, so tae speak. And the inspector asks can ye come along and say which is the murderer. We think we know which it is, but we need you tae say for certain."

"That's good work, Constable," Charles said, though he felt a tightening at the pit of his stomach. "Congratulations. But then I suppose it's all in a day's work for you."

"Well, to tell ye the truth, sir, in my twenty-five years on the force, he'll be my first. The first murderer that Ah've brought to justice mysel, that is. Mrs. Doig will be that proud."

Back at the small police station, a grave Inspector Ferris read to Charles and Maggie the appropriate cautions from the police manual on identifying suspects, and announced that those detained for questioning would be presented to Charles in what Ferris called "a parade."

"Miss Skene, this is hardly a business for ladies. I'm sure you'll be more comfortable in my office."

"No, Inspector, if you don't mind," Charles said, looking at Maggie. "We're a team. We've come this far together and we'll see it through together."

Ferris arched one eyebrow at Maggie and then nodded. "Very well, sir. Bring them in, Sergeant."

The door from the small whitewashed cell block opened and three men in chains filed in.

"Right, stand still," Ferris barked. "Now, turn and face this gentleman. Lift your heads up, please. That's better." He turned to Charles. "Now then, Mr. Lauchlan, which of these is the man?"

Charles had drawn in his breath in anticipation and stood tall, lifting his chest, confronting the moment of recognition. His eyes slid over the three shackled men and a furrow appeared between his brows.

"Huh? Well, that's—I'll be…" He turned to Maggie and saw the same turmoil of emotions he felt reflected on her face.

"Mr. Lauchlan?"

"None of them, Inspector. These men are all strangers to me."

It turned out that the three men, though similarly dressed to Taplow and approximately his height and body type, were exactly who they had claimed to be: a solicitor from Norwich; a dealer in brewery fittings from Ripon; and a grammar-school history teacher from Berwick-on-Tweed. Nor were they any too happy about having been ignominiously detained, handcuffed, and frog-marched out in front of Charles and Maggie. Mr. Playter, the lawyer, thundered at Ferris for a full five minutes before departing to rejoin his distressed wife.

"I'm so sorry, Inspector," Maggie said, once Playter had finished. "We were so sure!"

"Not your fault, Miss. But certainly not our finest day of policing," Ferris said, throwing a file down on his desk. "That's the trouble with a verbal description. We've not had time for an artist to do us a drawing of the suspect and we've no photograph or other likeness to go on. Without that, any fifty men are bound to fit the description. Add to that the fact that Taplow may well have changed his clothing and we're grasping at proverbial straws."

"What next, Inspector?" Charles said.

"We keep looking. We'll watch the canal steamship carefully tomorrow, in case he slipped through, as well as the road to Inverness. And we'll have the drawings up from Perth soon. Every police station in the country will be posting them in public places. Also, there's a special constable engaged by the Perth County Police who's gone down to Cambridge with two experts to search through Taplow's lodgings in his college." Ferris flipped open the file on his desk and trailed his finger down a page. "It's a little unorthodox if you ask me, but we'll hope to get more information from that search as well."

"How interesting, Inspector," Maggie said. "Do you know who these experts are?"

Ferris looked bemused. "Well, you'll not credit it, Miss, but according to Inspector Storrs, they are…" He consulted the file again. "A Mrs. Thorburn and a Miss Gairdner."

"Aha!" Charles whooped with delight and clapped his hands together. "The Burning Bush sisters are on the case! Now we'll get to the bottom of things. Wait a minute. Did you say a special constable?"

"Em—yes."

"What's his name?" Maggie said.

"I don't—Just a minute." Ferris looked again at his notes. "Yes, a Mr. Setter."

Ferris's further identifying information went unheard as Charles and Maggie erupted.

When they had stopped laughing, Charles said, "It looks as if you're closing in on Taplow, Inspector. We weren't lucky tonight, but it's hard to imagine that he'll evade you for much longer."

"Yes, and we'd like to see it through," Maggie said. "How can we help you?"

"By resuming your regular holiday plans, Miss. You've already put yourselves at risk in order to keep Taplow in your sights. We do appreciate it, though we don't recommend such activities on the part of the public. Best you leave it to us from now on."

Charles shook hands with the inspector, bid a rather

crestfallen Constable Doig goodbye and led Maggie out onto the street.

"I suppose that's it then," she said.

"Yes, I suppose so. But where do you suppose he's gotten to now? Did he take a different route than the Devil's Staircase? Or did he head somewhere else after Kinlochleven?"

"I don't think there is anywhere else to head after Kinlochleven. What if he just slipped by unnoticed somehow? He could be here this minute and we're the only ones who would recognize him," she said. "I just feel we could still be of use."

"No, darling girl, you heard the inspector. We should tend to our own knitting, of which there is considerable." He swept his arm around her waist and started walking her in the direction of her hotel.

"Back to Dunnlinton Lodge then?"

"Exactly. Back to Dunnlinton. I suppose we could take the coach down to Oban tomorrow and then train it to Rannoch Station."

"Yessss," she said, thinking out loud. "But you know it would be just as easy—and it would be so much more picturesque—to take the steamer up the Caledonian Canal to Inverness and then take the train back down to Struan. I'm sure Harald wouldn't mind sending a cart to Struan for us."

He stopped and looked at her with narrowed eyes. "Coincidentally, the steamer to Inverness is the major route a fugitive who was in a hurry to leave the country might take from here."

She was all innocence. "Why, yes, it would be. But we're tourists, aren't we? It's not as if we're going to be in Scotland every year. Shouldn't we take every opportunity to see what we can before we go home?"

"Well, that's a very reasonable case you've just put to

me. It features maximum scenery. And if we should happen to keep one eye open for Taplow, who's to know?" Charles raised his hand to his forehead, shielding his eyes, and did a melodramatic, swooping, 360-degree turn, looking high and low. When she gave him a shove, he took his cap off and slapped it against his thigh. "Blast! I was so sure he'd be one of those three men. And—oh—the look on their faces!" They laughed and she wrinkled up her nose, which she always did when embarrassed.

"But, blast again!" Charles said, "He must be out there somewhere. We just need one little shred of a lead to get back on his track."

39.

The two-decked side-wheeler *Gondolier* sailed only once per day and departed Fort William shortly before nine in the morning, making its way northeast at a leisurely pace up the Caledonian Canal, until it arrived at Inverness at a quarter after five in the afternoon. Charles and Maggie were on the quay at eight o'clock sharp in order to book their tickets, and watched the passing scene while they waited to board. There was considerable bustle as coaches and wagons delivered tourists from all the hotels of the town. Freight and heavy baggage destined for Inverness were loaded first, hauled on wheeled pallets and dollies by sweating navvies up a special wide gangway and lowered on a hoist into the belly of the steamer. Charles sighted Constable Doig in plain clothes, his large belly parting the crowd to this side and that as he made his way through the crush. He carried a battered leather satchel under his arm and was doing his best not to be too obvious, but his eyes sought out each person he went past.

"Good morning, Mr. Lauchlan, Miss." He doffed his hat to Maggie. "You'll be going up to Inverness then?"

"Right enough, Constable," Maggie said. "To Inverness and

then down by rail to rejoin our party near Kinloch Rannoch."

"As it happens, I'm away to Inverness myself."

"So we see. Still looking then?" Charles said.

"Not so loud, sir." Doig moved closer to Charles. "Officially, I'm away to deliver some files tae Superintendent Corbett at District Office. But for the rest—" He pointed to his eyes.

"Understood, Constable," Maggie said. "We won't breathe a word. And if we see—" she noted Doig putting a finger to his lips, "a person of mutual interest, we'll be sure to let you know."

"That would be much appreciated, miss. Meantime, just treat me like any other passenger, if you please."

They watched Doig's wide back recede into the crowd. Charles was a bit surprised at Ferris assigning Doig to do surveillance on the *Gondolier*. Did it mean that Ferris, having failed to nab Taplow the previous night, doubted that he was really in the vicinity? Then he felt guilty for making an assumption of lesser competence just because of Doig's age and girth. Maybe Doig was one of those people whose abilities are not obvious on superficial acquaintance. The purser interrupted these thoughts by walking to the foot of the gangway, removing the rope that barred the way and calling out, "All aboard! Tickets ready, please."

The day was overcast but not unpleasant as the *Gondolier* turned its back on the brooding outline of Ben Nevis and made its way across to Corpach, through the salt water bay where Loch Eil and Loch Linnhe meet at the south end of the Caledonian Canal. Here the ship turned north and entered the first of the series of ascending locks called "Neptune's Staircase" and began its step-wise progress up the canal toward Loch Lochy, the first of the chain of lochs lying in the bottom of the giant diagonal slash in the granite firmament of the Highlands that is the Great Glen.

Once the ship had cleared the last lock of the staircase, Charles and Maggie walked arm in arm and used a combination of charm and feigned ignorance to bluff their way below decks and into the cargo hold, where they idly checked out nooks and crannies among the boxes, steamer trunks, bales and wooden barrels, until a large sailor with tattoos running up each bare arm, chased them out. They had seen no sign of Taplow, but also no sign of Constable Doig.

The water was calm on Loch Lochy as the narrow ship's bow cut into the reflection of the green mountains lining the shore. Charles and Maggie continued their methodical reconnoitring of the ship, which they disguised by appearing to be enthusiastic tourists, dutifully pointing out bits of scenery and fittings of the ship to each other. Halfway through the enclosed passenger lounge of deck one, they came upon Doig, who had evidently run into an acquaintance and was deep into a conversation about fishing tackle. He was still talking when they ascended the winding stairs to deck two. At the stern of deck two, which was open to the sky except for the wheelhouse and a smaller lounge for passengers, they took a break and stood by the railing next to the davit from which the lifeboat hung, protected from rain by a tight canvas cover stretched taut over its gunnels.

"No sign of him," Maggie said. "I really had hopes for the cargo hold. Maybe we should try to go down there again. We really didn't have quite enough time for a thorough search."

"I doubt we can play ignorant again. That sailor would be on to us in no time. Let's face it, Taplow has slipped our grasp. And I doubt Doig will be any luckier."

Maggie laughed, then caught herself and looked around. "Yes," she said in a quieter voice. "Constable Doig may have the ship searched by the time we get to Inverness, but only if there are no more of his friends on board."

By the time the ship had gone through the Laggan Locks at the north end of Loch Lochy and entered the beautiful narrow channel that leads to Loch Oich, closely bordered by a dense, green wall of larches, Taplow had been forgotten and they became the gaping tourists they had until then only impersonated. When the ruins of Invergarry Castle came into view, on a rocky knoll overlooking Loch Oich, Charles was lost in the Scotland of his boyhood reading. Though no site better encapsulated both the aspirations and the defeat of Prince Charles Edward Stuart's cause in 1745, Charles could not help humming, "Wha Wouldna Fight for Charlie," as the boat passed by.

By now it was close to lunchtime and they made their way down to the confectionary, bought ham rolls and bottles of milk soda and sat happily in the lower deck passenger lounge, content to let the scenery drift by as the steamship navigated the locks on the River Oich that led to Fort Augustus. Others on board were not so patient. The progress of the ship was so slow through these locks and the canal so narrow that some of the passengers jumped easily over the railing and onto shore, and walked along the towpath, taking the air.

As the ship was docking at Fort Augustus, they were joined at the railing by Constable Doig who, true to their prediction, had not yet finished his search of the vessel. They soon passed on to chatting with him about other things, for Doig had grown up very near there. The village of Fort Augustus was underwhelming in itself, but Charles and Maggie had been intrigued to read in their guidebook about what looked like a remnant of the Middle Ages, or rather a fantasy of that; too new and perfect to be genuine. It was the Benedictine College and Monastery, built only seven years before, a modern homage to its forebears of the thirteenth century.

According to the book, the buildings were no longer open to the public, but since the ship was scheduled for a half-hour stop there, Maggie wanted to take a quick look at the exterior of the monastery, and so they were waiting to debark while some cargo destined for the village was unloaded down the cargo gangway. Charles noticed in an idle way that one of the sailors disengaged from the group that had manhandled the large crate onto the quay. This man, dressed in well-worn moleskin trousers, a tatty tweed waistcoat and a sweat-stained linen shirt, seemed to be carrying a rucksack, which registered as odd to Charles's mind. The man did not return to the ship with his mates, but strode off quickly, making his way through the crowd on the quay as if he were late for something. There was something about the way the man carried himself, about his demeanour that held Charles's eye, even though Maggie was talking to him. Then it hit him.

"Oh, my Lord! There he is!"

"Who? What do you—?"

"Taplow! He's been on board this whole time. I thought he was a navvy at first!"

"What's that, Mr. Lauchlan?" It was Doig.

"Constable, there! Charles grabbed Doig's shoulder and pointed emphatically.

"That's him?" said Doig. "That's the man? Strewth, I'll have to—"

Charles took one look at Doig and realized that the older man had no chance of catching a fit and desperate man.

"Constable! You and Maggie contact Inspector Ferris and tell him which direction Taplow's headed in. I'll follow him and try to see where he goes."

Before either Doig or Maggie could get another word out, Charles lunged down the gangplank, excusing himself as he pushed people out of the way.

40.

Cordwainer sighed and took up his position again outside Mr. Taplow's rooms. At least that Canadian constable had given him permission to sit down. He didn't see why it had to be himself who'd been given the job of barring entrance to Mr. Taplow's rooms to anyone but police authorities. Why couldn't one of the kitchen boys be spared? He thought of the lunch he was missing and of the quick pint—or three—at the Quail and Quince. Still, he had to smile at the college being all at sixes and sevens because of ladies, of all things, demanding to be allowed into the college precincts. And ladies accompanied by a Red Indian at that! Though Constable Setter wasn't giving much away, it seemed that Mr. Taplow was in some kind of trouble. Why, the Master was fit to be tied. He had sent one of the scouts to the chemist for a new supply of his stomach powders. Cordwainer stood up quickly when he saw Special Constable Setter striding down the hallway toward Taplow's rooms.

"Everything all right, Mr. Cordwainer?"

"Right as rain, Constable. I done as you said and turned everyone away until further notice."

"Good work. Carry on."

Setter slipped past Cordwainer, entered the room, and closed the door behind him. Before him was Taplow's sitting room, spare and well ordered, but with a leathery comfort suitable to its occupant. The room was dominated by a fireplace and mantle around which two calf-hide armchairs and a sofa were ranged. At the other end there was a round table and four wooden chairs at which Taplow drank his morning tea or led tutorials with students. His own search of the rooms had yielded nothing that seemed to pop out at him as important to the case. It was the apartment of a man who led a quiet and rather abstemious life. Setter wasn't able to make much out of the substance of that life, the letters and papers that Taplow had accumulated from his teaching and research. He hoped the sisters would fare better.

He found Janet and Annie sitting at Taplow's table. In the bedroom that opened onto the sitting room, they had found a large wooden desk with cubbyholes and drawers full of files and papers. The contents of that desk were now spread into neat piles on the table.

"Well, Sergeant," Annie could barely contain her excitement, "we think what we've found is important, but we're rather puzzled as well."

"Puzzled? In what way?" Setter, immediately intent, sat down in the chair opposite them and leaned forward on his elbows.

"We found a file marked 'Library'," Janet said. "In it we found a copy of the submission to the library trustees for the purchase of Radulescu's manuscript fragment, just as the Master described it." She ruffled through a pile of papers in front of her. "Here it is." She read out, "'Parchment fragment, Gospel of St. Mark, uncial, possibly dating from the fourth century AD.' Then he goes on to describe the verses contained in the fragment, the colour of the ink, condition of the parchment and so on."

"Is this the kind of description that is standard in your field?"

"Well, it's the kind of description that a scholar would write if they were in some doubt about several points in relation to the manuscript," Janet said.

"Do you think that's because Taplow wasn't sure the manuscript was genuine? The Master said Taplow was reluctant to make a final authentication until he'd had a chance to examine it in more detail."

"Well, that's one of the odd things," Janet said. "Mr. Taplow was cautious about saying that it was authentic when talking to the Master, and also in his submission to the trustees."

"But we've found some notes he made for his own use," Annie said. "Really, we were very excited when we read them."

"Yes? What do they say?"

"The notes indicate that Mr. Taplow had no doubts about the fragment at all; he was sure it was genuine. And you'll never guess..." Janet said.

"Yes—no, that's right I won't."

"If Mr. Taplow is correct, and we have no reason to doubt his view, Radulescu's fragment was originally a part of Codex Zwingliae, a fourth-century bound volume held in the University of Basel Library; one of the most important sources, though partial, that we have of the Gospel texts in Greek."

"And that's not all," Annie said. "The manuscript fragment that we bought from Radulescu—the one that he was so eager to get back—is also, we are reasonably sure, from Codex Zwingliae. We think that the two fragments may be closely related!"

Setter sat back in his chair and blew air out slowly between pursed lips while he thought. "So, if the two fragments are related, that would explain why Radulescu was interested in your fragment. And, presumably, why Taplow wanted to buy Radulescu's fragment, and yours as well?"

"We think so," Janet said. "Ever since we found Mr. Taplow's notes, we've realized that he did show a great deal of interest in our fragment, wanting to know what our plans were for publishing about it, and so on, though he never actually made us an offer for it."

"Wait! So, if he was convinced Radulescu's fragment was genuine and that it came from this Codex Zwingliae, why would he not say this to the Master, and why would he not include this information in his submission to the library trustees? Wouldn't this additional information have impressed the trustees and make them want to buy the manuscript?"

"That's what we thought, too," Annie said. "It doesn't make sense."

"He wanted this manuscript very badly, yet he would not reveal the information that would have been most persuasive in securing it for the college," Janet said.

"And subsequently, the trustees declined to buy the manuscript," Annie said.

"Have you any idea at all why he would want to keep this information to himself?"

"We do not, Sergeant," Annie said, "But see here." She handed Setter a letter. "Shortly after the trustees refused to buy Radulescu's manuscript, there's a note from a friend in Norfolk commiserating with Mr. Taplow about the illness that supposedly prevented Taplow from going to Norfolk for the shooting as he had planned, as well as other evidence that he made rather hurried plans to go to Edinburgh instead."

41.

Charles was afraid he would lose Taplow on the crowded quay and rushed off to the point where he'd last seen him. When he reached the roadway that ran parallel to the east bank of the River Oich, he stopped in confusion. Which way? He looked north and then south and just caught a glimpse of moleskin trousers and tweed headed south out of the village. Maggie and Doig were still visible on the deck of the *Gondolier*. He turned to them and did a comic-opera big-gesture, pointing in the direction that Taplow was headed. Maggie waved to signify that she understood. Then Charles turned to follow Taplow. He wrestled his ordnance map out of his rucksack as he continued to walk and tried to read the map while walking. Taplow was setting a brisk pace but Charles was confident he could keep up. He would have to try to look inconspicuous if Taplow looked back in his direction. Just then a man passed by him, walking in the opposite direction. The man wore a heavy tweed coat and carried a shepherd's crook. Charles walked on for several yards, and then stopped and turned.

"Hey! Excuse, me, sir. I need your coat."

"Eh? What? Are ye daft? Go on with ye." The shepherd continued on his way. Charles followed him.

"No, really. How much do you want for the coat? I'll give you my jacket, plus three pounds."

The shepherd stopped and shook his head in wonder. "Americans! What next, I ask ye?"

"Actually, I'm Can— Oh, never mind. I'm in dead earnest, sir. Look, I'll give you four pounds." Charles pulled the bank notes out of his billfold.

The shepherd reached out to touch Charles's jacket, rolling the fabric against his calloused fingers. "Mind, now, that's a nice bit of cloth. Well, sir, if you're mad enough to pay so dear, Ah'm mad enough tae gie ye ma coat!"

"If you'll give me your hat, I'll pay extra for your that as well."

In an instant the deal was done. Charles pressed the money into the shepherd's hand, emptied the pockets of his jacket, handed it off and hurriedly shrugged his way into the heavy tweed, thigh-length coat. All the while he kept his eyes southward along the road. He handed the shepherd his cap in exchange for the beaten-up old slouch hat, thanked him and set off after Taplow.

He pulled the old hat down over his eyes, did up the coat and hoped that Taplow would not recognize his gait. He pulled out the map again, folding it to the right area and taking little glances at it as he walked along. It seemed that Taplow was heading south. Why would he do that? If he had boarded the steamer to get to the northeast coastal ports, perhaps to find a ship to take him to Germany, Holland, or one of the Scandinavian countries, why was he now headed in the opposite direction?

Taplow was about three hundred yards ahead of Charles; a small figure, not running, but walking in a determined fashion, as if he knew where he was headed. With the main part of Fort Augustus behind them, Taplow stopped, looked around and pulled something out of his rucksack—a map. Charles pulled his hat down lower and slowed down, but kept the other man in view just under the brim of his hat. After a moment of looking at the map and looking at the lay of the land, Taplow folded the map and stowed it away with a definitive gesture and struck out into a field in a southeasterly direction toward a hill in the distance. Charles resumed his former pace again but had no idea what Taplow was up to. When he got to the place where Taplow had left the road, he stopped, crouched down and pretended to adjust his boots with his back to Taplow's direction so that Taplow would not be able to see him consulting his own map. Shepherds, after all, would know all the roads and paths here by heart. It took a few moments for Charles to find the right section of map and orient himself. He found that Taplow had turned off onto a path that followed a pass through the high hills to the southeast of Fort Augustus and down toward Laggan on the other side. He followed the path along the map to Laggan and there, he thought, was where Taplow was headed. The railway station at Newtonmore: the train up to Inverness and the fishing ports of the Moray Firth.

After missing the train at Rannoch Station, Taplow had seemed to avoid train travel. Charles thought he understood why: too many officials checking his ticket and looking him over in a place where he couldn't easily get away if someone wanted to ask him too many questions. But Taplow had been at large for a day and a half and he must sense the noose tightening. Now he had to take more chances. *But wait. Why did he get off the boat, when he could have stayed hidden all the way to Inverness?* Charles doubted that a sighting of Constable Doig would have convinced Taplow to run. Doig was in plain clothes and anyway, Taplow had somehow evaded capture the day before and may not even have seen the portly constable. But Taplow had been spooked into bolting off the ship by something. And that something was more than likely the presence of Maggie and himself on the *Gondolier*. Charles fingered the rough tweed of his coat. *I paid more than four pounds for this blasted coat and Taplow wasn't fooled for a minute. That furtive look behind him while he was consulting his map was to see if I was gaining on him.*

He stuffed the map back in his rucksack, took a deep breath. Taplow was tiny in the distance. Charles strode off in pursuit at a pace calculated to be slightly faster than Taplow's. He didn't quite know what to feel. He was excited, certainly; the quarry was in sight. But then the dampening hand of caution. He might just be able to catch up to Taplow, but if he did, what then? Be sensible and simply shadow him? Inspector Ferris had warned him not to make actual contact. But Charles found himself increasingly thinking about the state Taplow must be in not just of body, but of soul—the exhaustion, the desperation and above all the enormous weight of his sin. *He should give himself up. Surely it would go easier if he did. Shouldn't I try to talk to him?*

Once the trail began to mount the hills, the way became more forested and he lost sight of Taplow as the path entered the trees. Charles picked up a nice, stout sapling to use as a walking stick and was thankful for it as the path wound upward with gentle switchbacks. After twenty minutes of this the path opened onto upland meadow and moorland, forming a saddle between hills. The feeling of being up high and yet to be so small on that breadth of rolling treeless hillside was exhilarating. He saw Taplow ahead of him and realized that he had closed the distance between them slightly. Then up ahead and to the left of the path he saw a group of men splayed out in twos and threes, lying along the downward slope, and a pony and cart parked just off the path. This strange grouping made more sense as he passed the cart and in it saw a few rifles, ammunition and wicker baskets of food. These men must be a party of well-heeled hunters deerstalking with their ghillies, perhaps from one of the large estates nearby. The men paid no attention to him. They were facing away and focused entirely on the hill lower down. If Charles had not been in a hurry, he would have liked to have watched this strange and fascinating competition between stag and man; not at all like the squirrel shooting he had done in his childhood. Almost reluctantly he turned and followed the path upward.

The path followed a straight course now through tufts of scrubby bush and grasses until it emerged onto a higher, more windswept plateau of heather moorland strewn with boulders. On the crest of the hill there was a massing of stones that looked man-made. He expected to see Taplow ahead of him as before. But there was no sign of him. Charles hadn't seen any indication of a forking to an alternative trail and anyway, if Taplow had taken another path, the moor was so open he would still have been visible. The weather had turned colder now and a light rain had begun to fall. He continued on the trail past groups of boulders encrusted with lacy patches of green and black lichen, glad of the heavy tweed coat, which he now buttoned up to his throat as he walked.

A loud CRACK and a whistling of air jerked his head up and threw him sideways. Now he was sprawled behind the boulders he had been observing a second before. *Blast! Idiots! Do they think I'm a deer? Are they blind?*

What to do? It was so quiet now that he wondered if he had just imagined it. His heart was pounding and his breath roared in his ears. Still quiet, though. After a few moments, he moved to his knees, and peeked warily above the boulder. Couldn't see anything. Down again for a think. *Maybe the hunters have moved on? Can't stay here forever. I'll lose Taplow. Still quiet.* He clambered to his feet, still sheltered by the boulder, then moved out gingerly onto the path.

CRACK! Whizz! This time he was thrown backward and scrambled on all fours behind cover again. *What's going on? They must be able to see me!* He tried to master the pounding in his ears. *Breathe slower. Slower. Slower. Now. That's better.* A realization began to form as his breath slowed. He saw the pony cart again and what it had carried. The picture burned into focus. *Yes. The hunting party wasn't paying attention; they had seen a deer down on the lower slope. It would have been easy; I could have taken one myself and some ammunition, too.*

He was far away from help. The hunters down below would think nothing of shots heard higher up the pass. Doig and Maggie would have been able to alert the police in Fort William and maybe in Newtonmore or Kingussie. But the police would need more time. It was getting late in the day and few fellow travellers could be expected on this trail.

Just me and Taplow. I should stay low and run back down the slope. He won't follow me. He needs to get to Inverness. I should let him. That's what I should do. But—Blast! If I could just talk to him! Where the devil is he hiding up there anyway? There was only one way to find out. A deep breath. *God, my strength and my salvation.* He sprang up, and, moving into the path, started loping forward, but with quick zigzags to left and right. His dive for cover and the shot were simultaneous, but as he landed hard behind a higher outcropping, the picture was clearer. Taplow, alarmed at Charles's sudden plunge forward, had moved out to fire from behind the cover of a small, low hut about a hundred yards up the gentle slope.

All Charles's senses were unbearably intense. The air,

still vibrating from the sound, the rain softly falling, the colours—purple, grey, brown, green—the granular feel of the boulder against his cheek and his breath steaming the air. He became aware of another sound, a gurgling, water over rock, pooling and rushing. There was a stream flowing down the hill, a stream that had bitten its ways into the hillside over hundreds, maybe thousands, of years and had eroded for itself a channel, perhaps three feet deep incised into the hillside and bordered by coarse thickets of heather. Charles focused all of his senses and his rational mind on that stream-bed. The stream ran quite close to the hut as far as he could tell. He raised his head above the boulder and looked directly up, saw enough and ducked down again. *Is it possible?* He calculated the distance between his position and the stream-bed. About ten yards. He would only just have enough cover from the heather, occasional boulders and sedge grasses if he pulled himself toward the stream lying prone on the ground and playing lizard. He tried to think of another way but there wasn't one.

By some miracle he had held onto his walking stick and the sight of it clenched in his fist gave him another idea. He stuck his head just enough above the boulder for his shapeless tweed hat to be visible. Then pulled down again, shrugged his way out of his coat and took off his hat. The hat he propped up on the stick so that just the top of it would be visible to Taplow as before. A flimsy diversion, but it might work. Then he began his crawl toward the streambed, praying that Taplow would not catch sight of him moving. As the rain mixed with his sweat, he was able to scuttle carefully down into the streambed. He had no choice but to go right down into the water. He had to reach a point in the stream that would take him slightly beyond the hut so that he would emerge behind Taplow. There was usually enough cover from the heather and grasses along the streambed to crawl on all fours, but at points he had to return to his lizard position. He tried to keep his head clear of the water, but it was not easy.

He was crawling against the force of the water, which soaked his clothes and numbed his muscles with cold. He had to navigate around or even over the larger stones in the stream, and the closer he got to Taplow the quieter he had to be and therefore the slower he had to go. It seemed to take forever to make any progress. When could he risk looking over the bank of the stream to get his bearings? If he were way off, the game would be over. Whatever he did, it had to be done immediately once he got up to a standing position. The cold was getting unbearable and he wondered whether he would even be able to move properly. *Can't take much more. Have to see.* He raised himself up on his knees and peered above the bank. *Now!*

Charles exploded over the bank and with a guttural roar took two bounding steps toward the place where Taplow had last been. *Crack!* The shot stopped his forward momentum, spraying mud and gravel as it hit the ground only a few feet in front of him. He fell sideways, absurdly and hard.

"Stop this foolishness at once! Stay down, I warn you!"

Charles looked up to see the barrel of the rifle pointed at him a few inches from his nose. "Oh, um. Hello, Taplow."

"What do you mean, 'Hello Taplow'? For God's sake, this isn't a garden party, Lauchlan! What the devil are you doing following me?"

Charles was wondering that same thing as the barrel of the rifle jerked around unpredictably. He swept his wet hair off his forehead and moved onto his knees. "I'm not sure, really. I suppose I thought you might need to see a friendly face."

"A friend!" Taplow snorted. "Is that what we are?"

Charles very slowly got to his feet, holding Taplow's eyes. "Well, leaving aside for the moment the fact that you've treated me like an illiterate colonial parson of no account, we've been friendly. There's no reason why we can't go the whole way. You could use a friend, especially in a storm."

It was true. What had started as a gentle rain was now working up to a full deluge.

Taplow, still pointing the gun at Charles, twisted his mouth into a weary smile. "I must shoot at people more often. Think how my social life would improve."

Charles had no idea what was going to happen next, but one thing was clear: If he didn't find a way to get warm and dry, he was going to freeze to death.

"I'm going back to get my things. I don't know what you intend to do, but I'm going to see if there's a way to make a fire in that hut."

"Bothy," said Taplow.

"What?"

"They call it a bothy." He did not lower the rifle completely, but his chest hollowed and his shoulders sagged.

Charles took a deep breath and, turning, began to walk as slowly as he could make himself, down toward the place where he had left his things.

"I could have hit you, you know, if I'd wanted to," Taplow called after him and Charles stopped, stock still at the sound of his voice. "Believe it or not, I'm quite a good shot."

Charles turned, nodded to the other man, then turned and walked again, quicker, down the slope.

When he returned with his coat, hat and rucksack and bent low to enter the small hut he saw that Taplow had found some firewood and was building a fire in a small stone fireplace. When standing upright, their heads grazed the roof joists and there was only just enough room for two. The only furnishing in the hut was a small, scratched wooden table with a heavy pewter candlestick on it and a wooden box beside the fire, well stocked with firewood. The table had a drawer and when Charles opened it, he found candles and matches. He lit a candle and, realizing that his only chance for comfort was to dry his clothes somehow, took everything off and hung the sodden clothes over the fireplace on a cord that must have been strung exactly for that purpose by the benevolent hand or hands that had provided this shelter. Naked, he wrapped himself in the scratchy folds of the old woollen coat, the inner layers of which were still dry, and breathed a silent prayer of thanks to the shepherd who now wore his own coat.

"You saw us on the boat, then, Maggie and me?"

"Yes, if you'd stayed in the cargo hold a little longer, you would have found me." He undid his own coat and put it on the line beside Charles's clothes. "Believe me, the navvy's life is not one to aspire to. The smell alone was unbearable—*is* unbearable." He lifted the front of his collar and took a slight sniff of his sweat-encrusted shirt. "I'm afraid there's no space for you to sit downwind here."

Charles was surprised at the change that only two days of flight had brought about in Taplow. It wasn't just the tatty clothes. The lines of his face were etched deeper with weather and distress, and the colour raised by wind and rain was only a gloss on the underlying greyness of deep exhaustion. As he got up to put another log on the fire, he seemed thinner, worn away. He had stopped actually holding the rifle, but had been careful to prop it within easy reach at a place where Charles could not grab it.

"I couldn't make out why you would follow me."

Charles laughed a little at that. "At first, I think it was a case of too much Sir Walter Scott when young."

That brought a chill smile to Taplow's face.

"But there was practicality, too. We knew what you looked like and the police were far away. We just wanted to see where you were going. Until they could catch up."

"Perhaps you've missed your calling."

"Oh, no. I'm too soft to ever make a policeman. Just ask Andrew Setter. For instance, for the longest time, I couldn't convince myself that you'd actually done it."

Taplow sat back against the wall of the hut with his face in shadow. He poked at the fire with Charles's stick, causing sparks to fly upward, but said nothing.

"And then the false name in the hotel register at King's House; taking the less-travelled ways; seeing that you'd deliberately changed your appearance." It hurt him almost physically to draw the conclusion and he dropped his voice. "Well, you're quiet now, but these actions speak."

The silence continued for several moments. "Now that you've found me, what do you intend to do?"

It was a crucial moment. Charles knew his safety hung in the balance. "I don't intend to turn you in, if that's what you mean, even if that were possible. But I equally will not willingly do anything to prevent that happening." These words surprised even himself, as they came out of his mouth. He hadn't really formulated that thought beforehand. "So, you don't have to tie me up or hit me over the head."

"What, then?"

"I'm not sure, exactly. But, you know, even if you hadn't started shooting at me, I think I would have tried to catch up to you."

"Why?"

"You'll laugh, I suppose. I wanted—needed—some explanation. Of how that catastrophe in the hills above Dunnlinton could possibly have happened."

A sound somewhere between a sigh and a groan came out of Taplow and when he turned to set another log on the fire, Charles saw a face that he would remember for a long time. It was the face of utter hopelessness.

"Look here, I'm starving," Charles said. "I've got some ham rolls and cheese in my bag to contribute. Have you got anything?"

Taplow seemed a little stunned but finally roused himself to reach for his rucksack. "Ah—well. Let's see." He stirred around. "I've got some sausages. And some whisky."

"Sounds like supper."

42.

With their supper done, they sat back feeding the fire and listening to the rain pelt down on the slate roof. It was clear to both of them that neither was going anywhere and that they would have to spend the night in the little bothy. Apart from a few small leaks, the hut was surprisingly snug. They found two dented metal cups in the drawer of the wooden table. After washing them by holding them out in the downpour, Taplow filled each with a generous measure of whisky. The rifle was still leaning against the wall close to Taplow, a jarring note in their otherwise cozy after-dinner mellowness. Taplow made sure to guard it with his body as he handed a cup to Charles.

"What do you think your life will be like now? If you get away, I mean," Charles said.

Taplow sat down on the floor on the opposite side of the fire, placed the rifle on the side of him furthest from Charles and leaned back against the wall. He picked up Charles's walking stick and laid it across his lap. "Oh, I don't know. Perhaps I'll find a place to work somewhere. I can still teach. My German is good. I hear that teachers of English are wanted in the Scandinavian countries. Some small place out of the way. Perhaps I could even continue my research, though of course, I couldn't think of publishing."

"I don't doubt that you could find ways to feed and clothe yourself. You have many talents. But what about… what about—?"

"Yes. I've had ample time to think about that, too. My sins go with me wherever I end up."

"Why not turn yourself in? It will be easier on you if you do. And God is merciful to those who truly have repentance in their hearts."

"I take it you discount the Revelation of St. John: 'The lake that burneth with fire and brimstone: which is the second death.'"

"How can I discount it when that surely describes your current state. You don't need to stay there. Christ in his mercy shows us the way to him."

Taplow closed his eyes tight, then opened them and fixed them on some distant place. "You don't know how I would like to believe that."

"Then believe it—with your whole heart—and relieve your soul of its burden."

"I suppose you mean that I should lay my sins before God." It was almost a whisper. Then there was a brief flash of the old Taplow. "You're a strange sort of confessor, Lauchlan. When I speak to my priest, he at least has trousers on."

Charles pulled the coat more closely around himself. "Yes, but I have the advantage of being here at this moment. And besides, you won't just be speaking to me."

Taplow was quiet. Charles decided to keep pressing. "Well then. Are you prepared?"

"My church does not recognize your ordination."

Charles sighed and shook his head in frustration. "Then

talk to me as a fellow believer. Can anything be worse than the way you feel now?"

The muscles of Taplow's jaw worked and he rubbed his hand against the two-day growth of beard, but said nothing.

Charles held up his hand in benediction. "In the name of the Father, and of the Son, and of the Holy Spirit."

Silence. Then, "Amen," Taplow said. He closed his eyes. The knuckles of his hands showed white as they gripped Charles's walking stick. "I pray God to have mercy on me."

"He will not fail you."

"I don't know where to start."

"Did the note from Radulescu ask you to meet him?"

"Yes."

"Why did he want to see you?"

"Hah. Yes, that's as good a place to start as any." Taplow took a swig of his whisky. "How to explain it…? He dangled the thought in front of me that our interests might coincide. But really, he was desperate to know what I was up to. He was afraid I was going to get my hands on that manuscript fragment of Mrs. Thorburn's and Miss Gairdner's. That I would get to it before he did."

"Was that what you were trying to do?"

"I had some thought of that initially. What the sisters did not know was that Radulescu also had a fragment from the same codex—Codex Zwingliae—and adjoining pages no less." Taplow shook his head. "A freakish occurrence. An unparalleled find. I still wonder at it, but yet it seemed to be true. I had seen Radulescu's fragment and seen a description of that belonging to the sisters. To my knowledge, Radulescu and I were the only ones who knew the fragments fitted together. Of course, together they are worth exponentially more than as separate items."

"I don't understand. You wanted to get your hands on

both fragments? For the money?"

"Oh no. I cared nothing for their monetary value. No, that was Radulescu's obsession. My concern was for what was written there: On the sisters' piece, the beginning of a marginal gloss by an editor casting doubt on the authenticity of certain verses; and then on Radulescu's piece, the continuation of this note and a symbol indicating the beginning of the dubious passage."

"Would it be—you mean—the last twelve verses of Mark?"

"Yes. The verses I've spent the last fifteen years of my life defending as original, as coming direct from the hand of Mark. The verses containing the promise of the Resurrection."

"Are—? Wait. Are you telling me you wanted to get hold of the two fragments so that you could prevent them from being made public?"

"Actually, I had given up on the idea of acquiring both fragments. My college refused to buy Radulescu's and I could tell that, in spite of Radulescu's efforts, the sisters would never part with theirs. No, my only remaining option was to prevent or delay the discovery of the two fragments and the realization that they fit together."

"So, you were prepared to compromise your most cherished scholarly standards for the sake of your professional vanity?"

"It sounds so self-serving when you put it like that. When I was on my way to meet Radulescu, I dressed it up in a lot of higher, nobler folderol. This one man, I said to God, this piece of human excrement is standing between me and the greatest service I could render to the Church. If he was somehow…em…not there, I could then reach a height of eminence sufficient to defend Holy Scripture from the ignominious assaults of parsing German critics. Those who want to reduce the sacred texts to a level no higher than the plays of George Bernard bloody Shaw!" Taplow banged his hand on the table for emphasis.

"But—but surely the evidence of one manuscript would not be enough to completely undermine your theories?"

"No, but you see, that one find—those two fragments together—would make a great splash at first. And, before cooler heads could determine the relation of these fragments to other manuscripts, that first big splash would be all that Renshaw would need to secure the Millbankian. Don't you see? I could do so much with the podium the Millbankian Professorship provides; so much to defend the Authorized Version and the whole vision of the Gospel of Mark."

"How would killing him have gained you this manuscript? Surely, he didn't have it with him."

Taplow stirred the coals in the fireplace to a higher flame with the walking stick. "That's true. He did not. But all I needed to do was to…to get Radulescu out of the way, so that the unified manuscript's arrival in the scholarly world would be delayed."

"Delayed? Wouldn't his fragment be found among his things and eventually the two fragments be found to be related?"

"Yes, eventually. But by that time, I would already have won the election to the Millbankian Professorship in Biblical Studies, and from that aerie I could very much blunt any negative impact. I planted sufficient doubt, at least within my own college, about the authenticity of Radulescu's fragment that my eventual argument that it was a forgery would have been well accepted."

"You killed Radulescu for this?"

The intense engagement in Taplow's eyes suddenly turned opaque, as if someone had abruptly pulled a blind down. He lifted his face toward the ceiling. Then he seemed to shrink and draw inward as he leaned back against the wall and his face fell into shadow. The small bothy amplified all that was trapped within it: the sound of the rain on the slates; steam rolling off the clothing on the line; the mingled smell of sweat and whisky; firelight, red and orange. The silence grew between them and Charles knew that the other man had pulled away. They sat captive in their separate thoughts.

43.

They walked along early the next morning, Charles ahead and Taplow following, holding the rifle in front of him with the barrel pointed upward. The sky was still overcast but the rain had tailed off. Though Taplow carried the gun with the safety lever engaged, Charles was all too aware that there were cartridges in the magazine and the gun could be readied to fire in an instant. It seemed that Taplow intended to keep him close at hand and under surveillance and, for the moment at least, Charles wasn't going to risk testing that assumption. At about five-thirty they had had a meagre breakfast of porridge made from oats that Taplow produced, which they boiled up over the fire in the metal cups and finished off with the last of the whisky. The bothy was located near the beginning of the descent toward Laggan and the trail now ran parallel to the River Spey which rose in these hills and began to make its way toward its outlet on the Moray Firth.

Charles believed that Taplow's agonized penitence of the night before was sincere, yet he had shied away from a complete confession. He had sheltered behind evasions and carefully avoided saying the actual words that would incriminate him, though the conclusions evident from what he had told Charles left little doubt about his guilt. And he had made no change in his ultimate plan to escape, all of which confirmed for Charles that Taplow's mind and heart remained in a state of sin. An equally grave thought followed that: he was now the only person besides Taplow himself who had certain knowledge of Taplow's crime. In the chill light of morning his decision to confront Taplow looked hopelessly naive. He thought of Maggie and of the life they had planned together. Why hadn't he simply run back down the hill toward Fort Augustus when Taplow started shooting? Surely any sensible man would have done that, and he had thought himself to be as sensible a man as the next. *You've got a fool for a lover, darling girl, and I'm so sorry.*

By late afternoon they were getting desperately tired and hungry. Signs of proximity to civilization were getting more numerous: sheep on the hillsides, bridges crossing streams, old fences falling down, and smoke rising from distant chimneys. They had encountered a few other walkers along the path. Charles was aware of Taplow eyeing him nervously as they saw a man approaching carrying a huge bundle of branches, deadfall collected from the forest below. He could feel Taplow's unease increasing, the closer they came to places where he might be recognized or challenged.

"This fellow may have some food we could buy," Charles said in a whisper. "Let's ask him."

"All right. But you ask him. And remember, I'll be watching."

Charles nodded and called out to the man. As he came abreast of them on the path, Charles remarked on the storm of the previous evening, then asked the man if by any chance he had any food he could spare. Taplow took up a position about five yards off the path and pretended to be adjusting the straps of his rucksack. The question about food was rewarded by the man producing some bread and cold mutton. Charles took out his wallet but the man shook his head and refused to take money. As Charles was thanking him profusely, the man cast a questioning glance toward Taplow.

"Oh, ah. My friend would like to thank you as well," Charles said, "but he doesn't speak English. Uh, German, you see."

Taplow bowed to the man in what he doubtless hoped was a German fashion. The man adjusted his bundle of sticks, touched his cap and moved on up the path.

They ate the bread and mutton immediately as they walked and washed it down with water from the river. About six o'clock, they were approaching the place where the path they had been travelling led into the village of Laggan and joined the main road to Newtonmore. Taplow stopped short and grabbed Charles's arm.

"Look, there. Do you see that?"

"What?"

"A fellow standing near the end of the path—and another sitting down on a stile on the other side of the road."

"Yes, yes, I see them. Hmm—they look like—"

"Yes, policemen. Quick! We'll have to go this way."

Charles hesitated, but Taplow said, "Come on!" and grabbed the collar of Charles's coat, pulling him off the path. "We'll have to rough it away from the main roads and paths from now on," Taplow said, tugging Charles along. "I can't risk being seen."

"I'm not sure that's the best plan, either, Taplow. It's quite open here. You can see for miles. If those policemen see us turning off the path suddenly, they're bound to be suspicious."

"I have to risk that. If I can just get to Newtonmore

station, I can catch the 8:15 to Inverness."

"Then what?"

"Find a place to hide on the train, I suppose."

Charles was about to say that sometime, somewhere, the game of hide and seek would be over and he was just prolonging the inevitable, but Taplow yanked him forward abruptly so that he was once again in front and forced him into a fast trot. They tried to head in a straight line across the breast of the hill parallel to the road below, but the going was not always easy. They had to pick their way through a clump of hawthorn bushes and the long spikes scratched at their arms and grabbed at their coats. Once through this, they crossed through a flock of sheep grazing lazily, who seemed to place their rotund bodies in the way deliberately and looked offended at having to move. Having finally threaded their way through the flock, they reached an area that was forested, but not densely, so that they could pass through quite easily.

With fewer impediments, Taplow set a desperately fast pace, forcing Charles along, both men labouring for breath. Though the hill became steep above them, they found a path that headed in the direction of Newtonmore and continued along it for what seemed like another half mile. Charles sensed that Taplow's whole being was now focused completely on that train in Newtonmore station. They emerged from the woods into an open field from which the ruins of a village were visible on the slope below, and below that, the main road. They could see a mill on the side of the hill at the end of a millrace that turned its massive wheel. In the distance was Newtonmore, less than a mile off.

Charles looked down toward the road to the village. "Hey, wait a minute. Look there!" Taplow plowed onward and Charles had to turn and grab his arm, pointing in the direction of the main road below them.

"Four men coming up the hill. I think it's the police!"

Taplow cast around, looking frantically in every direction. "There's a river over there, powering that mill. It's between us and Newtonmore." He dropped the rifle and started running toward the point where the millrace diverted water from the river.

Thoughts were jumbling up and falling all over themselves in Charles's mind. Follow Taplow? Stay and wait for the police? He scrambled after the running man. He caught up to Taplow at the edge of the water, where he was pacing like a wolf in a zoo, looking for a way across. The gentle stream that Charles expected had swollen with the rains of the night before into a boiling, roaring torrent, straining against the rough granite banks. Taplow loped toward a point where a series of wet, craggy boulders created a narrows before a steep fall into a heavily churning gorge. The distance across was about eight yards but at two points there were gaps of over five feet between boulders. Taplow looked intently at Charles and then behind him. They could now clearly make out the navy blue tunics of the two constables running uphill and the plainclothes officers trailing several yards behind them.

With a great heave and a rasping exhalation of breath, Taplow threw his rucksack across the chasm and watched it land on the far crags.

"For God's sake, Taplow. It's too dangerous! Don't—"

But Taplow stepped out onto the rocks. He jumped onto the first boulder, then the second with ease and came to the first gap. Coiling himself into a deep knee bend, he sprang into the air, sprawled on the landing rock, but grabbed hold and clambered to his feet. Charles watched with growing alarm. He called out again but his voice was lost in the sound of the water rushing into the gorge below. Taplow leaped onto the next rock and stared with burning intensity at the six feet of swiftly moving water between him and the next boulder. The jump after that gap was an easy one and then he would be across. There was a bit of room on the rock where he stood to take two steps backward. Then—one— two! Taplow whipped his body up high into the air with a scream that cut through the roar of the water. He hung in the air a moment pulling his legs forward with all his strength. He landed in the water two feet short and his legs glanced off the rock. The current snatched him instantly, dragging him downstream away from safety. Charles watched in horror as Taplow grabbed out desperately for something, anything, to stop being washed into the gorge. His hands slipped off one rock, then a second. He thudded against a third and in that fraction of a second's delay turned his body and grabbed onto the boulder with both arms. That stopped his forward motion into the gorge, but it was all he could do to simply keep himself suspended in the rushing current, holding on to the boulder with the last of his strength.

"Hold on. I'm coming to get you!" Charles frantically undid the belt on his trousers and pulled it out of its loops. He dumped out the contents of his rucksack and scrabbled through it with desperate hands. There! A length of rope, not quite long enough but with the belt attached, maybe.

"Hurry!" Taplow yelled.

"Not long now! Hang on!" His hands were shaking and it seemed to take forever to attach the belt to the rope. Finally, he finished and pulled the ends to test the join. He jumped to the first rock, then the second. Without even thinking he leaped across the first gap between the boulders and landed a bit short but with enough purchase to pull himself up onto the rock and scramble to his feet. He uncoiled the end of the rope and tied a loop onto it.

"Can't hold on!"

He was about eight feet away from Taplow. Just close enough. He moved down into a position that allowed him to brace his legs against the boulder.

"I'll toss the rope so that it lands on the rock. I'll get it as close to your right hand as I can." After a couple of tries, the looped end of the rope caught on the boulder and hung clear of the water about a foot from Taplow's hand.

"Keep your left arm around the rock and grab the rope quick as you can!"

Taplow gathered his strength and jerked his right hand toward the rope. Inches short of the rope, his left arm slid off the boulder.

Charles was in the water at the same instant that Taplow was swept into the gorge.

A jolt of cold; plunging, churning downward, blinded by foam; crushed by the unbearable weight of water on top of him, flung against rocks helplessly; swept along at terrifying speed; fighting to catch a breath and being pulled under again. Abruptly he was pitched like a skipping stone into a deep pool where the current once again pulled him under. Flaying, his hand brushed against something slithery. *Reeds. And light above.* He pushed his feet against the reeds, found solid bottom and pushed upward with all his might through a haze of bubbles toward the light, stroking with his arms, crashing through to the surface with a desperate intake of air.

Taplow! Where is he? Charles gave himself two more deep breaths of blessed air and then dove downward again, swimming with the current. The water was calmer here but turbid; he could only see for six feet around him. *He's got to be ahead of me, but where?* He stayed down searching, fighting the buoyancy, as he drifted with the current until his lungs nearly burst and he had to surface again. He scanned the water ahead of him and round about the shoreline. Nothing. Down again with the eerie, echoing sounds of the water pressing on his ears. He caught sight of something light-coloured off to his left and stroked toward it. Something more or less white and floating near the bottom in the reeds, like a torn flag. *A shirt!* He swam closer but was rapidly running out of air. He reached for the torn material and pulled it toward him. Taplow's face emerged from the reeds, his eyes closed, his face calm, unconcerned. Charles grabbed for his arms and pulled but where he expected Taplow's inert body to float easily upward with him, he met only resistance. Now his lungs were burning and he started to see silvery pin pricks of light shimmering in front of his eyes. He drove upward and exploded through to the air. Three huge breaths and then back down. For a moment he was desperately afraid that he wouldn't find Taplow again. But he saw the whiteness of the shirt and made for it, grabbing the other man by the arm. Taplow's torso floated up from the reeds, silt and greasy bubbles flowing up around him. But his left leg wouldn't come up with the rest of him. Charles dropped Taplow's arms and swam down to the bottom again. *What the——? It's his foot!* Taplow's foot was wedged between a rock and a smooth, triangular shape. Charles strained to see clearer through the disturbed water. The triangular shape resolved itself into the blade of a cast-off plow.

It had to be now. There was no time to go up for air. Charles grabbed Taplow's leg and twisted it. Still stuck. Twisted it the other direction. *Lord! Please!* With his lungs exploding, he pulled Taplow's foot with one hand, pulled at the plow blade with the other and the foot came loose. With one swift motion he pushed against the bottom with his legs and grabbed the back of Taplow's collar, pulling it upward with him as he kicked frantically for the surface. He broke through and supported Taplow's head above water while he sucked in huge breaths of air.

It was calmer water where they were now and he headed for a patch of reedy shoreline. Legs wobbling as he emerged from the water, alternately walking and falling down, he dragged Taplow behind him through the reeds and onto a flat, muddy stretch of river grass. He could hear shouts and clamour as he turned Taplow onto his stomach, sat astride his back and began alternately pressing down heavily on his rib cage and lifting his arms by the elbows. Water flowed out of Taplow's mouth but he was otherwise still as death. Charles kept pressing his rib cage and lifting his arms. Then a gagging sound, a large outrush of water and vomit and Taplow jerked upward, taking in a long, rasping breath, followed by racking coughs. Charles slid off Taplow's back and flopped down beside him, exhausted.

"Hey! You there! You two. Police. Stop where you are!"

The two plainclothes officers did not attempt the hazardous crossing but stayed watching on the opposite bank while the two constables ran back down the field toward the road. By the time the constables had crossed at the bridge below and come back up to where Charles and Taplow were, Taplow was sitting quietly on a boulder, his eyes looking far away, beyond taking any notice of Charles as he stood wringing out his shirt and socks.

44.

The visiting room of H.M. Prison Perth was not an inviting place. Janet looked around at the other tables in the stark, stone-walled room with its high barred windows and dim lighting. There was a family at the next table, a heavily pregnant wife decked out in her Sunday best, with two children in tow. The small boy pushed a drawing of a stick man and a large yellow sun across the table toward his father, who sat in his chains on the other side, watched carefully by a guard. The father took the drawing and, in so doing, lightly touched the hand of the boy.

"No touching, Muncey, or I'll have to remove you."

The prisoner, Muncey, pulled his hand back with a jerk and rubbed it, as if it had been burned, turning to give a searing look at the guard that Janet feared might get him removed faster than breaking the rules by touching his child.

The door that had admitted Muncey and his guard opened again and Taplow hobbled in, dressed in the same shapeless grey prison suit with cartoon-like arrows embroidered all over it. The guard was none too gentle and hurried him along faster than he could keep pace with his legs and arms chained to a metal belt around his waist. As a result, he fell into the chair opposite Janet.

"Is that strictly necessary?" Janet said. "Can't you see he can't walk any faster with those horrible things on?"

The guard looked a bit surprised at her tone, but all he said was, "Twenty minutes, Taplow. No touching and I'll have to search through anything she gives you before you go back to your cell."

"Very kind of you to come, Mrs. Thorburn. Although, I must say, I am a little surprised."

"Well, I—I was just on my way to visit Harald, and I thought I'd drop by."

"I see. Yes. He's a good man, Harald."

"Yes. A good man. He misses Ada most at this time of year. So—well, I did want to see how you're getting on. And I've brought you some books." She lifted the stack of six books bound with string from her lap, placed them on the wide table and pushed them toward Taplow. It became clear that even then he would not be able to reach them since his chains did not allow his arms to move more than a foot and a half in front of his body. The guard leaned over and picked up the bundle, scanning the titles on the spines.

"Strewth, Taplow, they're not even in English," the guard said. He cut the string with his penknife and looked through each volume, flipping the pages and turning them upside down to see if any escape instructions fluttered to the floor. Snapping the last one shut, he placed the stack in front of Taplow. "Suppose they're harmless enough, though I'm damned if I can make any sense of them."

Taplow's face glowed, as if, not having eaten for several days, a six-course meal had been set in front of him. He fingered the spines lovingly and turned to the title pages of each in turn. "Wonderful. Oh! Claremont on St. Augustine.

Marvellous. And the latest number of the *New Testament Review*. And Sophocles, *Oedipus at Colonus*, in the original. I shall have a crack at translating some of that." He looked up at Janet. "If I have time. Really. This is extraordinarily kind. It's—well—really, I don't know what to say."

He looked as if he might weep, which Janet found disconcerting. "Well, em—it really is no trouble and I asked myself what, were I in your place, might I want to have and so, books were top of the list."

"I don't think you would ever find yourself here, Mrs. Thorburn. I can hardly imagine that you can prevent your-self from despising me. When I heard that you were here, I thought you were looking for an opportunity to vent your fury at me. You would be justified in doing so."

"That's just it. I can't find it in my heart to despise you, though perhaps I should. Deplore what you did. Yes, that I do condemn. But, you see, I—I can't fit the two together. The man who fixed the straps on my rucksack. The man who was so congenial in refuting my every argument. The man who offered me a kind of combative friendship. I can't fit him together with the one who committed that vicious act." She shook her head in distress but then a coldness came to her face. She looked him straight in the eyes. "But then, I suppose your friendship was a sham, too. You wanted our manuscript. It was in your interest to be friendly to us."

"No, you're wrong about that. Well—you're right that I wanted your manuscript. And I am the sort of person who places his own desires first in almost every situation. But my actions toward you were sincere. Really, you are the last person that I would have expected to like, but I did—and I do. I hope you will believe that. I have no reason to lie now."

"I have wanted to believe it." She thawed a little.

He took a deep breath. "Good. Perhaps, in time…"

His voice tailed off as a thought occurred to him that made him frown slightly and lean toward her a little. "But I do want there to be no misunderstandings between us. I think you have sensed that I am not a marrying kind of man."

She sat back in her chair and considered this for a moment. "Yes, I think I knew that, but that was not what I was looking for from you."

"I'm relieved. I have so much to atone for without adding your disappointment to my score. But if circumstances were different, if I hadn't done what I did, I'd like to think we could have had a long and fiery friendship."

She smiled to think of it. "Yes. I picture us in our dotage in our bath chairs and lap robes, still disputing Paul's letters with the aid of our ear trumpets."

He laughed, picturing it with her. Then back to earth. "But circumstances are not different, Janet. And you must somehow accept—as I must accept—that I did what I am accused of in full knowledge of my act. God help me."

She looked, for a moment, as if he had slapped her. "But that is exactly what I cannot accept. How could you? How could you possibly think of it?"

"I can't explain it." He shook his head, and squeezed his eyes shut for a moment. "It's as if I was in some kind of altered state of mind in which I was able to convince myself that black was white, that what I was about to do would be for the best, that I could do it and get away with it and continue on the path I had set for myself. When I awoke the next morning, everything was different. The enormity of it! Like the coward I am, I started running."

She sat in silence for some time, trying to take in what he had just said. "Then…I shall pray for you. And for understanding."

"Thank you. Thank you for that."

"You intend to plead guilty?"

"Yes, and the trial will not be long as a consequence."

"I see."

"Janet, time is short. I—have a favour—a great favour to ask you, and you must feel free to decline. I would not blame you at all if you did."

"What is it?"

"Well, I have almost no family. And those I have refuse to have anything to do with me now. It would help me a great deal—that is, I think I could make a good end of it—"

"What are you asking?"

"We both know what the punishment is for those condemned of murder. I understand some provision is made for family or friends to attend, if they wish to—"

"Oh, dear God!" She brought her hand to her mouth.

"Yes, it is monstrous to expect this from you. I ask your forgiveness for this, as for so much else. But, the thing is, Lauchlan was right. I would like to see one friendly face."

Fear and apprehension registered on her face, but then she dropped the hand away from her mouth and nodded.

45.

After a grey and showery day the sun made a surprise appearance, filling the back garden at the Gairdner house with the caramelized light of a late summer evening. Janet herded the dinner guests outside to admire the new Cotoneaster dammeri bushes that had been trained onto the back wall and were just starting to form the red berries that would brighten the garden well into the winter. The guests filed out of the conservatory doors dutifully, glasses of juice in hand, to inspect the new plantings. Annie was not paying much attention to Janet's presentation but had taken Gordon gently by the arm to lead him around the side of the conservatory and was now showing him her double-pink Scots roses that had surprised her by a brave second blooming late in the season. It was clear to everyone that Gordon had been to the Greenhill Gardens house several times since the end of the tour and seemed comfortable in its massive embrace.

Violet, dressed in an especially elegant periwinkle silk and lace evening dress, cut to make the most of her lovely neck and shoulders, offered some considered remarks on the care of the garden but she kept casting questioning looks at the doors to the conservatory. Andrew Setter, who held his glass of kale and carrot juice without drinking it, was happy to stand on the red brick patio taking in the last rays of sun while surveying the others quietly.

This was a reunion of sorts. After Taplow's abrupt departure and the sobering knowledge of the reason for it, there had been little enthusiasm for more bicycling and Janet had wisely suggested ending the tour at Dunnlinton. The hitherto inseparable trio of Violet, Cavers and Ben had become all too separable, and Charles wondered if there was more to this than an emotional hangover after such heightened excitement. Dwight Cavers had already departed by the time Charles arrived back at Dunnlinton and Ben, too, rode off the next day on his way to Skye.

The dinner was also a farewell to Charles and Maggie. They were packed and ready to board the Allan Line steamer *Laurentian* from Glasgow two days hence, in order to be back in Winnipeg to make final arrangements for their wedding in October. Setter, too, had booked his passage on the same cattle freighter that had brought him to Scotland the previous month.

"I wonder what could have happened to Ben," Annie said. "I'm sure I put seven o'clock sharp on the invitation."

"Well, we can't wait dinner for him forever," Janet said. "Come, everyone. I hope you've brought a good appetite. Emmie and Cook have been slaving away all day and we've got fricandeau of veal and Emmie's famous currant flummery to finish with."

Setter brightened like a new penny at this and offered his arm to Janet, who took it and motioned the rest to fall in line behind her. In the dining room there was the usual chaotic gesturing, bumpings-into and colliding of hips while everyone sorted out and found their appointed places. There was an empty chair beside Violet, and Charles thought that there was just a hint of sadness to her face in unguarded moments when she wasn't engaged in conversation. Just as Emmie was bringing the soup in from the kitchen, the sound of knocking from the massive front door reverberated throughout the house. Emmie, flustered, set the tray of soup down on the sideboard and called in to the kitchen for Cook to distribute the soup plates while she answered the door. A moment later Emmie reappeared in the dining room.

"Mr. Riddoch has arrived, Miss Janet. He's just coming."

"Aha!" Charles said. "The late Mr. Riddoch."

Ben rushed through the door. "Janet, Annie, please forgive me! I'm awfully sorry to be late after you were so kind as to invite me. I seem to specialize in being late to dinner these days. Hello, everyone. I'm so sorry. I didn't realize that filing my papers would take so long."

"Welcome, Ben," Annie said. "We've only just started so you haven't missed anything. Please, come and sit down."

Gordon rose to shake Ben's hand and Charles and Setter followed suit. Amid all the welcomes and half-explanations Ben made his way to the empty seat beside Violet. He took the hand she held out in both of his own and could not help a long exhalation of breath and a wordless nod in appreciation of how she looked in her beautiful dress. He, himself, was dressed in a well-pressed grey suit with a matching waistcoat, bright white shirt with a high collar and cranberry-coloured necktie.

"Don't you look smart, Ben," Maggie said.

Ben looked sheepish. "Thank God I know a men's outfitter who was an old school chum. I'm buying this whole get-up on hire purchase."

"Why the investment in respectable attire?" Charles said.

"Aye, well. That's rather why I'm a wee bit late." He said and picked up his spoon while trying unsuccessfully to disguise a smile.

"Well, don't keep us in suspense," Violet said.

"Right. Hold on to your hats. You're looking at the Independent Labour Party candidate for the constituency of West Fife in the upcoming parliamentary elections. I've just submitted my nomination forms."

They all spoke at once. "Ben! How marvellous—didn't know you were thinking—heartiest congratulations—how do you rate your chances? —didn't have the least idea you were interested—"

"Well, I've got my work cut out for me of course. We weren't able to talk the Liberals into not running a candidate. I'm hoping for the miners' vote, of course—those that can vote. But if I could just skim off a few votes from the Liberals in the towns and the Conservatives in the agricultural parts of the constituency, just maybe I'll have a chance." This last he addressed primarily to Violet.

"Country people take a long time to trust someone who's not one of them," Violet said. "You'd have to be very honest with them about needing to earn their respect and learn about their concerns."

"You see! That's exactly the kind of advice I need to hear."

"I—I don't know much about electoral politics—apart from the suffrage issue, that is," Violet said, with a shy smile.

"Then you'll help me, Vi? Oh, that would be grand. When can you start?"

"Well, I—that is, yes, Ben, I think I could. Em, let me see. Would tomorrow be all right?"

"Tomorrow would be very much all right."

Everyone was soon lost in the intricacies of politics in

the coal-producing regions, offering free advice and disagreeing loudly over strategy. Charles smiled across the table at Maggie and felt the stab of that sweet hurt that came from knowing that he'd never again experience this exact moment with these exact people.

"By the way, I wrote to Father today," she said later, while they were walking back to Miss Semple's.

"Yes? Did you give him my regards?"

"Of course. And I told him to rent me a typewriting machine. I'm going to take the six-week Maple Leaf Business Academy typewriting course starting in November."

He stopped in surprise. "What? Why are you doing that?"

"You needn't fear. I'm not going to become a wage slave. It's a good skill to have, and I can help you in your work. I'll start by typing your notes for those YMCA lectures. And your sermon notes. No more squinting in the pulpit for you."

"Well. I am disarmed. You would do that for me?"

They resumed walking. "Yes, of course. It's part of the new plan," she said. "I asked you to support me in my ambitions and it wouldn't be fair if the support went just one way. You said it yourself. We're a team now."

"Darling girl." He raised her hand, which she had been resting in the crook of his elbow, and kissed it. "It's us against the world, then?"

"Yes, us against the world."

They had reached the front steps of Miss Semple's where, out of the corner of Charles's eye, he saw the curtains pulled discreetly aside in the bow window of the matron's office, from which there was a view of the front door. As they mounted the steps, he pulled a paper bag out of his jacket pocket.

"What's that?" she said.

"I think this is the appropriate moment. Sorry it isn't

wrapped. I had planned to at least put a ribbon on it."

She took the dog-eared bag from him, opened it and pulled out a small book. She flipped to the title page. "*An Introductory Account of Certain Modern Ideas and Methods in Plane Analytic Geometry* by Charlotte Angas Scott."

"See here," he leaned over and pointed, "Miss Scott— that is, Dr. Scott—is professor of mathematics at Bryn Mawr College in the States."

"Oh, Charles, it's wonderful! You're wonderful! I don't deserve you."

"Oh, you know me. Ever the misty-eyed romantic."

He tried to praise himself further, but she had thrown her arms around him, which was how the matron found them when she pulled open the front door.

"Mr. Lauchlan! Miss Skene! Really, this is quite outside the rules of Miss Semple's! In full view of the street, too. Stop this display immediately. Oh, heavens!"

Indeed, Charles and Maggie had stopped kissing. But Charles then planted a large and sloppy kiss on the matron's cheek.

"But, matron, isn't it wonderful? It's the twentieth century!" He skipped down the stairs and swung jauntily around the corner, whistling.

Author's Note

Some of the things I learned while doing research for this book are too interesting not to share.

The Scottish sisters, Agnes Smith Lewis and Margaret Dunlop Gibson, were the real-life inspirations for my characters Janet and Annie. Mrs. Lewis and Mrs. Gibson mounted two expeditions to St. Catherine's Monastery in the Sinai desert and discovered in the library there an important fourth-century manuscript, in Syriac, of the four gospels. I've had my fun with Janet and Annie who, apart from a few biographical similarities, evolved to be themselves and bear no other resemblance to Mrs. Lewis and Mrs. Gibson.

The dispute over the last twelve verses of the Gospel of Mark, 16:9-20, was a hot issue among Biblical scholars during the early twentieth century and continues to be an unsettled question. The style of Greek in these verses is more refined than the language in the rest of Mark and several of the earliest manuscripts—including that found by Mrs. Lewis and Mrs. Gibson—don't include these verses. So, were they an original and integral part of the Gospel of Mark?

Or were they a later addition tacked on to lend authenticity to the story of the resurrection? Most scholars subscribe to the latter view, that the earliest texts end at 16:8 and that this is the most reliable ending. But if this is true, many more questions arise as to how and why Mark appears, at least to modern eyes, to end so abruptly and without the inclusion of the resurrection of Jesus. Recently the idea that the original ending was lost and was somehow recovered later has been gaining support. I made my character Taplow a proponent of that idea.

I spent a very pleasant week in the National Library of Scotland reading about the history of bicycle touring in Scotland at the turn of the twentieth century. The Scots did amazing things on their bikes during that period. For instance, the Reverend James Paterson rode from Stirling to Inverness in one day, a distance of 158 miles. I cribbed many details from the exploits of Paterson and other two-wheeled adventurers for use by my little band of touring bicyclists. But the path of true cycling did not run smooth; many roads in the Highlands were then little better than cattle trails and often were not sign-posted. J.W. Walker really did take the wrong turn at the Fincastle Burn bridge while Paterson and his brother John found themselves in the middle of Rannoch Moor and had to carry their bicycles on their backs or drag them through bogs for eight miles until they reached a road.

It was a surprise to me that some people rode chainless bicycles in 1900. But, indeed, by 1898, some manufacturers, particularly in the United States, were producing chainless models, also known as shaft-driven bicycles, to compete with the chained bicycles that subsequently became the standard. In the chainless bicycle, power was transmitted from the pedal crank to a set of interlocking gears that in turn drove a revolving rod connected between those gears and similar gears on the rear wheel, and lastly, from the rear wheel gears to the wheel itself.

Finally, I have a few cautions for readers. I have tried to stick to the geography of Scotland as it was in 1900 but sometimes castles are just not located where you need them to be. You'll find many ruined tower house castles in Scotland but Castle Allean isn't one of them; it is fictional. Codex Zwingliae is a fiction, too. (I modelled its physical description on the real Codex Sinaiticus, a fourth-century bound volume of the Christian Bible, including the earliest complete surviving text of the New Testament in Greek.)

Acknowledgements

I have many people to thank.

Alistair and Sheila Dow kindly drove my husband, Greg, and me over the route travelled by my fictional cyclists. And when I emailed Alistair and said, "I need a very steep hill in the vicinity of Dunkeld," he knew the exact one that would suit my purposes. Within days, I had photographs.

Bonnie Moore and Frank Prior put us up in fine style while I did research in Edinburgh and answered questions like, "Can palm trees survive the limited daylight of a Scottish winter?"

Moira Fentum gave me access to a large collection of research material she compiled on early bicycling, including a wonderful set of photographs and drawings showing the clothing worn by women cyclists at the turn of the twentieth century.

Clark Saunders shared with me his research on Agnes Smith Lewis and Margaret Dunlop Gibson, first gathered during his time as a student at Westminster College, Cambridge, the Presbyterian college that was founded in part by a generous endowment from these remarkable Scottish sisters.

An excerpt from Lancelot Andrewes' "An Evening Reflection," opens this book. My deep thanks to poet David Scott for permission to use his translation of this meditation, the full text of which can be found in *Lancelot Andrewes: The Private Prayers*, selected and translated by David Scott. London: SPCK, 2002.

I'm Canadian and I'm sorry. Thankfully, editor Gale Winskill removed bits of dialogue from my text that no self-respecting Scot would say and corrected unwitting errors in the Scottish setting.

The editorial attentions of both Sylvia McConnell and Douglas Whiteway have made this a better book. Both delivered their advice along with a much-appreciated serving of encouragement.

Copy editor Priyanka Ketkar's eagle eye caught many small and some larger problems, for which I thank her most sincerely.

It's a wonderful thing to be able to have coffee with your publisher. Thanks to Matt Joudrey of At Bay Press for believing in this book and for a very congenial publishing relationship.